James Cr... ...for more
than thirt... ...is previ-
ous Inspector Carlyle novels, *London Calling*, *Never Apologise*,

Also by James Craig

JAMES CRAIG
DYING DAYS

CONSTABLE

CONSTABLE

First published in Great Britain in 2019 by Constable

1 3 5 7 9 10 8 6 4 2

ISBN: 978-1-47212-222-3

Typeset in Times New Roman by TW Type, Cornwall
Printed and bound in Great Britain by CPI Group (UK) Ltd, Croydon CR0 4YY

Papers used by Constable are from well-managed forests
and other responsible sources.

MIX
Paper from
responsible sources
FSC® C104740

Constable
An imprint of
Little, Brown Book Group
Carmelite House
50 Victoria Embankment
London EC4Y 0DZ

An Hachette UK Company
www.hachette.co.uk

www.littlebrown.co.uk

For Catherine and Cate

This is the thirteenth Carlyle novel.
Thanks for getting it completed go to
Krystyna Green, Rebecca Sheppard,
Hazel Orme, Joan Deitch and Michael Doggart.

ONE

The world invariably seemed a happier place when things slipped out of focus. With his glasses perched precariously on top of his head, John Carlyle watched the blurry figures hustling up and down Shaftesbury Avenue until interrupted by the buzzing of his phone. This would be, the inspector guessed, a long-overdue call from his boss.

'Where have you been?' he enquired cheerily. 'On holiday? Or another of those expensive management training courses?'

'Mr Carlyle?' The irritated male voice at the other end of the line most definitely didn't belong to Commander Carole Simpson.

'Sorry, yes.' Carlyle placed his specs on his nose with his free hand, just in time to see a spotty teenage girl walk past the café window. She was wearing a ripped T-shirt bearing the legend *The Damned* and sported a large nose-ring. An electric-blue Mohican that must have required a whole pot of gel to keep it in place completed the look.

You're forty-plus years too late, love, Carlyle mused.

'This is Dr Scott.'

'Yes?' The name didn't ring any bells.

'From your father's medical centre on Dawes Road.'

'Of course.' Carlyle coughed.

'I'm the duty officer who's been in to visit Alexander at home this week.' The GP sounded annoyed that his valuable time was being wasted on an old man at the edge of death. Where

Carlyle's mother's exit had been sudden, as ruthlessly efficient as the woman herself, his father was taking his own sweet time about moving on from this life.

Is this it? Carlyle wondered. Game over?

'He's still hanging in there.'

'Yes.' Carlyle kept his gaze firmly on the outside world; he wanted to focus on life, rather than the alternative.

'I was quite surprised not to see you there.' The doctor's tone reminded Carlyle of Miss Teverson, back in the third year of St Horace's Primary School, when he was misbehaving and she was having a bad day. 'You know there's not much time left.'

Everyone had been saying that for quite a while. 'I get down when I can,' said Carlyle, defensively. 'Work is keeping me very busy.'

A dismissive *I've heard it all before* grunt rolled down the line.

'I'm a police officer. We've got a couple of big cases pending.' His statement was less than half true, at best. Things at Charing Cross were unusually quiet. The inspector had taken to praying for a nice complicated murder – or some other outbreak of serious criminality – in the Central London area to relieve his boredom and also save him from having to go down to Fulham to watch his father dying in slow motion.

'Well, from what I can see, Alexander's care is adequate,' Dr Scott continued.

Adequate was probably the best you could hope for from the NHS. 'Thank you.' Carlyle wondered what the good doctor made of Stine Hassing. Alexander's 'death doula' had appeared on the scene several months ago. At first, he had been deeply sceptical of what he considered to be the Danish woman's New Age flakery. However, Stine's commitment to helping Alexander Carlyle through his last days had grown to the point that she had taken up residence in his father's flat as the endgame approached. Right now, the doula was the only thing standing between the old man and a last few tragic days in Fulham Park Trust Hospital. For the inspector, the useless, helpless, hopeless son, the mixture of gratitude and relief was almost as powerful as one of his father's morphine drips.

'And we've made sure that he has plenty of pain relief.'

About bloody time. 'Good.' The NHS had finally come through with a decent supply of drugs to ensure that the old man could go out high as a kite. For more than nine months previously, the inspector had been supplying his father with a selection of immensely effective but totally illegal opiates, sourced via his good friend and contact, a former drug-dealer by the name of Dominic Silver. But Dom's own suppliers had proved erratic. There had been no black-market pills available for more than a month. As a policeman, Carlyle was pleased that his illegal drug-dealing activity had been curtailed; as a concerned son, less so.

'When did you last visit your father?' The question was abrupt, almost accusatory.

'Probably a couple of days ago,' Carlyle lied. The truth was closer to a fortnight. 'Like I said, the thing is—'

Not interested in his excuses, Dr Scott cut him off: 'Alexander's done very well to last this long,' he said flatly. 'He's a very strong man. If it wasn't for the cancer, he would have many years in front of him.'

That's good to know, Carlyle thought sourly. I'm sure that makes the poor old bugger feel much better about things.

'But now your father's definitely reaching the end. I would strongly advise you to go and see him in the next day or two. You need to spend some time with him soon, or it may be too late.'

On Shaftesbury Avenue, a taxi pulled up to the kerb, in front of the window. The inspector watched an elegant woman in an expensive-looking trouser suit get out of the back. Wearing a pair of outsized sunglasses, she glanced in Carlyle's direction before easing the taxi door closed.

Fuck death.

Choose life.

3

'Mr Carlyle?'

'Yes,' he said hastily. 'Thank you for letting me know, Doctor. It was very kind of you. I appreciate the heads-up.'

'One of my colleagues from the medical centre will be round to see Alexander tomorrow, but it really is close now.'

'I understand.'

The woman paid her cab fare and headed down the street. Watching her go, Carlyle contemplated the prospect of finally becoming an orphan in his sixth decade on the planet.

TWO

Sitting at the back of the café, Karen Jansen watched the crumpled middle-aged man gawping at the girls passing on the street as he mumbled into his mobile. That's a punter right there, she thought, *definitely* a punter. Not that it was the most stunning insight she had ever had. When it came down to it, all men were either punters or potential punters.

Finishing his call, the man stared out of the window for a short while before slipping off his stool and heading onto the street. Bored, she tuned in to the telephone conversation of the girl opposite her. Melody Rainbow (amazingly, it was her real name) was one of Jansen's most troublesome employees. A second-year student at the University of London's School of Oriental and African Studies, Melody was studying for a BA in Tibetan and social anthropology. Six months ago, to help fund a year studying at Lhasa University, the girl had signed on at the Nelly Ternan Escort Agency. However, getting Melody to take any jobs was a struggle: there was always an unfinished essay or a suspicious boyfriend getting in the way of her earning some money. Jansen had long since marked Melody down as a waste of time. Unfortunately, the agency's owner, an old-school gangster by the name of Vernon Holder, had taken a shine to the girl. Moreover, the agency was suffering a severe shortage of talent. Brexit, it seemed, was putting everybody off coming to London, even the hookers.

This set of circumstances meant that Melody Rainbow was

basically unsackable, at least until a decent set of new arrivals appeared on the scene.

'Stop it.' Melody played with a strand of her bubblegum pink hair while shouting into her iPhone. 'I told you, I have to work tonight.'

Jansen signalled it was time to wind up the call, but the girl ignored her.

'Why would I lie to you? I'm sitting in a café right now – that's what the noise is. When I finish my panini, I need to go to the library and finish off my essay on the Yarlung Dynasty . . . No, no, Yarlung.'

Jansen pulled a pair of reading glasses from her bag, along with her phone. Slipping on the specs, she googled 'Yarlung Empire'. Clicking on the third of more than a million results, she read a potted history: *Yarlung was home to the first king of Tibet . . . The Yarlung Dynasty reached its peak during the military successes of the seventh and eighth centuries and came to an end after the assassination of the last king of the Tibetan empire, Langdarma . . .*

I probably know more about it now than you do, Jansen thought sadly. Knowledge isn't what it was. Chuckling to herself, she took another sip of her tea. Melody was a pretty girl but if she stopped hiding behind the persona of a naughty schoolgirl and just grew up a little she'd be truly beautiful.

'I told you . . .' Cradling the phone between shoulder and ear, Melody turned her attention to toying with the remains of her food. 'You never believe me. Tomorrow? . . . Maybe. Let's see. Look, I've got to go now . . . Yeah, sure.' Ending the call, she dropped the handset onto the table and let out a world-weary sigh.

'Which one was that?' Jansen asked, more than a little irritated that she had to pay more attention to Melody's boyfriends than her own.

'Chris.'

Jansen racked her brain but couldn't come up with a Chris

from the constantly swelling ranks of the Melody Rainbow Appreciation Society.

Looking up from her plate, Melody recognised the confusion on Jansen's face. 'He's new. Well, newish. I met him at the Constantinople Ballroom a couple of weeks ago.'

'Uh-huh.' Jansen had never heard of the Constantinople but she didn't bother to ask. The girl collected boyfriends like other people collected loyalty-card stamps, although there was no doubt that the latter offered considerably better value for money.

'He's becoming quite possessive.'

'Already?'

'He says I'm his dream woman.' The look on Melody's face suggested she considered that a perfectly reasonable assertion.

'Maybe you should ditch him.' In Jansen's experience, the average bloke had a shelf life of about a month, max – less if they started going all gooey on you.

'But he's got a Maserati. And he took me to Malvaceae the other night.'

'What's that? A new club?'

'It's a restaurant,' Melody explained. 'It's got two Michelin stars.'

'Hm. I've always wondered, what is a Michelin star, anyway?'

'It means it's good,' Melody said airily.

'It means it's expensive,' Jansen translated. 'Anyway, about tonight.'

'You heard me on the phone,' Melody squealed. 'I've got to do my essay. I need to write a minimum of three and a half thousand words, or I could flunk this part of my course.'

'They're not going to flunk you.' Jansen parroted the Americanism in an attempt at empathy. 'They want the fees.'

'But if I have to go back and do it again, that's *more* fees.'

Jansen gritted her teeth. She hated it when the girl surprised her by saying something that made some sort of sense.

'Three thousand five hundred words.' Melody seemed mesmerised by the number. 'That's a lot.'

'Quite a lot.'

'It's a hell of a lot when you're sitting there staring at a blank page.'

'Can't you just buy an essay online?'

Melody looked offended. 'But that's cheating.'

'I thought everybody did it these days,' Jansen quipped. 'Sounds like a good idea to me.'

'It's expensive.'

'So, you've done it before?'

'Once or twice,' Melody admitted, 'like, you know, when I was under a bit of deadline pressure.'

'Like now.'

'I suppose so. This is a big essay, though, and they normally charge by the word. It'll probably end up costing a grand or more.'

'That's less than you'll make tonight,' Jansen pointed out. 'You'll still come out ahead.'

'I suppose so,' Melody repeated. She could see the logic.

'I wish they'd had something like that in my day.' Jansen – an MBA from La Trobe in Melbourne – recalled the thirty-thou-sand-word dissertation she'd had to write as part of her final exams: *The role of censor strategies to prevent a clash of cultures through advertising: applications and implications.* Very bloody useful that had proved to be. She was surprised she could even remember the title.

'What's so funny?'

'Nothing.'

Jansen occasionally wondered if Melody Rainbow was a complete fantasist. Maybe the girl was just making it all up about her degree. She'd once quizzed Melody on why she had chosen such an 'esoteric' (read: 'useless') subject to study. The girl had responded by reciting the marketing brochure: 'Graduates leave SOAS not only with linguistic and cultural expertise, but also with a portfolio of widely transferable skills, which employers seek in many professional and management careers.'

'What transferable skills?'

'Written and oral communication skills, language skills, attention to detail, analytical and problem-solving skills, and the ability to research, amass and order information from a variety of sources.'

Sounds perfect preparation for being an escort, Jansen had reflected. 'What do you want to do when you gr–' She was about to say 'grow up' but skilfully managed instead to turn it into '– graduate?'

Running out of marketing babble, Melody blew her fringe out of her eyes. 'Dunno. Depends what comes along. Maybe management consultancy or merchant banking.' She thought about it some more. 'Private equity, maybe.'

Jansen stifled a chortle. 'Why not?'

'If one of those doesn't work out, there's always PR as a last resort.'

Truly, Jansen had thought, we're all prostitutes. 'Making use of your excellent communication skills.'

'Exactly.'

'Well, at least you seem to have given it some thought.'

'You have to plan ahead,' Melody opined. 'The world is so competitive – you can't just make it up as you go along, like you did in your day.'

'I suppose not.' Jansen was only twelve years older than Melody but it seemed like they belonged to different centuries, different worlds. They probably did.

Now Jansen put her glasses away. 'We need to get moving.'

'I've got to do my essay.'

'Mel—'

'I'm not lying to you,' Melody squawked, a bit too loudly. At the next table, a couple of middle-aged women, fresh from a matinee performance of a nearby musical, gave them irritated stares from behind their souvenir programmes.

Maybe they don't like the pink hair, Jansen thought. I bet it'll go down a storm in Lhasa, though. Despite everything, she had a bit of a soft spot for Melody. At least the girl was trying to do something unusual. 'You can do it in the morning.' Squinting, she began flicking through the dozens of messages stored on her phone. Conscious of the nosy women at the next table, she lowered her voice: 'The client's flat is only five minutes up the road. You can go straight to the library afterwards.'

'I'll be too tired.'

'Not at all,' Jansen persisted. The girl was sorely trying her patience but the client – Martin Grom – had, on the recommendation of Vernon Holder, asked specifically for Melody. Jansen had long wondered about the connection between the two men. A professor specialising in development studies and an East End gangster were not the most obvious bedfellows. But Holder had never been forthcoming on the matter and Jansen knew better than to ask too many questions. 'It won't take too long. Martin's an older gentleman, a long-time client of Mr Holder's.'

'Urgh.' Melody's face screwed up in disgust. 'I hate the older guys. Disgusting bodies. Shrivelled cocks. They make me gag.'

One of the nearby women embarked on a violent coughing fit.

'Keep your voice down,' Jansen hissed. 'He's a nice guy, very . . . polite.'

A wearily sceptical look crossed Melody's face, ageing her about twenty years in less than a second. 'How old?'

Seventy-three. 'I don't know.'

'Over sixty?'

Even Jansen couldn't lie that far. 'I would assume so,' she said blandly. 'He's retired. But he was an academic, so you never know.'

'An academic?'

'A professor. He used to teach at the university. You know what it's like with those people – they work ten hours a week, take six months' holiday a year and retire on some ridiculous pension when they're forty-five.'

That sounded like an ideal career plan for a girl with a BA in

Tibetan and social anthropology. 'He's got to be older than that, though, right?'

'I don't know.'

'I've decided,' Melody stated solemnly. 'No more men over forty-five. I was thinking about making it forty, but forty-five seems more realistic.'

Yeah, right.

'It's a new rule. My psychologist says I need to start making more rules.'

Psychologist? Jansen knew better than to go there.

'I've got to set myself boundaries, if I'm going to organise my life properly and achieve my goals.'

'And this is your first, erm, goal?'

'Not the first,' Melody said brightly. 'I'd already decided to stop drinking alcohol – and also no more cheese.'

'Cheese?' What is this? A philosophy for life or a diet programme?

Melody shook her head sadly. 'It doesn't agree with me. Unsettles my stomach. Plus, it's just all fat, basically.'

We're getting off the point, Jansen admonished herself. 'So, the no-over-forty rule—'

'No over-forty-*fives*. I made it after you sent me to see that IT guy last week.'

Jansen searched through her mental checklist of past appointments. 'The guy in the Docklands?'

'Nah. The Docklands guy was a banker. He was okay, a bit shy. Not very experienced, I don't think. Gave me a nice tip, though. The IT guy was the American who had the penthouse suite at the Landmark.'

'I remember,' said Jansen. 'But he wasn't that old. Only thirty, something like that. I read a profile of him on ft.com. He collects lizards.'

'Snakes,' Melody corrected her.

'Yuck.'

'Anyway, when I got there it turned out he was a

11

twenty-eight-year-old virgin who didn't have a clue. He spent more time trying to film me on his mobile phone than doing the deed.' Melody raised her eyes to the ceiling. 'I really hate that. No videos – that's another rule.'

Jansen, who had seen enough of herself on the internet to last a lifetime, gave a sympathetic cluck.

'But his father must have been something like eighty.'

'His father?' Jansen belatedly recalled that the booking had been one of Victor's BOGOF specials for first-time clients. Buy One, Get One Free.

'Yeah.' Melody gave her a crooked smile. 'You forgot to mention him, didn't you?' She shuddered at the memory. 'It was horrible, like fucking a corpse. A corpse with a very dirty mind. And incredible stamina for a man of his age. All in all, not a happy combination.'

The women at the next table looked like their eyes were about to pop out of their heads. Having given up on any pretence of holding their own conversation, they were hanging on the pink-haired freak's every word. One of the women had her mouth open so far that her tongue was almost on the table. The other clasped a mobile phone to her ample bosom, as if she was recording the whole conversation for posterity.

Which, of course, she might well be doing. That would be something to tell the folks back home: '*Well, we went to see a show but, then, the people who live in that place . . . a complete den of iniquity . . .*'

'Melody, for Christ's sake keep it down.' I sound like the girl's mother, Jansen thought. Irritated beyond belief, she glared at the two women as hard as she could, before returning her attention to her truculent employee.

'You just don't vet these people properly,' the girl scowled, 'do you?'

'There will be no surprises with the professor, I can promise you.'

'Send one of the other girls.'

'I would if I could.'

'I made my mind up,' Melody said. 'The rule is the rule. Non-negotiable.'

'You don't – *we* don't get to make the rules,' Jansen reminded her. 'Vernon would have a total fit if he could hear this conversation.'

'Vernon can do one,' Melody suggested. Cue more coughing from the next table. The gawkers really were getting their money's worth – this had to be a million times more entertaining than the revival of some eighties musical. 'He can just sod off.'

This was not an unreasonable point of view, Jansen had to admit, but not one that helped pay the bills. A sudden wave of self-pity washed over her. Middle-management was such hard work: everything was a protracted negotiation. These days, no one would ever just do what they were damn well told. She racked her brain, trying to come up with another argument that would encourage the girl to do her bidding. 'What about that Irish guy?' she asked finally. 'You like him.'

'Mr Durkan?' Melody's face brightened up. 'He's a sweetie. He only takes about ten minutes. He can be a bit rough sometimes, when he gets carried away, but he always gives me a massive tip.'

'He's ancient, though, much older than forty-five.'

Melody couldn't deny that basic truth. 'I think that Gerry can be the exception that proves the rule.'

'Compared to Gerry Durkan,' Jansen pointed out, 'Martin Grom is a *real* gentleman.'

'That's what you think.'

'Trust me.' It was a feeble plea, an admission of defeat.

'Gerry says you shouldn't trust anyone.'

Especially not Durkan. Jansen changed tack: 'This job's been booked in for a week. It's a bit late to be having this kind of conversation. The client's expecting you.'

'Do you know him?' Melody asked. What she meant was: has he fucked you?

Jansen ignored the question. 'He has a thing for undergraduates.'

'Dirty old man.'

'He's interested in your studies.'

Melody idly scratched her left breast through the silk of her shirt. 'Yeah, right.'

'He is. He wants to discuss them with you over dinner.'

'Dinner?'

'He's preparing dinner at his flat. Apparently, he's a great cook.'

Melody looked vaguely interested but decidedly less than convinced. 'Where did he teach? At SOAS?'

'I think so. He might be able to help you with your essay.'

'I've got to get it done,' Melody repeated. 'It's already almost a week late. Three thousand five hundred words. That's a lot.'

'Well,' Jansen suggested, 'another day isn't going to make too much difference, is it?'

THREE

Carlyle clocked the strikingly pretty girl as he left the café. Pink hair was better than a blue Mohican, he decided, but if Alice ever did anything like that, there would be hell to pay. Thankfully, his daughter had never shown any inclination for such a crass display. It was just as well: City School for Girls, where Alice was currently studying for her A levels, considered hair-dyeing an expellable offence.

Outside, you could smell the rain in the air. Unsure about his direction of travel, the inspector paused under the glowering sky. Alice was having a study sleepover at a friend's house while Helen had an emergency meeting at work. His wife worked for a medical aid charity called Avalon. Over the last few months, emergency meetings had become the norm. The charity was a good cause and all that, but its seemingly permanent state of chaos was beginning to take its toll.

Faced with the prospect of returning to an empty flat, the inspector decided that he really should take Dr Scott's advice. A visit to his father was long overdue. A fat raindrop landing on his head encouraged him to get moving. Scuttling in the direction of Leicester Square, he hoped to reach the sanctuary of the tube station before the heavens opened completely.

FOUR

The Maserati or the Porsche? It shouldn't have been such a difficult decision. Balthazar Quant had set his heart on the Maserati.
Unfortunately, his long-held fantasy of walking into the Maserati
showroom, handing over a briefcase containing seventy grand in
crisp fifty-pound notes and driving out in the blood-red Ghibli
S that he had twice taken for a test drive round Canary Wharf,
was now in tatters. When that total bastard of a boss, Gerry
Durkan, had handed over his bonus, Balthazar had been genuinely shocked and totally horrified to discover a number that was
so far below his expectations that it would barely cover a deposit
on a Macan from the Porsche dealer down the road at the India
Docks.

Of course, leasing the Maserati was still an option. However,
he had told the salesman of his intention to buy, and to backtrack
now would be profoundly embarrassing. A sense of deep frustra-
tion burned inside Balthazar's guts. An MBA from the Technical
University at Padua, followed by fourteen years working like a
slave in this grim, soulless city, should have brought far greater
rewards than this. His original plan had been to work hard, squir-
rel away twenty mil, US, and retire to a quiet life in Tuscany or
Switzerland. After a decade of missed targets, broken promises
and clawed-back bonuses, he had massaged this figure down to
ten. Now even that was looking like a stretch. Whoever had said,
'The first ten million is the hardest,' had certainly known what
he was talking about.

Finding long-term planning increasingly wearisome, Balthazar found himself needing to splurge, just to get through the daily grind of working in the financial markets. This time around, however, a new watch or a long weekend in Cannes with one of the girls from Ternan's wouldn't be enough to beat the hamster-wheel blues. This time he needed a special treat if he was going to be able to keep on getting out of bed in the morning.

So – back to the matter in hand: the Maserati or the Porsche?

Fuck it, he'd swallow his pride and lease the Maserati. For the moment, though, he would have to make do with the tube. Balthazar hurried past the almost completed Crossrail station, heading for the entrance to the Jubilee Line. Coming across an empty Coke can lying on the pavement, he gave it an angry kick in the direction of the gutter. 'Goddamn Gerry Durkan.' How had he ever managed to hook up with such a total cowboy? More to the point, how had such a total cowboy ever managed to make it to number 197 on the London Rich List, with a fortune estimated at more than £450 million?

Balthazar knew that such a figure – cobbled together by a journalist with little more than the back of an envelope and a couple of clippings from the *Financial Times* to go on – was total nonsense. Once you stripped out Gerry Durkan's various mortgages and other debts, you could knock a zero off it, for a start. But, whatever the real number, it was a hell of an achievement. Even Balthazar had to admit that. For a man who had started out as a terrorist, a player in the Irish Republican Army who had tried to kill a prime minister, Gerry Durkan had performed some pretty major miracles to get as far as he had.

Back in the day, Gerry Durkan had been part of the IRA crew responsible for blowing up Margaret Thatcher in a hotel room in the crappy seaside resort of Brighton. Fortunately for Durkan, the prime minister had survived. Otherwise he might still have been in jail. Or in the ground, courtesy of the British Army.

After a time on the run, the Brits had caught him and put him in prison. There, instead of smearing shit on the walls or going on hunger strike, he had got his head down and started studying. Over the course of a dozen years, he managed to collect degrees in economics, accountancy and business management. Released as part of a general amnesty, he dabbled in Dublin property before arriving in London just in time to ride the wave of one of the capital's financial-services booms. Say what you like about the City, if you can make a decent ROI no one cares very much where you've come from or, indeed, where you're going. Within a remarkably short space of time, it became rudeness personified to make any mention of Durkan's early CV.

'I've had two lives,' the man himself liked to say. 'The first Gerry Durkan was an immature, uptight, know-nothing little gobshite. He died in prison, thanks be to God. If I saw him walking down the street today, I'd cross the road to avoid him. I wouldn't piss on the little wanker if he was on fire.'

The second Gerry Durkan liked to think of himself as a fully paid-up member of the metropolitan elite: season tickets at the Emirates, bespoke suits, wine auctions and private jets for weekends away in Cannes or Barcelona. 'My old self,' he admitted, 'wouldn't recognise me now.'

Sadly, when it came to sharing the love, Gerry Durkan 2.0 was just as tight as the original version. Balthazar had been his third hire at MCS, the great man's hedge fund, Macroom Castlebar Salle. Now the business consisted of more than four hundred people. Aside from Durkan himself, Balthazar was the longest surviving member of staff, by some considerable margin. But, unlike his boss, he wasn't rich, nowhere near.

He didn't even have a decent car.

The unhappy financier continued towards the Underground station. Behind him, the glass, steel and concrete of Thatcher Tower No. 1 rose into the troubled night sky. Feeling the weight of failure on his shoulders, Balthazar slouched past a giant billboard advertising another three towers bearing the name of the former prime minister. Thanks to the never-ending aftershocks from the last banking crisis, they had yet to get off the drawing board. But they would, one day. Meanwhile, Durkan would still be sitting pretty behind the desk of his massive thirty-first-floor office in Tower No. 1, most likely looking at websites for either bookmakers or escort agencies. Or both. The new Gerry Durkan had retained more than a few of the peccadilloes of the old one.

Dealing with Balthazar had been a doddle. It was the same every year. The boy just didn't know how to negotiate. For Gerry Durkan, it was almost no fun any more.

'The numbers are only provisional. Things might change. A little. But not too much. Plus, we need to take account of the pipeline, which, I have to say, is giving a little cause for concern at this stage. Not because there's nothing in it, you understand, but there's a lack of visibility about the timescales involved in things coming through.' Durkan paused for breath. It was so easy spouting this crap by the yard that he had to make a conscious effort to stop talking. He gave his underling a look that said, *That's the end of my spiel. Feel free to get your arse back to work.*

'Yes, yes,' Balthazar snapped, 'I understand that.'

'Of course you do. You know this stuff better than I do.' Durkan glanced at the chunky timepiece on his wrist. Right on cue, Delia Sansom, his executive assistant, poked her head inside the room. Even from five yards away, it was clear that she had slapped on the old war paint in readiness for a big night out. Durkan shook his head. Mutton dressed as lamb. Even though Delia was easily the wrong side of forty, she still chose to party like someone in their early twenties. It really was a sad carry on. Shuddering to think where she might end up, he made a bet with himself that she would shamelessly throw a sickie tomorrow.

'You've got the O'Flaherty call in a minute, sir,' she advised solemnly. 'I've told them you'll be calling direct.'

O'Flaherty? Jeez, woman, couldn't you have come up with a better name than that? 'Thanks, Delia. I've got the number.' He gave her a flash of his generous Celtic smile. 'Off for a night on the town? Have a good one.'

'Thanks.' The PA headed for the door. 'I'm leaving now. See you tomorrow.'

We'll see. 'Have fun.'

'I will,' Delia promised, before disappearing behind the heavy door.

'Sorry about this.' Durkan reached for the phone sitting on his desk. 'I've got to make an important call. The Argentinian situation.'

Balthazar nodded sagely.

The Argentinian government was planning one of its periodic debt defaults. MCS ran one of a number of so-called 'vulture funds', trying to get them to pay out in full. Durkan had taken a big bet that 'the Argies' would fold, giving him a massive profit. 'An important call,' he repeated, waving the receiver in front of his face.

'It's just that I had certain expectations,' Balthazar stammered. 'Certain assurances were given at the end of the first half of the year.'

'"Assurances" would be overstating it. You know that as well as anyone in this building.' Or, at least, you should. Randomly pushing different buttons, Durkan lifted the receiver to his ear. 'We give indications. Forecasts are not the same as results.'

'I made some plans, based on what I'd been told . . . I was given some pretty clear *guidance* about what to expect, all in all.'

'Guidance is always tricky.' An irritating smirk passed across Durkan's face. He placed the receiver back on its cradle, making an ostentatious display of giving his employee his undivided attention for a few further precious seconds.

'Yes, but—'

Like an old-fashioned copper directing the traffic, Durkan held up a hand.

Time for some calm.

This is important to you, so it's important to me. These days,

Gerry Durkan liked to think of himself of something of a Zen master. There was hardly a relaxation, meditation, neutrality or wellbeing retreat within fifty miles of London that he had not visited at least once. Twice a year, he would spend a fortnight at a spa in Évian, enjoying the mineral baths, the mountain air and the lack of cellphone coverage. Of course, the twelve years he had spent in Long Kesh, five of them in solitary, were probably a contributing factor to his never-ending search for peace and tranquillity. So, too, was the ageing process. Well past sixty, it had been a long time since he had been able to tap into the reserves of energy that had driven him as a young man.

'It was clear,' Balthazar repeated, 'and definitive.'

'You know how guidance can change.'

'Up to a point,' Balthazar grumped.

'The second half of the financial year was quite volatile,' Durkan persisted, warming to his theme. They had reprised the same basic conversation several times over the years and the CEO knew that he held all the cards.

The basic message never changed: Fit in or fuck off.

If Balthazar didn't like the size of his bonus, he could walk – try to find a job somewhere else – and they both knew he didn't have the balls to do that. The reality was that Balthazar had passed his sell-by date quite a while ago. His market value was small, and it was diminishing all the time. As far as the City was concerned, poor old Balthazar was well past his peak. That was the thing about the markets: there was always someone younger, smarter, hungrier and, crucially, *cheaper* begging to be hired; someone happy, willing and able to step over the broken bodies of people like Balthazar to take their shot at the pot of gold at the end of the rainbow. 'Things took a disappointing downward turn in the third quarter. You know what I mean.'

'Even so—'

'It was unfortunate, but revenues dipped just as costs were going up.' Bored, Durkan began tapping at the keyboard sitting on his desk. There was some American racing coming up and a horse he had heard about – Candystripe – was supposed to be a bit of a ringer. Durkan liked ringers. 'Of course, it didn't help that we made a couple of expensive new hires.'

'Expensive flops,' Balthazar grumbled.

'Then there was the money we had to throw at the IT network to stop it falling over.' Durkan stifled a snigger – IT spending was an easy excuse come bonus time.

'Everyone's seeing their bonus cut,' Durkan continued, his eyes fixed on the screen as he contemplated the latest odds from Emerald Downs. 'Hell, I'm not even getting *any* bonus this year.' Candystripe was still available at an attractive 8–1. 'I have to lead by example, after all.'

FIVE

A large seagull sauntered across the street and began nibbling at a crisp peeking out from a refuse sack dumped by the base of a lamppost. 'Shoo.' Balthazar aimed a desultory kick in its direction. The gull paid no heed, continuing to snack until a Daimler rolled past, causing it to take flight with an unhappy cry. As the limousine headed towards the Limehouse Tunnel, Balthazar's thoughts returned to his four-wheeled woes. One thing was for sure, his boss had no problems in the car department. According to a recent *Classic Car Collector* profile, Gerry Durkan's collection extended to more than seventy cars, including two Ferraris, six Aston Martins, various Mercs, a 1930s Rolls-Royce Silver Shadow, a Humvee rescued from the desert after the first Gulf War, and four Maseratis. All this, although the man didn't even hold a driving licence.

'What will you do when petrol cars are banned?' the interviewer – a washed-up former model busy reinventing herself as a petrolhead – had asked him.

'Not my problem,' was Durkan's reported response. 'I'll be long dead by then.'

'Hey, Balthazar.'

'Excuse me?'

'Balthazar Quant.'

Shaken from his thoughts, Balthazar instinctively moved away from the voice. As a rule, you did not 'bump into' people in the Docklands, certainly not on the street. Here, everyone went about their business at an accelerated pace, avoided eye contact and never, ever stopped to chat. The whole place was rather like *The Invasion of the Body Snatchers* made real, which was one of the few things he liked about it.

'Surprised to see us?'

Reluctantly, the financier turned to face his inquisitor. The giant in front of him was instantly recognisable but Balthazar feigned ignorance as best he could. 'Sorry, do I know you?'

'Now, now. Is that any way to greet old friends?' The small man who had stepped out from behind the giant was also familiar, despite the mess of scars that criss-crossed his face.

What the hell happened to you? Balthazar wondered. The guy looked like that Latin American dictator, the one they called Pineapple Face. Noriega was his name. Balthazar vaguely remembered reading his obituary not so long ago. He had been thrown into jail by the Americans for drugs-trafficking and tried to sue a publisher for using him as a character in one of their computer-game franchises. Balthazar liked the game: he played it now and again on his Xbox.

'More to the point, is that any way to greet valued clients?' The man with the messed-up face held an antique-looking walking stick with a bulbous silver top. He smacked the end of the cane into the palm of his free hand. 'Is it?'

'Erm?' Balthazar looked around for help, but the streets were empty. His brain screamed at him to move but, before his legs could act, the giant grabbed his arm and began dragging him back in the direction from which he had come.

'Come with us,' the small man commanded. 'It's time to get re-acquainted.'

SIX

Carlyle arrived at his father's flat just as the rain started to ease. Dripping wet, he made his way down the corridor and into the living room. Stine Hassing was standing on the small balcony, smoking a cigarette in the thickening gloom. Scowling, he watched her blow a lungful of smoke into the sky.

'We all have our little weaknesses,' the death doula said, pre-empting his query. 'Anyway, as you know, I'm not scared of death.'

Just as well, Carlyle thought. More than half an hour doing battle with the District Line – along with his subsequent soaking – had done nothing for his *joie de vivre*.

'Your father's asleep. He's been quite peaceful today.'

'Good.' Carlyle looked out across Lille Park, on the other side of the road, wondering how quickly he could leave.

'Your father has been here a long time.'

'In the flat, you mean?'

'In the flat.' Stine shrugged. 'In London.'

'A long time,' Carlyle confirmed. 'He and my mother arrived from Glasgow in the 1950s after they were married.'

'Scotland.'

'Yeah.' In Carlyle's mind, the country of his ancestors was just part of the amorphous mass that wasn't London, not a location, just an absence of location, the badlands of the grim north. 'They came to find work, basically. There wasn't any up there and they had enough gumption to get up and go.'

Stine looked at him through a smoky haze. 'Gumption?'

'It means . . .' Carlyle fumbled for the word '. . . initiative. They had enough determination and drive to move away from their friends and family in search of, I dunno, a better life.' It sounded corny but it was true and their son was suitably grateful.

'You owe them a lot.'

Carlyle felt himself blush slightly. 'Doesn't every child owe their parents?'

'Some parents are just not very good,' Stine observed.

'Mine were good,' Carlyle said quietly. Good enough, anyway. 'I can have no complaints.'

'That's good.'

'I suppose so.'

'Do you ever go back there?'

'To Scotland? Not very often.' Carlyle tried to remember the last time he had been north of the border. Not since his grandmother's funeral. Uncomfortable talking about himself, he asked, 'What about you? Have you ever been there?'

'I went to the Edinburgh Festival once,' Stine ventured. 'It was cold. And it rained all the time.'

'And that was the summer.'

'I know.' She giggled. 'Everything was so dark and grim. I had a boyfriend who was doing a one-man show at the festival about Danish heroes of the Holocaust.'

'Sounds interesting,' Carlyle lied.

Stine took another puff on her fag, careful to blow the smoke away from the inspector. 'He was performing in the basement of a church in the middle of nowhere, for a week. On the first night, only one person turned up. And he was there by mistake. When he realised that the show was in Danish, he sat in the back row and read a newspaper while Jesper went through his entire show. The thing lasted more than three hours.'

'What happened on the second night?'

'I don't know,' Stine admitted. 'One night was enough for

26

me. It was probably enough for poor old Jesper, too. His dream of being the next Per Gundmann died that night.'

Carlyle looked at her blankly.

'Per Gundmann was a Danish actor,' Stine explained. 'Jesper wanted to be an artist, much to the annoyance of his parents.' She took a final drag on her smoke before flicking the stub over the balcony. Carlyle watched the tip flare against the night sky before disappearing into the street below. 'His father hated the fact that Jesper was an actor. He wanted him to go into the family insurance business.'

'Urgh,' Carlyle groaned, 'how boring. But I can understand – my folks weren't very happy about me joining the police.'

'Being a cop is a bit anti-social.'

'Anti-social?' It suddenly struck the inspector that he really knew very little about the woman who was looking after his father in his dying days. Perhaps some kind of anti-establishment radical lurked behind the hippie-ish façade.

'Well,' she said, 'not everyone likes cops, do they?'

Carlyle said nothing.

'People see the violence, the corruption and the abuse of power and they don't like it.'

'This is Britain,' he responded feebly. 'In my experience, most people respect the police. Or, at least, give them the benefit of the doubt, most of the time.'

Stine's eyes twinkled with amusement. 'That makes you the good cop, does it?'

'I'm just a cop,' Carlyle said. 'It's up to other people to decide whether I'm any good or not.'

'And your parents, what did they want you to do?'

'I dunno. Something that involved working in an office. Safe and secure. For their generation, I suppose, in their eyes, getting paid for sitting behind a desk and talking to people represented progress.'

'Living the middle-class dream.'

'Something like that.' Carlyle finally came up with a question that would move the conversation on to someone else. 'After you left Edinburgh, what happened to Jesper?'

'Now he is living a different dream.'

'His parents' dream, selling insurance?'

'Not exactly. After finishing his shows at the Edinburgh Festival, Jesper packed in acting and went home to Copenhagen. He took the job working for his dad. He sold the insurance business to a German company a few years ago and invested in a start-up company making games for mobile phones. You know, chopping up fruit or blowing up animals, the kind of thing people play while they're waiting for the bus to come. One of their games took off and they made billions. Now he's one of the richest businessmen in Denmark. His picture's in the paper just about every week.' She shook her head in disbelief. 'And to think, back then, the boy could barely manage to cross the road on his own.'

'Do you keep in touch? It's always useful to have friends in high places.'

'I haven't seen Jesper since that time in Edinburgh. We had a massive row after his first show and I dumped him. Or he dumped me. Or maybe it was a mutual decision. The details are a bit vague after all this time.'

'You should get in touch,' Carlyle suggested. 'Maybe he's sitting at home right now, counting his money, wondering how to find you.'

'Hardly. He's got the trophy wife – a blonde ex-skier – and four picture-perfect kids. He's definitely not thinking about me.'

'You never know.'

'Oh, I know. Anyway, more to the point, I'm not thinking about him.'

Oh, no? Carlyle mused. It sounds to me like you're not thinking about him quite a bit.

'Even all the way back then, it was obvious that the relationship was never going to work. I said to myself, "Stine, what are you doing sitting shivering in a damp basement in the middle of August, watching this rubbish? There's a whole world out there for you to explore." I packed up my stuff and hitchhiked down to London. I worked in a bar in Chelsea for a couple of months, scraped together enough cash for a flight to Ibiza and spent the next two years bumming around the Mediterranean.'

It all sounded far too adventurous for the inspector, who had never managed to find the time – or money – to bum his way around anywhere. 'You never made it to Glasgow, then?'

'No.' Stine reached for another smoke before thinking better of it. 'Edinburgh was enough of Scotland for me.'

'Well, you're not missing much,' the inspector observed. 'In many ways, Glasgow's just Edinburgh's poor relation. Back in the days of Queen Victoria, it liked to call itself "the second city of the British Empire". Since then, it's all been downhill. The city's glory days are long gone, and they ain't coming back.'

'Don't you feel a little bit Scottish?' Stine asked.

'No,' he said firmly. 'I'm a London boy. I was born just up the road from here and I've lived in the city all my life. I'd be lost anywhere else.'

'It's good to have a place called home, but you need to see the wider world.'

'London *is* the world.'

'I don't know about that,' Stine said. 'For sure, you won't know if you don't take a look.'

'You sound like my mother.' Carlyle didn't mean it as a compliment. Lorna Gordon (she had never abandoned her maiden name) had always been a difficult woman.

'Alexander told me about your mother.' Stine paused. 'What was it he said?'

Carlyle knew what was coming but he waited patiently for her to find the phrase.

'She wore the trousers.' She smiled. 'It is a nice form of words, I think.'

Not really. The idea of his father confiding in this Danish woman rankled momentarily. But, on the other hand, why shouldn't he? At least she was present for him to talk to.

'A strong woman.'

'Yes.'

'I think he liked that.'

'Perhaps.' Carlyle had never considered the possibility. As far as he could recall, his father had always seemed vaguely oppressed. 'The main thing was the divorce. It really disappointed him.'

Stine stuck out her lower lip. 'Disappointed. Yes, that's a good word. He is still quite sad about it.'

'He just didn't see the need for it. Not at their age. And then when Mum got herself a boyfriend, I think that really knocked the stuffing out of him.'

'Not that there's anything we can do about that.'

Carlyle glanced at his watch. Would Helen still be in her latest emergency meeting? He wanted to go home.

'What did you think about it?' Stine asked.

'Me?'

'It must have been upsetting.'

'Not really. I mean, it wasn't like I was a kid when it happened.'

'No, but even so, no one likes to see their parents split up.'

The truth was that Carlyle had never lost any sleep over either his father's infidelity or the subsequent divorce. 'I suppose I understood where my old man was coming from. I mean, it seemed fairly pointless, to be honest, breaking up over something that had happened decades earlier.'

'Alexander had an affair with a neighbour. That's what he said.'

'Yes, briefly. But my mother couldn't overlook it.'

'She divorced him on a point of principle.'

'Yes. But I don't see how that negates the fact that they had what I suppose you might call a successful marriage for such a long time, both before and after my old man played away.'

Stine gave him a quizzical look. 'Played away?'

'Before he had his fling with the neighbour,' Carlyle explained, glancing nervously over his shoulder, as if his father might somehow appear in the doorway to hear their conversation.

'Ah, yes.'

'Keeping a marriage together for almost your entire adult life is a hell of an achievement, on both sides. There are bound to be ups and downs.'

'I wouldn't really know.'

'They were both adults. It was up to them to sort it out among themselves. My mother was always one to stick to her guns once she had decided on something. I remember her telling me that she was going to get a divorce. There was never any suggestion that it was just posturing, I knew straight away that she would go and do it.' Carlyle gave a rueful grin. 'I inherited that determined streak from her – it's served me well in the Job.'

'Maybe your mother could have been a cop,' Stine speculated.

'I don't know about that.' Carlyle chuckled. 'I think maybe too many suspects might have fallen down the stairs in the police station. She would have beaten them black and blue.'

'Did she hit you? Or your father?'

'No, no,' Carlyle said hastily, 'nothing like that. With us, her sharp tongue was the thing.' Surprised by his willingness to talk, Carlyle made a conscious effort to shut up, letting his gaze drift into the middle distance. In the gloaming, he could just make out a couple of small boys kicking a football to each other as they made their way home across the park for some tea and perhaps an ear-bashing from a concerned mother. He recalled his father's desultory attempts at football back when he was a kid and there was no one else around to play with, the old fella refusing to go in goal and losing his rag whenever his son kicked the ball into the bushes. The bushes were long gone now, gardeners being a luxury that the local council had long since axed. Otherwise, the place hadn't really changed all that much over the decades; it certainly hadn't changed as much as he had.

'Has your father spoken to you about the funeral?'

'No.' Carlyle watched the boys reach the edge of the park and disappear between a row of parked cars.

'He wants a simple ceremony.'

'Sure.' Carlyle would deal with the details in due course. He didn't want to talk about it now.

'No Catholic priests.'

Carlyle thought back to his mother's funeral, the ceremony conducted by a priest who'd had no idea who she was. It was hardly the poor guy's fault but he might as well have been reading the eulogy from the back of a cereal packet. 'I'm with him on that one.'

Stine gestured inside. 'Maybe you would like to sit with him for a while.'

Not really. 'If he's asleep, I wouldn't want to wake him.'

'He's sleeping soundly.' Stine stifled a yawn. 'You can just be with him. It will let me go for a walk and get some air. I haven't been out of here all day. And I need to buy some more cigarettes.'

Unable to come up with any further objections, Carlyle slowly made his way to the old man's room. More than thirty years ago, it had been his own. After the divorce, Alexander had been unceremoniously kicked out of the family home. Returning after Lorna's death, he had decided to set up camp in the spare bedroom, rather than return to the marital bed.

A solitary lamp standing on the bedside table shone a weak light on the scene. Alexander, gaunt and unshaven, the duvet pulled tightly under his chin, was breathing evenly. A morphine drip hung from a stand, a tube running into the old man's arm.

What kind of dreams are you having? Carlyle wondered.

On the other side of the bed stood a chair redeployed from the kitchen. Taking a seat, Carlyle looked around the small space. The wallpaper hadn't been changed since he'd moved out. It was an early seventies brown and orange pattern that had probably acquired a sense of retro chic over the decades. In the gloom, the inspector imagined that he could just about make out the faded patches on the walls where a couple of Clash posters had hung, circa 1978. He heard the front door close as Stine went out in search of her cigarettes. Alexander did not stir.

SEVEN

High in the sky, the red light blinked twice. Flat on his back, Balthazar Quant licked his lips and blinked twice in reply. Three thousand feet above him, the plane, heading for an unheralded airport in Sweden, took no notice of his attempts at communication as it slid from view.

Trying to assess his surroundings, Balthazar let his head fall to one side. It appeared that he was lying at the bottom of a concrete-lined circular tunnel something like twenty metres deep and five in diameter. There were a couple of hard hats and various pieces of drilling equipment. A crumpled Coke can lay near a discarded copy of the *Sun*. A set of temporary stairs offered a theoretical means of escape.

Building works. The shaft would be part of the new railway station, a hub for the new train line that was expected to cost London's taxpayers a chunky fifteen billion pounds, even before the latest bail-out. At least they're not going to bury me in the foundations, Balthazar reflected dolefully, seeing as they were completed years ago.

Somewhere off to his left came the sound of shuffling feet, followed by the ominous sound of metal on concrete, a length of piping being tapped gently against the wall. 'I should have been in St James's by now,' said an irritated voice. 'I've got to go and pick up my new Ting Sasse print.'

Is the bastard complaining because I'm interrupting his shopping schedule? Balthazar tried to push himself up on his

33

elbows but all his strength had fled. Too exhausted to panic, he made a mental inventory of the injuries he had sustained: one leg fractured, a dislocated thumb, various badly bruised or even broken ribs, blurred vision in one eye, two lost teeth. He spat a gobbet of blood onto his shirt and took a succession of shallow breaths. 'I have money.' He slowly manoeuvred his head, better to see the two men standing over him. The pain was excruciating and he had to bite hard into the lining of his mouth to stop himself fainting. 'My bonus,' he rasped, 'it's just been paid.' That was a lie: Gerry Durkan wouldn't place the money in his account for another month, at least, but what did he have to lose? He added a couple of zeros for good measure. 'Seven figures.'

There was a pause before his attackers conferred in a language Balthazar didn't recognise. Their conversation lasted maybe a minute before the smaller man stepped closer.

'Seven figures,' Balthazar repeated. A wave of nausea washed over him and he started to gag.

The small man took a jump backwards. 'Don't puke on my damn shoes, you total thieving bastard.'

'I didn't steal anything,' Balthazar gasped, waiting for the nausea to pass. 'I have money. You can have it all.'

'This is not about money,' the man snapped.

'It's always about money.' Balthazar's voice was barely more than a whisper.

'Not this time. Not any longer.'

'But it's always about money.' Balthazar sobbed. 'I was going to buy a Maserati.'

'I have to get my print.' Speaking to his giant goon, the small man with the scarred face retreated towards the ladder. 'And you've got that other thing to attend to, don't forget.'

What other thing? Balthazar felt outraged. Here he was, facing a brutal end, and his killers were just limbering up for the rest of their evening. He wasn't even going to be the main event at his own death. 'Wait,' he croaked.

The only reply was the sound of the boss man slowly ascending the steps. Near the top, he paused, before issuing a final instruction: 'Finish him.'

EIGHT

Melody Rainbow sat at the breakfast bar, playing with her mobile phone. 'I didn't know you were going to make dinner,' she lied, not caring about the obvious petulance in her voice.

Martin Grom looked up from the green pepper he had been carefully chopping into thin slices. 'Am I taking too long with the preparations?' The professor pushed his glasses further up his nose. 'Or perhaps you have eaten already.'

'No.' Melody put down the phone and reached for the glass of white wine in front of her. Tentatively she brought the glass to her mouth, barely letting the alcohol coat her lips. Normally, she liked to get drunk – or, at least, quite tipsy – when she was working. Tonight, however, that wouldn't be such a good idea. The matter of her overdue essay on the Yarlung Dynasty was still causing her stress. Melody told herself that she really would have to come up with three and a half thousand vaguely relevant words in the morning and a hangover most certainly wouldn't help.

Getting through the night sober wasn't going to be easy either. Melody looked at the wine and then at the old guy hunched over the chopping board. He had to be seventy if he was a day. So much for her freshly minted no-over-forty-fives rule. Once again, Karen Jansen had talked her into doing something she didn't want to do. The woman was a total witch. Melody wondered why she couldn't stand up for herself. She thought of the second-hand paperback she'd bought for two quid from a stall in

Camden Market. It was the title that had grabbed her attention – *How to Say 'No' and Get Other People to Do the Dirty Work Instead.* She really should read it soon.

A television screen on the wall to her left was showing a football match with the sound down. Melody reached for the remote, which was sitting on top of a bunch of bananas in a fruit bowl on the bar. 'Do you like football?' It was the kind of conversational gambit that was standard in her line of work. Clients who appeared unable to string two words together could usually manage a five-minute conversation about the latest comings and goings in the Premier League. Apart from the Americans.

'Not really.'

So much for that. 'Do you mind if I change the TV channel?'

Grom didn't look up. 'Go ahead.'

'You're not watching the game?'

'Not at all.' Grom waved at the TV with his knife. 'I just have it for company . . . usually. Be my guest.'

'Thanks.' Melody began aimlessly flicking through the channels. Despite being totally ancient – and unable to talk about football – she had to admit that Professor Grom didn't seem so bad, relative to most punters. A small, dapper man with badly dyed hair and gold-rimmed glasses, he appeared desperate to please her and, more importantly, he smelled okay. Melody never ceased to be shocked and disappointed by the poor personal hygiene of so many of her clients. Grom's cleanliness marked him out as a true gentleman.

Gentleman or not, he seemed surprisingly nervous for someone who, according to Jansen, was one of Vernon Holder's long-time clients. The professor had already worked his way through half the bottle of Pinot Grigio and Melody hoped there had to be a good chance he would fall asleep before they ever got to the business part of the evening.

Unable to find anything interesting on the TV, she switched it off and returned the remote to the bowl.

'It's all rubbish, isn't it?' Grom finished slicing the pepper, scooped up the pieces and transferred them to a heated frying pan on the ceramic hob. 'Stir-fried vegetables,' he said, as the pepper pieces began to sizzle in the heated oil. 'Is that all right for you?'

'Sure.' Melody shrugged. If the old guy wanted to pay her to watch him cook, that was fine by her. She wasn't going to point out that she didn't really eat that much. Her diet rarely stretched beyond tomato soup, chocolate chip cookies and the odd hamburger or sandwich. Still, her extensive skill set meant that she could manage to move a few vegetables around her plate for a while, if circumstances demanded it.

Grom gave the peppers a stir and carefully turned down the heat under the pan. 'Are you hungry?'

'A little, maybe.' Trying to forget about her essay, Melody gulped a mouthful of wine. Perhaps she'd get pissed after all. Placing the glass next to her phone, she slipped off the stool and padded over to the window in her bare feet. 'Nice view.' She pointed across the rooftops towards the river. In the distance, you could make out the London Eye, lit up against the night sky.

'Yes.' Grom set about attacking a selection of carrots. 'The view is one of the best things about the flat. When I first saw it, I thought, This is the place for me. At the time, it was some way above my budget but the view sold it.'

'Hm.'

'That was almost forty years ago, now. I've been here ever since.'

Drifting over to a bookcase, Melody found herself looking at a faded photograph in a silver frame. It showed a Japanese woman standing in front of the Eiffel Tower on a summer's day. She was holding a guidebook and smiling into the camera.

'Who's this?'

'Who?' Looking up from his carrots, Grom squinted over the top of his glasses.

Melody held up the photograph. 'The lady in the picture.'

A look of embarrassment passed over the old man's face. 'That's Mika. She was my wife.'

'Was?' Melody raised an eyebrow. 'Are you guys divorced?'

Grom went back to his chopping. 'She's dead.'

'Oh.' Putting the picture carefully back on the shelf, Melody began studying the rows of books, all university texts of one sort or another.

'It happened a long time ago.' Dropping the carrots into the pan, Grom added some more oil.

'And you didn't remarry?'

'No.'

'No kids?'

'No.'

'It must be lonely.'

'Sometimes.'

'I can imagine.' She caught a glimpse of the professor's name on the spine of one of the books. Carefully taking it from the shelf, she scanned the blurb on the back cover: Sustainability: A Beginner's Guide *gives an introduction to the interdisciplinary field of sustainability. The focus is on equipping the student with the necessary conceptual understanding to enable them to develop effective solutions for the workplace.*

Stifling a yawn, Melody held up the tome. 'Did you write this?'

Grom gave her a smile. 'That's one of mine, yes. But I've written a few others.'

'How many?'

'Let me see,' Grom waved his knife airily. 'Four . . . No, five – if you include one that I co-edited.'

That doesn't seem very many, Melody thought, for a whole career, four and a bit books. 'Wow,' she said, 'that's cool.'

'Vernon tells me you're studying at SOAS. Maybe you'll write a book one day.'

'Maybe. I don't know about that.' Putting the book in its place, Melody took a step backwards, trying to work out the total number of titles on the shelves. 'You have so many books. Hundreds.'

Grom went back to his chopping. 'I've never counted them but, yes, I suppose that there are quite a lot.'

'Have you read all of them?'

'Just about. I don't like the idea of buying a book and not reading it. That seems like an insult to the author, don't you think?'

Melody had no idea. She returned to the stool. 'Don't you have a Kindle?'

Grom gestured vaguely towards the far side of the room. 'I do, but I don't really use it all that much.'

'You could hold all these books on a single tablet,' Melody observed, 'and much more besides.'

'I suppose so,' Grom agreed. 'But I just prefer to hold a physical book. It's a generational thing, I suppose.'

'But why do you keep them all?' Reaching for her wine, she emptied the glass in two quick gulps.

'I'm sorry?' Grom refilled her glass.

'Why don't you get rid of them? I mean, if you're only going to read them once. They take up so much space.'

'Some I've read more than once.' Grom recharged his own glass and took a mouthful. 'And some are textbooks I use for work.'

'But you're retired, right?'

'I retired more than a decade ago.'

'I don't think I would keep them if I was finished with them.'

'I like having them around. They comfort me.'

'One of my other clients said reading a book is like fucking a woman. There's no point keeping them once you've finished.'

Grom looked at her blankly.

'He says we live in a society where everything is disposable. You should use it once and throw it away.'

'Well, I suppose, erm, that's an interesting point of view.'

'He never hired the same girl twice.'

'No?'

'I certainly saw him only the one time.' It was a simple lie. The client did not exist; Melody had lifted the line from a film she had gone to see with Chris. Taking a break from his usual multiplex fare of space monsters and comic-book heroes, her boyfriend had made a bid for sophistication, insisting that they see a subtitled foreign film at an arthouse cinema in Notting Hill. Melody had squirmed in her seat when she had realised the story involved a student moonlighting as an escort. Chris, unaware of how closely art was imitating life, had sat drinking his beer, trying to pretend he was interested in the bits between the sex scenes.

'Did he have any books?'

'What?'

'Your other client. Did he have any books in his house?'

Melody thought about it for a moment. 'No,' she said finally. 'At least, I didn't see any while I was there. Well, maybe there was a big book of photographs on the coffee-table but that was it.' She mimed thinking some more. 'He had some nice pictures, though.'

'I remember reading an interview with a film director a few years ago.' Grom mentioned a name that meant nothing to Melody. 'He said something to the effect that if you go home with someone and find out they don't have any books, you should make your excuses and leave.'

Now it was her turn to look at him blankly.

'The idea,' Grom explained, 'was that you shouldn't sleep with anyone who doesn't read.'

'Yeah, right.' Melody thought about it for a moment. 'That's not such a great rule, these days, unless you want to be, like, totally celibate all the time.'

'You may be right,' Grom conceded. 'I'm glad that my teaching days are over. In my last twenty years at the university, I rarely found any students who were genuinely interested in learning.'

'I am,' said Melody, earnestly. 'I have a passion for my subject.'

41

'Good for you. Most of my students seemed just to be sliding through, using the degree as a stepping stone towards a job, a mortgage and a car.'

'I have to work hard to pay for my studies,' Melody told him. 'It's not a game for me.'

'No, no.' Grom turned off the hob. 'Anyway, the food is nearly ready.'

Melody tried to look enthusiastic. 'Before we eat, can I have a look at the rest of the flat? You never showed me around.'

Grom gestured towards the passageway leading to the back. 'Help yourself. I'll just set the table.'

NINE

Grom stood in the doorway to the bedroom, glass of wine in hand, contemplating the various items of clothing and under-clothing scattered on the floor. 'What're you doing?' His confusion seemed genuine.

From under the duvet, Melody gave him a sheepish grin. 'The bed just looked so nice and comfortable. I'm very tired.' A theatrical yawn underscored the point. 'And I've got a really tough day tomorrow.'

'But I've made dinner,' the professor proclaimed. 'Stir-fried vegetables with rice. It's on the table.'

'I know, I'm sorry. It was a very nice thing to do. I'm not used to people spoiling me like that but I'm not really hungry. Plus, it's never such a great idea to eat so late. I hate going to sleep feeling bloated, don't you?'

'You could have tried a little of what I made.' Grom leaned against the doorframe. 'You look so thin, you have to eat something.'

Melody giggled. 'There is plenty of flesh on my bones.' Pushing back the duvet, she let him see for himself.

Grom blushed but did not look away. 'I thought we would eat,' he said quietly, 'and talk. Am I too boring for a little din-ner-table conversation?'

'No, not at all. It's just that I'm exhausted. You know what it's like. Conversation can be such hard work when you're tired.'

'I'm interested in your studies.' Grom sipped his wine. 'What you think about the university.' He waved his glass in front of his face. 'The quality of the teaching, that sort of thing.'

'The teaching is very good.' Acting on autopilot, Melody let a hand slip between her legs.

The professor ran his tongue along his bottom lip.

'We can always eat afterwards.' Melody nodded in the direction of the kitchen. 'Why don't you go and get the rest of the wine?'

TEN

Sitting in his living room, Carlyle poked at the brochure on the coffee-table with his toe. 'Oxford University?' Having finally made it back from Fulham, the inspector had been looking forward to vegging out in front of the television. Instead, he found himself plunged into a detailed conversation about Alice's evolving university plans. 'When did she decide that she wanted to go there?'

Beside him on the sofa, Helen cradled a mug of white tea. 'She hasn't *decided* that she wants to go anywhere yet.'

'I stand corrected,' Carlyle said sourly.

'But she's *thinking* about PPE.'

'Politics, philosophy and economics.' Carlyle snorted. 'The degree of the useless ruling classes.'

'Don't be such an inverted snob.' Helen gave him a gentle poke.

'Me? Never. It's just that it's so – I dunno, it seems such a *boring* choice.' Secretly, he hoped that his daughter would decide on a London university. And stay at home. He was in no hurry to see his only child fly the nest. Such an arrangement should be easier on his wallet, too.

'Well, I think it's a good idea,' Helen declared. 'Oxford is the best place you could do PPE. Just be happy that Alice isn't thinking of going to somewhere further away, like . . .' she groped for somewhere suitably northern '. . . Newcastle.'

'Don't worry about that,' Carlyle deadpanned. 'I don't think they even have universities up there.'

'You're just a bag of random prejudices,' Helen scolded him.

'Not at all. It's just that I take a very metropolitan point of view.' He waved a hand in the air. 'Why would anyone move from *here* to *there*?'

'Well, at the end of the day, it'll be Alice's choice. And, dear me, there's certainly a lot of choice. What are you going to do if she decides she wants to go abroad?'

'Abroad?'

'You never know, she could end up with a scholarship to an American university, or something like that.'

Carlyle's heart sank. Did they really have to discuss this now?

'Anyway, it's good that she's starting to think about what she wants to do.'

'Sure.'

'I'd get behind the PPE idea, if I was you. It could be a lot worse.'

'I know,' Carlyle moaned. 'But how much is Oxford gonna cost? You've gotta be loaded to go there. It's okay if your dad's a lord or an oligarch or something, but I'm just a cop.' Glancing in the direction of Alice's bedroom, he lowered his voice. 'How would we afford it?'

Helen gave him a consoling pat on the knee. 'Don't worry, Officer. If it comes to it, we'll sort it out.'

'Easy to say.'

'She can get a student loan.'

'And be in debt for the rest of her life?' Carlyle was genuinely appalled at the prospect.

'It might not come to that,' Helen suggested. 'I talked to Alexander about it a while ago. He'll help us out.'

'Which should cover the cost of a notepad and a couple of biros,' Carlyle scoffed.

'That's not very nice,' she scolded. 'Your father wants to support Alice.'

'Good for him,' Carlyle huffed, 'but the old bugger doesn't have two beans to his name.'

'I wouldn't say that. He might not be the Duke of Westminster, but Alexander was always careful with his money.'

'Tight old sod.'

'John, for God's sake.' Helen smacked his arm.

'Ow.'

'You need to get a grip on yourself. What is wrong with you tonight? Why're you in such a terrible mood?'

'Well, come on, face the facts. It's not like we'll be sitting round rubbing our hands, waiting for the will to be read, is it?' He pushed the university brochure further away. 'For all I know, he hasn't even got a will.'

'He has.'

'Oh?' Carlyle raised an eyebrow, suddenly curious. 'And how do you know?'

'Like I said, we discussed it a while back.'

'He didn't talk to me about it.'

An amused smirk crept across Helen's face. 'I think Alexander thought I would be a better bet when it came to dealing with money matters.'

'Oh, he did, did he?' Although irked, Carlyle knew that was a perfectly reasonable assumption. Helen had always managed the family finances with a mixture of planning and prudence that had always proved beyond her husband. 'And you're only telling me this now? Just as he's about to snuff it?'

'You know what it's like. The conversation was overtaken by events. And you were fairly busy at the time.'

'I'm always busy.'

'In fact,' Helen chortled, 'you might even have been in jail at the time.'

'I was wrongfully detained,' Carlyle reminded her. 'As you know, once things were sorted out, I got a formal letter of apology from some assistant deputy commissioner or other.'

'And an M&S voucher,' Helen reminded him, 'for fifty quid.'

If Carlyle remembered correctly, Helen had used the voucher

to buy him some new underpants, along with various other essentials. 'It was a nice gesture.'

'It was a cynical ploy by your employer to stop you suing them.'

'Yes, well, it worked. I always was a cheap date.'

'Anyway,' Helen returned to the matter in hand, 'Alexander *has* made a will. And he and I went over the details.' She gestured towards the kitchen. 'I've got a copy in one of the drawers. There's another with his solicitor in Fulham.'

'Let's hope there's enough to cover the legal fees, then.'

Helen ignored his snide remark. 'It's all very straightforward. Everything goes to us, in trust for Alice, to be used for her education. Anything that is left over, she gets when she graduates.'

'Anything that's left over?' Carlyle looked at his wife suspiciously. 'How much are we talking about?'

Helen mentioned a surprisingly large sum. 'It's already been transferred into a bank account that I'll have control over once the will is executed.'

'Bloody hell,' Carlyle spluttered. 'Where did the cash come from? The old man didn't have a sideline knocking off sub-post offices that I didn't know about, did he?'

'Like I said, he was careful with his money. So was your mother for that matter. When did you ever see them spend any on themselves? They never went on holiday. Not even to Brighton for the day.'

'Looks like I did the poor old bugger a disservice,' the inspector conceded. He turned the numbers over in his head. 'It won't cover the cost of a PPE degree, though.'

'No, but then there's the flat.'

'The flat?' Carlyle pondered this latest piece of the puzzle. 'Doesn't that go back to the council?'

Smiling, Helen shook her head. 'Nope. Your parents took advantage of the right-to-buy scheme.'

'They bought it?'

'Just after you left home. They had a small mortgage but that got paid off a while ago when your dad inherited some money from your grandma.'

Carlyle scratched behind his ear. 'They never mentioned any of this to me.'

'I don't think they liked talking about money,' Helen observed. 'It's a generational thing. My parents were pretty much the same. It was considered rude, boastful.'

'Ah, well, I suppose it's better to be surprised in the upside.' Carlyle wondered how much an ex-council flat in Fulham might sell for. Quite a lot, he concluded, even in the current sticky market.

'Obviously, it will take a while to sell the place,' Helen continued, 'but we've got time.'

The inspector suddenly brought himself up short. 'All this talk about money, isn't it a bit mercenary? I mean, the poor old sod isn't even dead yet.'

'It's just one of those things you have to sort out.' Helen shrugged. 'There's lots of paperwork when someone dies – no reason to be squeamish about it.'

'I suppose.'

'The same will happen to us, in due course.'

'That's a happy thought.'

'Like I said, Alexander wanted to leave as few loose ends as possible. I think it's very commendable of him.'

'Yes.' Carlyle bit his lower lip as he thought back to earlier in the evening – his father, breathing evenly, dreaming his drug-fuelled dreams in Carlyle's childhood bedroom. Hopefully the old man was long past worrying about loose ends.

'Dying is an art, like everything else,' Helen said cryptically.

'I suppose it is.'

'Alexander's done it exceptionally well.'

'He's not dead yet.'

'You know what I mean. Alexander's done well by us on this. Other people wouldn't have bothered. They'd just have left their mess behind.'

49

'You're right, of course,' Carlyle agreed. 'I'm sure it'll make things a lot easier over the next few . . . when it happens.'

'I hope you're as organised, when the time comes.'

'Erm, yes.' Carlyle didn't want to think about his own demise, or the associated paperwork.

'I mean, it's so complicated. Your dad was sorry he didn't think about things earlier. With a bit of planning, we could maybe have avoided inheritance tax.'

'What?' Carlyle's eyes grew wide. 'You mean we're going to end up having to pay inheritance tax? How much has the old bugger salted away?'

'Maybe a little,' Helen said. 'It depends how much the flat goes for.'

For a moment, Carlyle was speechless. 'Bloody hell,' he said finally, 'who'd have thought it?'

ELEVEN

The news from the Emerald Downs racetrack was disappointing. Candystripe, the supposed ringer, had faded badly in the final furlong, finishing out of the places. A glance at the balance of his online account suggested the evening's gambling had left him out of pocket to the tune of a decent weekend break in Cap Ferrat. As he checked out the day's remaining racing, Gerry Durkan consoled himself with the fact that he was still slightly ahead for the year to date.

Finding nothing else worth a punt, Durkan – ever conscious of the need for proper cyber security – carefully logged out of his account and switched off his computer. Apropos nothing, it crossed his mind that Delia, his mutton-dressed-as-lamb PA, would probably be totally pissed by now, sitting in a booth at the Red Chihuahua bar with her tongue down the throat of an equally intoxicated intern of barely half her age. He really should be thinking about getting a new assistant.

He reached for the tumbler of single malt on his desk and took a healthy mouthful, letting the spirit linger in the back of his throat for several seconds before swallowing. Never mind Delia, he was feeling fairly pissed himself. Looking at his watch, he let out a low groan. Rose was hosting one of her soirées this evening, introducing a French installation artist she patronised to some potential clients, and he was way past late.

'Installation artist?' He raised his glass in a mock salute. 'We never had those in my day.' As with Delia, he wondered how it was that he was still lumbered with Rose. When it came to women, he was just too soft. The truth was he should have traded them both in years ago. A man of his standing and resources should have a stunning PA. And, just as important, he should be wandering round town with a twenty-something model on his arm, hobnobbing with Russian oligarchs at exclusive parties and getting his picture in the party pages of *ES* magazine. Instead, he found himself growing old with a woman who had been spending his money and generally driving him crazy for more than three decades.

Somehow, Rose Murray had become his life partner on a journey that had taken him from the alleyways of Belfast, via the Grand Hotel in Brighton and Long Kesh, to the thirty-first floor of Thatcher Tower No. 1. Not such a great distance in miles, perhaps, but a hell of a long way in every other sense. On the other hand, Gerry Durkan wasn't a man for regrets and he certainly wasn't going to regret his relationship with Rose. To be fair to the old girl, she had stood by him while he languished in prison. Such loyalty, in his experience, was unique.

Reaching for the whisky bottle, he refreshed his glass. One more drink and then he would head off to his club for dinner. If the place had any rooms free, he'd crash there for the night – he could always concoct some story about troublesome American clients keeping him in the office late. As long as the party went well, and her pet artist came away with a few commissions, Rose wouldn't miss him.

The landline on his desk started to ring. Durkan looked at it suspiciously. Not many people knew the number. And those who did knew better than to call so late. If that's Balthazar bloody Quant, he thought, reaching for the handset, crying for more money, I might just sack the little wanker on the spot.

'Look, Balthazar. I told you earlier—'

'Mr Quant is indisposed.'

The voice at the end of the line had a sobering effect. Durkan sat up straight in his chair. 'Indisposed?'

'That's right.' The crackle might have been static . . . or a dry chuckle. 'I hope you haven't actually paid out his bonus yet.'

'No.'

Silence.

'Why do you ask?'

'Suffice to say, the poor fellow won't be needing the money now.'

'He won't?' Durkan tried to process this information.

'That's the good news. I've saved you a seven-figure sum there.'

Seven figures? What seven figures? Durkan slowly realised that wasn't the right question. 'If that's the good news,' he asked warily, 'what's the bad news?'

This time he definitely heard a giggle. 'The bad news is that you won't be needing it, either.'

TWELVE

Standing at the bottom of shaft L16, Bartosz Bereszynski pulled on a pair of protective goggles. The sooner you started, the sooner you finished. That's what Bartosz's father had always said, God rest the old man's soul. The construction worker crossed himself. He didn't feel on top of his game. If it wasn't for the fact that his previous absenteeism already had him on the management's 'amber' watch-list, he would have called in sick and stayed in bed. What did the locals call it? A duvet day.

The previous evening had turned into something of a session. While some of the boys, heading back to Poland on holiday, would be sleeping off their hangovers on the flight home, Bartosz was facing the misery of an eight-hour shift shotcreting the walls of the ventilation shaft. Six beers and a couple of double vodkas were not conducive to a six for-ty-five a.m. start. Neither was Nico, the crazy Dutchman who had been paired with him for the job. A gangly youth from a town called Uden, he claimed to be twenty-five but looked about fourteen. Aside from a chronic addiction to Gladstone cigarettes and Motörhead, Nico had no known vices. Staying with an aunt in Camden Town, he always seemed to arrive for work ten minutes early. Worse, he invariably had a smile on his face.

Standing on an elevated metal platform about three metres above the floor of the shaft, Nico zipped up his boiler suit and looked down at his co-worker. 'Big night, was it?'

'I've had worse,' Bartosz grunted, fiddling with his ear protectors.

'Are you ready to go? We're already behind schedule.'

Bartosz glared at his partner. Why don't you come down here and do the hard work? And I can stand up there, pressing buttons and generally doing bugger-all.

'We're supposed to have this whole shaft done by the end of the day,' Nico reminded him.

'All right, all right.' Bartosz pulled the protectors over his ears and stepped up to the spraying machine.

'Don't forget I must be out of here on time – I've got my programming class tonight.'

Fuck your class. Bartosz couldn't care less that Nico was training to become a software engineer. The last thing the world needed was another IT geek.

'Ready?'

Bartosz grabbed the hose and waved it in the direction of the grinning Dutchman. 'Okay, let's go.'

'All right.' Nico smacked a green button on the control panel. There was a momentary silence followed by the growl of the mixer-pump struggling into action. Bartosz pointed the nozzle off to his left. 'Start further over,' Nico shouted, above the angry noise of the cement mixer's motor.

'Fuck off,' Bartosz muttered, doing as he was told. If nothing else, the boy would get the job done as quickly as possible. As the liquid concrete began to emerge from the machine, he directed the spray over the wall in a smooth, steady arc.

'Hey, hold on. Stop a second.' Almost as quickly as it had started, the flow of concrete had dwindled to a dribble.

Bartosz looked up at the platform. 'What the hell are you playing at? I was just getting going.'

'There's something there.' Nico pointed at the spot Bartosz had just been spraying.

Dropping the hose, Bartosz stepped over to the wall and dropped onto his haunches. The concrete had already started to set, but the tips of two fingers could clearly be seen sticking out about half a metre from the base of the shaft. Extending an arm, Bartosz cautiously began prodding around the area.

There was the sound of boots on metal steps before Nico appeared at his shoulder. 'Is it a body?' Bartosz could hear the excitement in his voice. 'Should I call the control centre?'

Bartosz stood up and backed away from the wall. 'Take a look.'

Falling to one knee, Nico reached out and cautiously prodded at one of the fingers. 'Aw, I thought—'

'You've read too many crime books.' Bartosz snorted. 'Someone just left their glove there.' He skipped over to the stairs and headed up to the platform. 'Anyway, let's get back to work. You can do some shotcreting for a while and I'll press the buttons.'

'But—'

'Keep an eye out for any more bodies.' Bartosz smirked.

'It was an honest mistake.' Blushing, Nico reached for the hose.

'Those are the worst kind.' Waiting for the boy to take up his position, Bartosz smacked the start button. The cement mixer once again rumbled into action.

After another moment, it fell silent.

Damn, what now? Bartosz scanned the control panel, finally deciding to give the start button another thump.

The machine gave him no response.

'There's no concrete,' Nico shouted up, stating the obvious. 'What's wrong?'

'No idea.' Pulling off his ear protectors, Bartosz skipped back down the steps of the platform. The mixer consisted of a hopper, a small inverted pyramid, mounted on the back of a trailer, next to a motor-driven pump. It had been winched down to the bottom of the shaft yesterday and was due to be taken out tonight once the job had been completed.

Jumping up onto the frame of the trailer, Bartosz peered inside the hopper and gasped. 'Holy shit, Nico. Come and look at this.'

THIRTEEN

Why did I ever return to work? Alison Roche stared at the raindrops landing in a puddle at her feet. From somewhere above her head came the sound of hearty laughter. I'm glad someone finds this funny, the sergeant thought morosely. On her feet all day, her back ached and her legs felt like lead. After the best part of a year at home, looking after her baby, being back on the Job was beyond exhausting. Checking the time on her phone, Roche muttered a curse. Unless she suddenly developed the ability to fly like Superman, she was never going to make it to the nursery in time for a lunchtime pick-up. It was time to call – or, rather, text – for back-up.

Stuck at the bottom of a big hole (literally). Can you pick up David? xx

She barely had time to send the message before the scowling figure of Detective Inspector Jay Wrench appeared in front of her. 'Not interrupting anything, am I?'

'Not at all.' Roche took a step backwards, trying to escape Wrench's eye-watering body odour.

'Good.' Wrench pointed towards two workmen sitting on a couple of upturned plastic crates on the far side of the ventilation shaft. Smoking cigarettes, they were chatting away in a language Roche didn't immediately recognise. 'Those two found the body.' He headed for the stairs. 'Take their statements and meet me back at the station.'

'My half-shift ends in less than half an hour.' Roche felt the words die in her mouth as Wrench, profoundly disinterested, began climbing towards ground level. She was already wearily familiar with the detective inspector's motto: *You chose the Job, the Job didn't choose you.* They had been almost the first words out of his mouth when she'd arrived at Limehouse police station. That had been the second day after she'd returned from maternity leave. On day one, Roche had turned up at her home shop, Charing Cross, to find a memo from HR informing her that she was being reassigned to Docklands, on maternity cover. Not amused in the slightest, she had tried to complain – first to HR, then to her erstwhile boss, the rather temperamental Inspector John Carlyle and, finally, to their ultimate boss, Commander Carole Simpson. It had been a futile exercise. No one in HR ever answered the phone and neither Carlyle nor Simpson could be found. The commander was rumoured to be on a Women in Policing course, probably about the hundredth she had taken during her career. Carlyle, meanwhile, was 'out on a case'.

Wherever he was, Carlyle still wasn't answering his phone. 'Nice to know some things don't change,' Roche muttered, before leaving the inspector another voicemail that she knew would probably never be listened to and would certainly never be answered.

In the absence of any further avenues of appeal, the sergeant had reluctantly presented herself for duty at Limehouse – a posting that helpfully added more than an hour to her daily commute – and found herself placed at the disposal of the oleaginous Wrench. For the first few days, the shifts had run to time, allowing her to pick up baby David from his nursery. Today, though, some bloke had been found stuffed into a concrete mixer and all bets were off.

Feeling profoundly sorry for herself, Roche fought back a sob as a chirp from her pocket indicated an incoming text: No worries, leaving now. Will work from home this afternoon X

'Yay. Good old Alex.' Roche could have cried with gratitude. Who would have thought that David's dad would turn out to be such a responsible adult? When Roche had first decided that she wanted a kid, Alex Morrow, a lawyer with the Police Federation, was a semi-regular squeeze, not high on the list of potential fathers. In the event, however, Alex had stepped up to the plate, so to speak, before, during and after the birth. Where Roche had always envisaged becoming a single parent, it quickly became apparent that the three of them were evolving into a proper little family unit.

Thx x

Putting her game face back on, the sergeant stepped over to the two workmen. 'Right,' she said briskly, 'maybe you guys can tell me what happened here.'

FOURTEEN

From the thirty-first floor, Gerry Durkan couldn't see the street-level crime scene in any detail. He could, however, make out the police cordon, ringed by a collection of vans, ID numbers visible on their roofs. A concentration of police anywhere nearby still made him feel a tad nervous.

As he watched the ants below, Durkan's mind wandered back several decades. The MacDermott Arms in Kilburn had been a regular haunt in his previous life. The day the TSG had turned up wanting a word was one he would never forget, however many lives he managed to get through.

The MacDermott Arms was a real no-nonsense, sawdust-on-the-floor, females-by-invitation-only type of place, the kind of old-fashioned establishment that was long gone, in London at least. For their part, the Territorial Support Group, despite numerous complaints over the years, was still going strong. The TSG was the heavy mob, specialising in 'public order containment', otherwise known as riot control. And if there wasn't a riot to control, the TSG would happily start one.

'It was like the fucking Alamo.' Durkan's mouth curled into a crooked smile as he recalled for the thousandth time how he'd escaped arrest, not to mention a monster shoeing, sneaking out through the pub's toilets. Coming out of a back alley, he had strolled past all the police vans lined up along the road, arse cheeks tightly clenched together as his heart threatened to explode out of his chest. Even now, the memory of it gave him a discernible buzz.

'I walked right past you wankers,' he crowed, 'right as you burst through the front door.'

'What?' The trip down Memory Lane was ended by Delia's appearance.

'Nothing,' he stammered. 'Just talking to myself.'

'Oh.' She placed a cup of tea on his desk.

A bit early for you to be in, isn't it? Durkan wondered. It's not even midday yet. The woman didn't look as grey around the gills as he would have expected. Last night must have been a bit of a damp squib.

'I thought you might like something to drink.' Delia pointed at the cup as she took a step back from the desk. 'And your lunch has just cancelled.'

Not moving from the window, Durkan frowned. 'Who was it with?'

Delia mentioned a less than important client.

'That's a relief. He's a right boring old sod. All he ever talks about is how he should never have ditched his second wife because she took him to the cleaners in the divorce courts.'

Delia had heard it all before. 'Shall I order something in?' she asked.

Durkan patted his stomach. Where had all the padding come from? One less business lunch had to be a good thing as far as his waistline was concerned. 'Maybe just a salad.'

'All right.'

'And some pasta.' Man cannot live by lettuce leaves alone. 'And maybe some of that carrot cake I like.' Order given, Durkan pointed at the window. 'What's going on down there? Is it a bomb?' Occasionally he would have a flashback to the Twin Towers and wonder about the wisdom of being so high up. On the other hand, Thatcher Tower No. 1 had gone up post-9/11: building regulations had been tightened and the chance of some terrorist being able to take it down had to be minimal. Blowing shit up was harder than it looked – he should know. Indeed, if he had made a better job of sending Mrs T into space, the sky-scraper he was now standing in would probably have a different name. 'It's gotta be some kind of terrorism alert, I'd've thought.'

Delia stepped over to the window and took a cursory peek. 'I don't think so. They were still letting people in and out of the building a couple of minutes ago. The security staff haven't said anything.'

'Get Camila to find out what's going on.' Camila Steinbrecher was Macroom Castlebar Salle's head of operations, the security chief. A recent hire from the Portuguese military intelligence service, Durkan hadn't yet decided if she was any good or not. Either way, he was hoping that the woman would at least stick around longer than her predecessors. For some reason, most of the ex-cops and former spooks who ended up in the private sector never seemed to stay for more than a few months.

Delia padded towards the door.

'And get me Balthazar, will you?'

'I haven't seen him this morning.'

That's probably because you've only just got in yourself.

'He's not been at his desk,' Delia added, as if reading his thoughts.

'No?' The bugger's probably throwing a sickie, Durkan told himself, still crying about the size of his bloody bonus.

'No one's seen him.'

Durkan recalled the unwelcome telephone call from the night before and felt a vague sense of unease. 'He's probably in a meet-ing somewhere,' he said, more for his benefit than Delia's. 'See if you can track him down for me. Tell him I want to see him in here ASAP.'

FIFTEEN

Nooooo. Catching a glimpse of the red numbers on the small travel clock sitting on the bedside table, Melody Rainbow leaped from the bed and began recovering her clothes. 'That can't be right,' she muttered to herself, wiping the sleep from her eyes. 'It's impossible.'

If the clock was indeed right, it was almost lunchtime. She must have slept for something like twelve hours. I must have been really, really tired, Melody thought. Maybe I should think about a holiday. Pulling on her shirt, she thought about booking a late-afternoon flight to Barcelona, or maybe Ibiza, heading straight to the airport and just forgetting about London for a while. That sounded good until she remembered her overdue essay. Letting out a small cry, she contemplated the effort required to come up with three thousand five hundred words on the Yarlung Dynasty. A feeling of hopelessness washed over her. If she didn't get the essay done today, she could flunk the entire term. So far, Melody had always managed to scrape through without having to retake any of her modules. Apart from anything else, having to repeat part of her course meant another round of fees, which meant more crappy jobs like this one. A chill passed through her abdomen. She vowed to get straight to the library and start writing the damn thing.

From the street outside came the angry sound of a car horn. Recalling her host's aborted meal, Melody realised she was starving. Perhaps food was a more immediate priority than visiting the library. But where was the professor? Biting her lower lip, Melody listened for sounds of activity elsewhere in the flat. After a couple of moments, she picked out the sound of the TV coming from next door. Hopefully the old guy was making some breakfast. If he wanted to feed her up, now was the time.

Her knickers would not be able to serve a second day. Tossing them onto the bed, Melody shimmied into her jeans, gratified that there was still plenty of spare capacity around the waist. At least she wasn't getting fat. Ever since Karen Jansen had threatened to put her on a diet, she had been obsessive about managing her calorie intake.

Wandering into the en-suite bathroom, she switched on the light. The windowless bathroom was tiny – a shower stall, toilet and washbasin crammed into a space not much bigger than a phone box. A shower would probably be a good idea. For a few seconds, Melody contemplated getting undressed again, then decided she didn't really have time. Instead, she turned to the basin, running the tap until the water turned the right side of lukewarm. Washing her face, she removed the remains of her make-up and looked at herself in the mirror above the basin.

'You look about twelve,' she mumbled to herself, unsure whether that was a good thing or not. 'And you need to get your roots done.' She looked around for a brush, or a comb, anything she could run through the pink bird's nest sitting on her head. Finding nothing, she used her hands to tidy her hair as best she could. Next, she squeezed some toothpaste on to her index finger and had a go at her teeth, then gargled with a shot of the professor's mouthwash.

'Urgh.' Appalled by the taste, she spat it out and rinsed her mouth with some water from the tap. After having a pee, she let herself out of the bathroom and made her way into the kitchen-cum-living-room area. On the TV screen, she recognised a daytime property makeover show that she liked to watch now and again. People taking on development projects that were way beyond their capabilities, then descending into a hell of unpaid bills, leaking roofs and marital strife was invariably entertaining viewing. Staring at the screen, Melody realised she had seen this episode before. A seriously deluded young couple imagined they were going to turn their bombed-out shell of a building into a palace worth millions. It was the point of the show where they were arguing about where to put their kitchen. The wife had a hammer in her hand and looked like she wanted to brain her husband with it. Standing just out of her range, the presenter, a smug American, was expertly stoking the fires of domestic discord.

'Just do what you're told,' Melody advised the husband, 'if you ever want to get laid again.' She tried to remember if the couple ended up getting divorced. It was probably for the best if they did. For her part, Melody couldn't imagine being married. Ever. The idea of a relationship lasting years, never mind decades, seemed impossible to contemplate.

The show went into an ad break. Melody stepped over to the breakfast bar and helped herself to a banana from the fruit bowl. Carefully unzipping the peel, she took a large bite and began chewing slowly and deliberately. Resting against the bar, she looked around the room. Nothing seemed to have changed from the night before.

Almost nothing.

Her gaze fell on the bookshelf by the window. Where was the photograph of the professor's wife? Closer inspection showed the silver frame lying on the floor. Melody frowned. Had she not put it back on the shelf properly the night before? Pushing the last of the banana into her mouth, she stepped forward and picked it up. To her relief, the frame didn't seem to have been damaged. There was a small crack in the glass. Melody was fairly sure it hadn't been there before, but the glass could easily be replaced. The photograph of the smiling Japanese lady, however, had gone.

Melody tried to recall the name of the professor's wife. Putting the frame back on the shelf, she wondered why he would have removed the picture from it. And, more to the point, where was the man himself?

Maybe he's gone out to get some coffee, she thought hopefully, and some croissants.

Croissants would be nice.

Returning to the breakfast bar, Melody surprised herself by coming to a sudden but clear decision. Forget the library, she would buy a damn essay after all. Sod the cost. If it ended up being all that expensive, she could hold off on the holiday. Her phone was still sitting next to the fruit bowl, where she had left it the night before. Picking it up, Melody was dismayed to see that the battery was almost dead. Using the last of her juice, she pulled up the website for White Knight Essays – *Only the best talent, only the best writing! No topic too obscure! 100 per cent non-plagiarised content and guaranteed discounts. Never beaten on price, never beaten on content* – and typed in her username and login.

SIXTEEN

The final cost of the essay was £1625.44, including VAT. Melody completed her order for the premium express six-hour service and hit the large green PAY button. Moments later a confirmation email arrived in her inbox, promising delivery by early evening. Feeling just about as pleased with herself as if she had actually written the thing, Melody pulled up Chris's number. Now that she had freed the rest of her day, there was no reason why her boyfriend couldn't take her to brunch. Hitting call, she listened to the phone ring once and then – nothing. Staring at the blank screen, it took Melody a second to realise that the battery had finally died. Cursing, she dropped the handset back on the bar. It looked like she'd have to sort out her own meal. Next to the fridge was a silver bread bin. Looking inside, she found a couple of bagels. Melody picked one up and gave it a squeeze. It seemed reasonably fresh.

'Perfect. Now, where's the toaster?'

Before she could answer her own question, there was the sound of a key being inserted into a lock, followed by the front door opening.

'Professor.' Melody anticipated the belated arrival of warm croissants and steaming coffee.

'Hello?' Through the door stepped a small woman, maybe five feet tall, with a mop of implausibly black hair on top of a deeply creased face, a plastic supermarket carrier bag in each hand. With a grunt, the woman placed the bags on the floor, then took off her coat and hung it on a hook on the wall. Keeping to her routine, she slipped off her shoes before finally turning her attention to the girl with the pink hair.

For a moment, the two women stared at each other.

'Who are you?' Melody asked finally.

'Cleaning lady.' The woman's English was heavily accented. She sounded like she was from somewhere in Eastern Europe but Melody couldn't place it any more precisely than that.

'Oh.' Melody guessed that the woman had to be in her sixties, at least.

'Today is cleaning day.'

Obviously, Melody thought.

'Who are you?'

'Erm, I'm one of the professor's students.' Melody carefully placed the bagel back in the bread bin. 'I was just going.' Grabbing her phone, she shoved it into the back pocket of her jeans.

Stepping into the middle of the room, the woman glanced at the tiny dinner table, still set for the night before. 'Where is the professor?'

'He went out,' Melody edged towards the door, 'to get some coffee, I think. He'll be back soon.'

'He likes to go swimming,' the woman said, apropos of nothing.

'Maybe he's gone swimming, then.' Stepping into her shoes, Melody hovered in the doorway. 'When he gets back, tell him I had to go. I'll call him later.'

Not waiting for a reply, she hurried out.

'You are a dirty old man.' Niza Curkoli watched the girl skip out of the door and shook her head. 'She could be your granddaughter.' Having cleaned for Martin Grom for twenty-three years, Niza was used to coming across the professor's female visitors now and then but she had never seen one with pink hair before. And so young-looking, too. The old fool would get himself into big trouble one day. That was for sure.

Niza's disapproval of her employer's behaviour ran deep – after all, she had a daughter herself – but it was not so strong that she had ever seriously considered ditching the job. As a refugee from the Balkan wars of the 1990s, she knew only too well that men were capable of far worse than taking advantage of silly girls. And, anyway, she needed the money.

Closing the door, Niza looked round the room. If the professor's guest had left the place in a mess, the extra work could put her behind schedule. Grom was the second of four jobs she had scheduled for today and time was always at a premium. On the other hand, assuming he was at the leisure centre, she would have the place to herself for the next couple of hours.

Niza hoisted the shopping bags onto the kitchen bar, then resumed her regular routine. Filling the kettle with water from the tap, she dropped a peppermint teabag into a mug. Once the kettle had boiled, she filled the mug and carried it over to the sofa, along with her spectacles, a small bar of chocolate and a copy of her favourite celebrity magazine. Twenty minutes for herself and two hours forty minutes for the professor: that was the deal.

When she had finished reading the sorry tale of a comedian who had hanged himself from a tree, Niza cleared up her rubbish and set about getting down to work. Taking a bucket from under the sink, she filled it with the remaining water from the kettle and added some camomile floor cleaner. Placing the bucket on the floor, she padded over to the utility cupboard by the front door to recover the mop. Still fretting about the deceased comic, she pulled open the door and was immediately head-butted in the face.

'Pfffff.'

Stumbling backwards, a dazed Niza found herself on the floor. A body was lying on top of her. It took her a moment to realise it was Grom's.

'Professor,' she groaned, 'what are you doing? What's going on?'

When Grom didn't respond, she gathered her strength and pushed him off, then struggled to her feet.

'Professor?' Dusting herself down, she looked into his eyes.

The man was clearly dead. Back home, Niza Curkoli had seen more than her share of corpses, including that of her only brother, a gentle soul who had been shot in the head by a drunken militia man as he walked down the street. Death was no stranger to her, so Grom's fate provoked little response beyond a slightly elevated heart rate and a mild sense of annoyance that she had lost a reliable long-term client. Scratching her nose, she took a moment to consider who might take over Grom's cleaning slot. The old man paid her monthly, in advance, so at least she wouldn't end up out of pocket immediately. But even a temporary short-term drop in income would be a major problem for someone with no bank account and accumulated savings of less than two hundred pounds. Quickly, Niza ran through a list of her remaining clients, picking out a couple who might be able to give her more work or, alternatively, refer her to friends or contacts. She would speak to them as soon as possible; hopefully the professor's slot would be filled in the next week or two.

Grom looked on, nonplussed.

'Sorry, Professor, but the living have to look after themselves first. That's just the way it is.' Stepping away from the body, Niza took her mobile from the pocket of her coat. 'Don't worry, though. I will get some help for you now.'

With her thumb hovering over the buttons, she stared at the screen, trying to recall the number for the police. Back home it was 92. But here? The number had never lodged in her brain.

'Almost half your life in this country,' Niza admonished herself, 'and still you can't remember a simple thing like that. That is not good, not good at all.'

She glanced back at the body. 'Sorry, Professor, I just have to find the number.' The old man had kept a telephone directory, even after getting rid of his landline. It was a massive yellow book that must have weighed more than a couple of kilos. Niza remembered putting it out with the recycling not so long ago.

'Damn,' she muttered to herself. 'The one time it would have been useful and you have to go and throw it out.'

71

After making one last attempt to retrieve the number from her brain, without success, she called Hana, her elder child.

The girl answered on the second ring. 'What is it, Mum? I'm just about to go into my class.'

'Sorry, sweetheart.' Despite the girl's irritated tone, Niza smiled. Both of her children had made it to university. Truly, it was something to be proud of. And, unlike her brother, Hana had stayed in London. The girl still lived at home, too, which was another bonus.

'I'm going to have to switch my phone off before I go into the lecture theatre.'

'Yes.' Niza quickly explained what she needed.

Hana gasped. 'Are you all right? What do you need the police for? What's happened?'

'Nothing, nothing.' Niza felt flustered. This conversation was turning out to be more stressful than being attacked by the dead professor. 'I'm fine.' She glanced at the body on the floor. 'I just need to check something for the professor. He, erm, had his mobile phone stolen.' Niza was pleased at her quick thinking.

'And he doesn't know 999?' The panic in Hana's voice had subsided, to be replaced by suspicion.

999. She must have known that. 'He's not here. He just asked me to call to check if they'd found it.'

'I don't think you ring 999 for that,' Hana advised. 'It's only for emergencies.' There was the sound of chatter in the background. 'I think they give you a card with a special victims-of-crime number on it. One of the girls on the course got one the other month when she was mugged on Oxford Street.'

'Don't worry about it. You go to your lecture. I'll sort it out. I shouldn't have disturbed you.'

'Anyway, why can't he do it himself?'

'You know what it's like. He's an old man. He's going a bit soft in the head.'

'You do too much for him, Mum,' the girl scolded. 'He doesn't pay you for this kind of thing.'

'It's fine.'

'Let me speak to the girl who was mugged, see if she still has the number.'

'No, don't worry. I'll sort it out. Now that you mention it, I think I've seen one of those cards on the professor's desk. I'll give you a call after your lecture if I still can't find it.'

'Okay.' The girl sounded happy enough with that compromise.

'You have a good class.'

'Sure.'

'And I'll see you at home later.'

'Okay. I might be going out tonight, but I'll let you know.'

'With Peter?' Niza knew she shouldn't be nosy, but she couldn't resist. Hana had been seeing the boy for – what? – more than three months now. Maybe this one would turn out to be serious. Niza hoped so. Peter wasn't particularly handsome but, from what she had seen, he was thoughtful and polite. Also, he was training to become an engineer. A good career was far more important than how the boy looked. All in all, he appeared an acceptable candidate for a son-in-law.

'I've got to go. Bye, Mama.'

'Bye.'

After Hana had rung off, Niza spent a minute daydreaming about becoming a grandmother. Then she shook herself back into the present and called the police.

SEVENTEEN

'Who found the body?'

Sergeant Adam Palin pointed towards the small woman sitting on the sofa, reading a glossy magazine. 'The cleaning lady.'

The woman sipped from a mug of tea, seemingly disinterested in the activity around her as she flipped the pages.

'She looks to be taking it in her stride,' Carlyle observed.

Palin shrugged. 'She says she's seen a lot worse in her time.'

'Good for her.' Carlyle had been on his way to see his father in Fulham when the call had come in. A suspicious death wouldn't necessarily lead to a criminal case but it would generate more than enough paperwork to tie him up for the rest of the day.

Before entering the dead man's flat, he had called Stine Hassing. The death doula seemed unsurprised by his latest no-show. Accepting his excuse without comment, she informed him that his father's condition hadn't really changed. Alexander was still hanging in there, but no one expected it to be that much longer.

'He's doped up to the eyeballs,' Stine observed drily. 'Meanwhile I'm running out of cigarettes again.'

'I'll get down there as quickly as I can,' Carlyle promised, recalling her chosen brand, 'and pick a packet up on the way.'

'Thanks,' she replied, in a tone that suggested she wasn't holding her breath.

'I'm sorry about this.'

'Don't worry. This is just how these things play out. It's why

I do this job. While other people run around like rats in a maze, I have the luxury of time. And freedom. I am very lucky.'

'I suppose you are.' Carlyle did indeed feel like a trapped rodent. He knew that he should be in Fulham, sitting with his father. Being able to say he was there at the end was a rite of passage of sorts. On the other hand, he had no desire to see the old man draw his final breath. The truth was he was quite happy to focus on work while nature took its course.

Helen argued he should apply for compassionate leave. At his wife's insistence, he had tried to get hold of his boss, Commander Carole Simpson, to get the necessary approvals. Simpson, however, was nowhere to be found. Carlyle tried to recall the last time he had seen her, or even spoken to her about a case. Disconcertingly, nothing came to mind. Over the years, he had spent much of his time ducking and weaving, trying to keep below Simpson's radar and out of sight. Recently, however, she had become more hands off, to the point where, now, he couldn't get hold of her. Even the commander's PA seemed to be uncontactable. It was a strange situation, but not one he particularly disliked.

As things stood, he remained on duty until he could find someone with the authority to relieve him. Helen, of course, would not be best pleased at him taking on this new case. In recent months, she had increasingly accused him of ignoring his family responsibilities.

'It's just the Job,' was Carlyle's standard defence.

'You have to get your priorities right,' Helen would shoot back. 'The Job can wait.'

'The Job pays the bills.'

'Not all of the bills,' she reminded him.

'I have to follow protocol.'

'Protocol? Ha. That's rich, coming from a man who only ever does what he wants.'

'Hardly.' They were exasperated at replaying a familiar conversation, each convinced that the other didn't want to listen. 'I would hardly have survived this long if I didn't play the game.'

'Only when it suits you.'

'Yes, well.' That was a different argument.

'Just tell them you need some time off,' Helen demanded. 'Head down to see your father and sort out the paperwork later.'

'It doesn't work like that.'

'Well, it should.' Running a medical charity, Helen had a rather different take on what constituted 'professional behaviour'. Years of working with difficult employees – headstrong medical professionals who were, basically, impossible to control – had left her with a rather laissez-faire attitude towards management. Ironically, she had even less faith in the 'chain of command' than Carlyle, who had always shied away from any kind of managerial responsibility.

The tearing sound of a cadaver pouch being unzipped woke him from his unhappy reverie. Hands on hips, he watched the paramedics carefully working the body into the bag. 'What do we know about the victim?'

'Professor Martin Grom.' Palin kept his voice low. 'Retired widower. Taught at the School of Oriental and African Studies for more than thirty years.'

'Oh?' Mention of the SOAS sparked Carlyle's interest. Another possible university that would keep Alice in London. 'What did he teach?'

'Don't know. I can find out, though.'

'Doesn't matter. Hardly likely to be relevant.'

'Right. Anyway, the wife died some time ago and he lived alone. They didn't have any children.'

'The poor sod must have been lonely.'

'I suppose.'

'What happened?'

'Well,' Palin coughed, 'in short, he fell out of the cupboard when the cleaner went to get a mop.'

'What the hell was he doing in the cupboard?'

'No idea,' Palin admitted. 'Maybe he was looking for something and had a heart attack.'

'And closed the door behind him?' Carlyle shook his head. When Palin didn't offer any alternative theories, he changed tack. 'Who's the pathologist?'

'Phillips.'

'Good.' Carlyle had known Susan Phillips for many years; she was one of the few colleagues he actually liked working with.

'An interesting one for her farewell.'

'What d'you mean,' Carlyle snapped, 'her farewell?'

'This is gonna be one of her last cases,' Palin explained, somewhat surprised by the question. 'She's taking early retirement at the end of the month.'

Bloody hell, Carlyle thought. Phillips was quite a bit younger than him. 'Voluntary?'

'Yeah. She took a deal as part of the latest round of cuts.' The look on Palin's face suggested a certain degree of surprise that Carlyle wasn't going as well. 'Didn't you read the email?'

Carlyle considered his untended inbox. 'No.'

'Apparently, it wasn't such a good deal, not compared to previous offers, anyway.'

'It'll only be worse next time,' Carlyle groused.

'If there is a next time.'

'There's always a next time,' said Carlyle. 'I've lost count of the number of downsizings there's been over the years.'

'You could talk to HR,' Palin suggested, his tone a bit too hopeful to Carlyle's ear. 'They might still have some money left in the current pot.'

'I can't afford to call it a day.' Not wishing to get into his finances with Palin, Carlyle changed tack. 'What's Phillips going to do after she retires?'

'Dunno.' Palin scratched behind his ear. 'But she's having her leaving do at the Monkey in Orbit next week.'

The inspector gave no impression of knowing the establishment in question.

'It's a new gastropub in Smithfield,' Palin explained.

Just what the world needs, Carlyle reflected.

'Basically, it's themed on Taiwan's space monkey programme—'

'Don't take the piss,' Carlyle growled.

'No,' Palin protested, 'seriously. Rita told me about it. We went there just after it opened. It's not bad.'

Rita Vicedo was a crime-fighting nun, who had helped them out on a previous case. To say that Palin had the hots for her would be a massive understatement. 'Are you guys going out, then?' Carlyle asked, not at all innocently.

'Not really.' Blushing, Palin looked at his shoes. 'I mean, she can't date, can she?'

'I suppose not.' Carlyle smirked.

'We just hook up, now and again.' Palin allowed himself to be distracted by the paramedics manoeuvring Grom's body out of the flat.

Can a nun hook up? Carlyle decided it was better not to ask. 'Phillips must be demob happy,' he mused, returning, almost, to the matter in hand.

'She wouldn't have taken this case, but her replacement hasn't turned up yet,' Palin explained. He mentioned a name that meant nothing to Carlyle. 'The guy's thrown a sickie in his first week. Phillips was complaining about him before you arrived. She's quite pissed off about it.'

'I bet she is.'

'Understandable, though. That's taking a bit of a liberty if you ask me.'

'Depends on how sick he is,' Carlyle opined. Everyone knew that sickness levels in the Met were ridiculously high.

'You'd have thought he'd make more of an effort in his first week.'

'You'd have thought,' Carlyle agreed. 'Is Phillips still around?'

Palin shook his head. 'She went back to Holborn.'

Carlyle contemplated a detour to the Holborn station on the way back to Charing Cross. Maybe he could treat Phillips to a farewell sandwich at one of the cafés on Lamb's Conduit

Street. Somehow, he didn't see himself making it to the Monkey in Orbit. Leaving dos were always faintly depressing. He certainly wouldn't be bothering with one when it was time for him to bugger off. 'Any initial findings?'

'She said it might have been a heart attack.'

'Before or after he went into the cupboard?'

'She didn't say.'

'Okay. Take a quick look round the rest of the flat. And get some uniforms to start canvassing the neighbours. I'll have a word with the cleaner.'

EIGHTEEN

Closing her magazine, Niza Curkoli moved along the sofa to make some space for the policeman to sit down beside her. Her first impression was of a small, shabby man of indeterminate age, who looked like he had other things on his mind. Niza could always tell when people were set to do a good job. This man looked like he wanted to do the bare minimum, fill in the necessary forms and go home. That was fine by Niza: she had already been forced to cancel her next job, much to the annoyance of the client, the very demanding and increasingly senile Mrs Constant, and was keen to get back on schedule as quickly as possible. If she didn't work, she didn't get paid.

'Simple as', as her son liked to say.

Looking over her shoulder, Niza realised that she and the policeman were alone. The room, so full of investigators ten minutes ago, had emptied. Even the professor had gone. The chalk outline on the floor was the only reminder of his presence. It was like he no longer existed.

What was she talking about? Poor old Grom didn't exist any longer. Decades living in this flat and now nothing. Niza supposed she should feel sorry for him. In reality, she didn't feel anything. An ex-client was just an ex-client.

Did such a lack of sentiment make her a bad person? Niza had no idea.

'Nice view.' The policeman gestured at the window as he handed her his card.

Niza squinted under her glasses, sitting up slightly as she read the words: *Inspector John Carlyle, Charing Cross Police Station*. Was that the same place as the train station? Despite living in London for more than twenty years, Niza had been there only once, the day when she'd gone to see the lions in Trafalgar Square. She didn't remember seeing a police station. 'Important policeman,' she said, in accented English.

'Just an ordinary policeman,' Carlyle corrected her.

Niza muttered something to herself in a language she knew he wouldn't understand. Even though her papers were in order, officials of the state always made her nervous. She might not be an illegal immigrant, but experience had told her that authority was always something to be feared.

Carlyle pointed at the window again. 'You can see all the way to the river.'

Niza placed the card on top of her magazine, on the arm of the sofa. 'The professor thought it was the best thing about the place. He said it was why he bought the apartment even though he couldn't afford it.'

Pulling a small notebook and a pen from his jacket, the inspector signalled he was ready to get down to business. 'Maybe you could tell me what happened?'

Keeping things simple, Niza nodded over at the cupboard. 'I pull the door and he fall out.'

Carlyle opened the notebook but didn't write anything down. 'And what happened then?'

'He fall on top of me.' Niza grimaced at the memory. 'Oh, my God. I get a big shock.'

'I can imagine.'

'I push him off and get up.' She did a reconstruction through the medium of mime. 'It is clear he is gone. Then I call the number for police – 999 – and I tell them he is dead.'

'When you arrived this morning,' Carlyle said gently, 'was there anything unusual that you noticed? Before you opened the cupboard, I mean.'

Niza shook her head. She had already decided that mentioning the girl with the pink hair would only slow things up. If she managed to get out of there in the next hour or so, she could still make her last appointment of the day.

'Nothing?'

'No.' Niza tried to look like she was thinking carefully about answering the question. 'Everything seemed normal. All quiet.'

'Weren't you surprised not to see him?'

'The professor is usually out of the flat when I come. He didn't like to get in the way.'

Carlyle glanced at the dinner table, set for two. 'He lived alone, as I understand it.'

'Maybe he was having someone round,' Niza ventured. 'I don't know.'

They were interrupted by Palin, emerging from the back of the flat, carrying a couple of transparent plastic evidence bags.

'What have you got?' Carlyle asked.

'A notebook of some sort,' Palin replied. 'And these.' Grinning, he held up one of the bags to display a pair of crumpled red knickers. 'They were lying on the bed. I don't suppose they belonged to the professor.'

Carlyle looked at Niza.

'No,' the cleaner said defiantly, 'they not his. The professor wasn't some weirdo. He was a nice old man.'

'Looks like the professor had some company, then,' Palin suggested.

'When you came in to work this morning,' Carlyle gestured at the bag, 'you didn't see the, erm, *garment* in question?'

'I don't get as far as the bedroom.' The woman shrugged. 'I do that last thing. When I come in, everything seem normal. I get ready to wash the floor, I go for the mop—'

'Okay, okay.' Carlyle held up a hand. 'I get the picture.' The woman had clearly decided on her story and was sticking to it. That was fair enough – he detected a basic fear of authority in

82

her tone rather than sensing that she had anything particular to hide. 'Go and see how the interviews with the neighbours are going,' he instructed his sergeant, pointing towards the door. 'Ask if anyone knew anything about lady visitors.'

'What shall I do with these?' Palin waved the bag in the air.

'Just log them in evidence for now.' If the professor's demise was just a heart attack brought on by a bit of bedroom action, Carlyle didn't want to waste more time – or money – on the investigation than was absolutely necessary. 'Let's see where we get to.'

'Right.' Seemingly content with his allotted tasks, Palin trotted towards the door and disappeared.

Having watched the sergeant leave, Niza evidently calculated that she could be a little more forthcoming to the policeman sitting next to her. 'The professor had lady visitors,' she said quietly, pushing her spectacles back up her nose, 'from time to time.'

'Visitors? As in female friends?'

'Lady visitors,' Niza repeated. 'They come to the flat.' She pointed at the dinner table. 'Sometimes he cook dinner for them. He needed . . .' She struggled for the words and settled for 'He not like to be alone all the time.'

Carlyle peered at the table set for two. 'It doesn't look like they had a meal last night.'

'They didn't come to eat.'

'No, I suppose not.'

'Talking with the professor was hard,' Niza explained. 'He was a very educated man. Some of the girls were very young. He would tell me they had nothing to say. But it was hard to understand what he was saying.'

'What did he teach?'

'Something complicated,' was the cleaner's only response.

That narrowed it down, then. 'These young girls,' he asked, 'did you ever see any of them?'

'No,' Niza measured her words carefully, 'but the professor

would sometimes mention them.' She gestured towards where Palin had been standing. 'As your officer found, there would often be things left behind. He would always apologise if there was a bad mess.'

A bad mess? The inspector decided there was no need to be too prurient, at least at this stage in the proceedings. 'Do you know where the girls came from?'

Niza bit her upper lip. 'No.'

'If we knew where to find some of these ladies,' he said gently, 'we might be able to discover what happened last night.'

'I thought that the poor man had a heart attack, no?' Niza shifted uneasily in her seat. The possibility that there was anything more sinister behind Professor Grom's death clearly hadn't crossed her mind.

'Perhaps,' Carlyle admitted, 'but that doesn't explain how he ended up in the cupboard.'

Niza conceded the point.

'At the very least, if there was someone here, in the flat, when it happened, they should have called 999, like you did.'

The girl with the pink hair. Niza wondered if she could have saved Grom. It didn't make much difference now. 'Is it a crime,' she asked, 'not to call the police?'

'Sometimes. But I'm not looking to get anyone into trouble.'

'No,' Niza agreed, 'police is different here.'

'I just need to understand what happened. If there is anything else you can tell me, it would be helpful.'

It's not going to help the professor, Niza reflected. 'I never know where the girls come from.' Looking out of the window, she noticed that it had started to rain. Time was running out if she was to make the last appointment and at least limit her losses on the day. 'When I arrive this morning, everything look normal.'

'All right.' Getting to his feet, Carlyle offered his notebook and pen to her. 'I think we're done here. If you write down your name, address and a contact mobile number someone will be in touch about coming to the police station to give us a formal statement.'

'I just tell you what happened.' Niza made no effort to take possession of either item.

'I know, but we will need something for the official record. I apologise for the inconvenience, but it will not take long.'

Niza sucked in air through the gap in her teeth. She didn't have time for visits to police stations.

'Or we could go there now.'

Glancing at her watch, Niza realised that this was her last chance to make the final job of the day. Grabbing the pen and the notebook, she scribbled down her details, making a mental note to screen any unfamiliar numbers on her phone for the next few weeks. She was sure that the police would only try to catch up with her for a little while. After a couple of calls, three at the most, they would give up and leave her in peace.

'Can I go now?' she asked, handing the inspector back his things.

'Yes. Thank you for your help.'

Struggling out of the sofa, Niza picked up both his business card and her magazine. Shuffling over to the breakfast bar, she placed them both in one of the shopping bags.

'Are you going home?' Carlyle asked. 'You must have had quite a shock.'

'Pfffff.' Niza lifted the bags from the bar. 'I have to get back to work. The professor is not my only client.'

'I hope the rest of your day is less eventful,' Carlyle offered.

Niza headed for the door and slipped on her shoes. Straightening up, she turned to face the inspector, a resigned expression on her face. 'An old man has died. It happens. Life goes on.'

'Yes, but still . . .'

The woman endeavoured to blow away his sentimentality with an expressive sigh. 'Where I come from there is a saying: *In something good there is bad, in something bad there is good.*'

'Where's the good in this?' Carlyle wondered aloud.

'Now, he can at last be with his wife.' Niza shuffled out the door. 'And the poor woman does not have to look down and watch her husband playing the fool with whores young enough to be his granddaughter.'

NINETEEN

After the cleaner had left, Carlyle stood in the empty flat, listening to the sound of the traffic from the street below. What would happen to this place? he wondered. Looking around, he made the kind of quick mental calculation that came naturally to any Londoner – a rough approximation of the property's market value based on location plus square footage – and came up with a number that caused him to emit a low whistle. Even after accounting for taxes, the professor's estate would easily make it into seven figures. If, as Palin had said, there were no kids, maybe some distant cousin or nephew was in for a nice surprise when the will was read and the place got sold. It would be a shame, the inspector decided, if there was no one to enjoy the windfall. It would be a terrible waste if the proceeds of the academic's lifetime of work simply disappeared into the ungrateful black hole of the public finances.

Whatever happened to the flat, the books would probably end up on the shelves of a charity shop. There were certainly enough of them. Carlyle scanned the titles in a vain search for anything he recognised. There was no Lee Child or Henning Mankell here. In front of a massive tome on *Ethnicity and Equality* stood a photograph frame. It was empty. Carlyle pushed out his lips. Who had an empty photo frame on display?

There was a sound behind him and the inspector wheeled

around to see Palin in the doorway. 'We're not having a lot of luck with the neighbours right now,' the sergeant admitted. 'Most people are out at work. We're gonna have to come back tonight.'

'Fair enough.' Carlyle's relaxed tone suggested that wasn't much of a surprise. 'Just make sure we don't run up any unnecessary overtime.'

'No.'

'In fact, let's wait and see what Phillips comes up with. If it was just a heart attack, we'll call it case closed, even if he was found in the cupboard.'

'You're the boss,' Palin responded, his tone suggesting that Carlyle could have made *that* decision before they had started knocking on any doors in the first place.

Ignoring his sergeant's petulance, the inspector pointed to the empty photograph frame. 'Where's the picture?'

'No idea,' Palin said. 'Can't say I noticed it before.'

'A bit strange, don't you think?'

'Maybe he'd just bought it,' Palin ventured, 'and hadn't put anything in it yet.'

'Maybe.' Carlyle peered at the silver frame. 'Looks old, though.' He noticed a small crack in the top right-hand corner of the glass. 'Maybe we should get it checked for prints.'

'Before we hear from Phillips?' The look on Palin's face was a mixture of confusion and irritation. 'I thought we were trying to avoid running up costs.'

'Good point. Let's hold fire on that and call it a day.' Signalling for Palin to lead the way, Carlyle headed out of the flat. Closing the door behind him, he followed the sergeant down the stairs and out onto the street.

'Going back to the station?' Palin asked.

'No.' The last thing Carlyle wanted to do was go back to Charing Cross. That would kill the rest of his day stone dead. 'I'll see you back there later on. I've got a few things to sort out in the meantime.'

'All right.' Palin was slowly coming to terms with the inspector's tendency to keep his movements to himself. He didn't ask for any more information before wandering off.

Watching the sergeant disappear down the street, Carlyle dawdled, considering his options. He could make for Holborn, to catch up with Phillips, or just bunk off for half an hour and read the evening paper in a nearby café. Either option was more appealing than the third possibility: going to Fulham to see if his father was still breathing. However, he knew that the pathologist would need more time to deliver a verdict on the causes of the professor's death. And guilt would erode his enjoyment of sneaking off for a coffee. Reluctantly, he let a feeble sense of duty tug him towards SW6.

On the opposite side of the road there was a newsagent. He waited for a break in the traffic, then jogged across and stepped inside. A few minutes later, he emerged with a packet of cigarettes and a Mars Bar. Stuffing the smokes into his pocket, he tore open the wrapper on the chocolate and took a large bite, chewing thoughtfully as he went in search of a bus that would take him in the direction of Parsons Green.

Got David. All good x

Smiling, Alison Roche typed in a reply consisting of a simple x and hit send. Shoving the phone back into her pocket, the sergeant stepped over to the floor-to-ceiling window and looked down. Thirty-one floors was a long way up. For an instant, she had a flashback to 9/11, those poor bastards throwing themselves out of the burning towers, and shuddered.

'Would you like something to drink?'

Roche turned to face the assistant who had shown her into the office. 'I'm fine. Thanks.'

'Mr Durkan will be with you in a minute. He's currently stuck on a conference call to Jakarta.'

Jakarta? That was Indonesia, right? Roche looked at her

watch. She only had the sketchiest idea of where Jakarta was on a map but, surely, it would be the middle of the night over there right now. She let it pass.

'If you need anything, just let me know.' Turning, the woman left the room.

In the event, it was almost fifteen minutes before the man himself finally appeared. 'Sergeant Roche?' Spreading his arms wide, Gerry Durkan made a show of looking her up and down, clearly liking what he saw. 'Sorry to keep you waiting. I was stuck on an important call with some investors.'

'In Jakarta, your secretary said.'

'We do a lot of business with Indonesia, these days. Amazing place. I've never been there myself, but Bianca, my chief marketing officer, practically lives there. Fighting them off with a stick, so she is. Great girl.' Finishing his spiel, he gestured towards the chair in front of his desk. 'Please, take a seat.' Roche obliged while Durkan installed himself in his fancy chair. 'Now, what can I do for you?'

'Balthazar Quant.'

Durkan's stomach lurched downwards. 'What about him?'

'He's dead.' After being kept waiting for so long, Roche was disinclined to soften the blow. At this rate, she could end up missing David's bath and his bedtime. The prospect made her want to scream.

'Dead?' The man's smile evaporated. 'As in . . .'

'As in murdered.' Roche made a mental note that the dismay on Durkan's face could not be mistaken for surprise. She gestured at the window with her thumb. 'Someone stuck him in a cement mixer in the building site downstairs.'

Durkan glanced towards the window. 'That's what the police vans were for.'

'Yes.'

Durkan shifted uncomfortably in his seat. It was clear that he had a number of questions but he kept his mouth clamped firmly shut.

Pulling a notebook and a pen from her pocket, Roche started through her own list. 'When did you last see Mr Quant?'

'Last night.' Durkan scratched his chin. 'He was sitting where you are now. I gave him details of his bonus. He seemed very happy.'

Roche scribbled some notes. 'Happy with the bonus?'

'Yes, of course. We've had a very good year. And staff at MCS are always very well remunerated. But it wasn't just the money. Balthazar was happy in his work. He is – was – one of my longest-serving employees.' Lifting an arm, he waved in the direction of the trading floor. 'This is – was – a very stable working environment for Balthazar. He was a well-liked and well-respected member of our . . .' Durkan was about to say 'family' but realised it sounded too trite '. . . *community.*' He brought his hand back to rest over his heart. 'Personally, I liked working with him very much. He was a valued colleague.'

Spare me the blarney, Roche thought. 'What about his home life?'

'His home life?' Durkan seemed somewhat perplexed by the question.

'Was he married?' Roche prompted.

'Oh, no.'

'Girlfriend?'

'I don't think so.' Durkan again gestured towards the trading floor. 'This is a punishing environment. It takes its toll on relationships.'

Roche looked up from her notes. 'Boyfriend?'

'Not as far as I'm aware.'

Roche shot him a look.

'I never really pried,' Durkan explained. 'I'm his boss, not his father.'

'Good point. Next of kin.'

'What about them?'

'Would you have their contact details?'

'Maybe,' Durkan offered unconvincingly.

'Do you think you might at least be able to give me a home address?' Roche asked.

Durkan thought about that for a moment or two. 'Human Resources should be able to do that for you.'

'For such a valued colleague,' Roche observed, 'you don't seem to know much about him.'

A rather unpleasant smile crossed Durkan's face. 'You've heard of work-life balance, Detective?'

'Sergeant,' Roche corrected him, 'but, yes, I have.'

'Well, at MCS we like to have more of what I like to call a work-work balance: we work hard, we play hard and we make money. We don't mess about with all the other stuff.'

Roche bit her upper lip. 'Does that mean Mr Quant's death must, in some way, be work-related?'

'Not at all. All I'm saying is that I knew Balthazar well, in the work environment, which, in our case, is fairly all-encompassing. Domestic chit-chat wasn't part of our normal discourse.'

'So, you don't think anyone in this building could have been in any way involved in his death?'

'Please,' Durkan spluttered, 'we're all on the same side here. We win together, we lose together. That's the deal, if you join MCS. You don't have to like all your colleagues, you don't even have to *pretend* to like all of them, but you do have to accept that we're a team. As some politician once said, we're all in it together.' For a moment, it looked like Durkan was about to giggle, but he quickly composed himself. 'Coming from one of those idiots in Westminster, it's nonsense, obviously. But here, we really are all in it together. No one has the time to bear any grudges, much less attack anyone else. Bottom line, there's no money to be made doing that and we're here to make money.'

'So,' Roche summarised, 'you're saying you have no idea who might have beaten Mr Quant to a pulp, smashed in his skull and stuffed his corpse into a cement mixer?'

Durkan brought the fingertips of both hands together in contemplation. Lifting his gaze to the ceiling, he mumbled a few words that might have been a prayer for his departed colleague. Equally, it might have been a shopping list of things he wanted to pick up from the convenience store on the way home.

Putting away her notebook, Roche waited patiently for her host to return to the temporal plane.

Finally, Durkan placed his palms flat on the desk. 'I'm very sorry, Sergeant,' he said solemnly, bringing his gaze back to Roche's face, 'but I'm afraid I really have no idea whatsoever.'

TWENTY

Bob Biswas tilted his head as he looked at his new purchase. The Ting Sasse print, sitting on a sideboard, propped up against the wall, was called *Death Smiles IV*. The grey smears supposedly represented the Four Horsemen of the Apocalypse galloping towards the viewer. According to the dealer's marketing spiel, it had been inspired by the artist's near-death experience during a particularly unfortunate surfing accident.

Standing in the Molby-Nicol gallery, with a glass of expensive wine in his hand and the gallery owner talking seductively in his ear, Biswas had felt that the composition made perfect sense. Back in his hotel suite, he wasn't so sure that it worked at all. If you didn't understand the surfing backstory, it could easily appear like little more than the random daubings of a rather disturbed five-year-old. He shuddered to think what Arumina would make of it. Biswas's wife was invariably scornful of his attempts to build a modern-art collection in their Brasschaat home. Three years ago, he had come home with an original Damien Hirst only for Arumina to banish it to the garage. God knows what she would do with his latest acquisition. He had been planning to put it in his study but now he feared that the guest cloakroom beckoned, at best. All in all, it wasn't shaping up to be the best twenty-five thousand he had ever spent in his life.

Maybe he should just take it back. He was a good client and the gallery owner surely wouldn't quibble. Deep down, though, Biswas knew he'd be too embarrassed to ask for his money back.

What kind of collector purchased something at one minute only to return it the next? He was no dilettante. Hopefully the print would grow on him.

Turning away from his unfortunate purchase, he contemplated the small photograph he held. It showed a smiling woman standing in front of the Eiffel Tower. 'What am I supposed to do with this?' he grunted. Emmanuel Bole gently took the picture from his hand and turned it over. Written on the back in faded blue biro were two lines of numbers: a sort code and an account number. Biswas scanned the numbers, then looked at Manny. 'This is where he has his money?'

The bodyguard nodded.

Manny's going through one of his silent phases, Biswas thought. It's his way of dealing with the fact that he's fucked things up. From past experience, he knew that Manny could stay mute for hours, days or even weeks, depending on the magnitude of his faux pas. It was like dealing with a giant sulking teenager. 'And it's got sufficient funds?'

Manny shrugged.

'Let's work on the assumption that it has.' Biswas felt like an idiot, having to hold both sides of the conversation. 'How are we going to get our hands on it?'

Manny looked at him blankly.

'How are we going to get the money out of this account,' Biswas repeated, his patience waning, 'given that you managed to kill the old man?'

'I didn't kill him,' Manny blurted out. 'He just kind of, well, died while I happened to be present.'

At least he's talking again, Biswas reflected, determined to be grateful for small mercies. 'You scared him silly and he had a heart attack.'

'I didn't do anything to him.'

Biswas shook his head in dismay. It was supposed to be a simple exercise in debt collection: how could it possibly have gone so badly wrong?

'These things happen,' Manny continued, his voice surprisingly gentle for such a big man. 'I never even touched him. It wasn't my fault, boss. He was old. For all we know, he could have been due to have the heart attack even if I hadn't been there.'

I like you better mute, Biswas thought. 'And no one saw you at the flat?'

'No one,' the giant confirmed. 'He lived alone. A lonely old man.' Manny pointed at the photo. 'That's his wife. She died years ago.'

'Okay, okay,' Biswas said wearily, 'so we know where the money is. But how do we access it?'

'We need to hack the account.' Manny made it sound like a statement of the obvious. 'Before anyone realises he's dead and closes it down.'

Biswas scratched his nose. 'Who do we know who can do that for us?'

Manny mentioned a few names.

'They're all in India,' Biswas pointed out. 'We need someone closer.'

'But this is the global economy, boss. Geography doesn't matter nowadays.'

'Thank you, Mr MBA,' Biswas said scornfully. 'Trust me on this, we want someone we can control, not some little devil sitting halfway around the world who can make our money appear *and* disappear before we can lay a finger on it. Someone who knows that they will lose all of their fingers – instantly – if they start tapping the wrong keys.'

'Yes, boss.'

Biswas shoved the photo into the back pocket of his freshly pressed jeans. 'And I think I know just the man.'

TWENTY-ONE

Based on a combination of extensive research, detailed analysis and gut instinct, Gerry Durkan had a strong fancy for Red Tassel in the nine fifteen at Suffolk Downs. He was just about to place a suitably large bet on his chosen horse when the office door swung open and an unannounced visitor walked in.

Durkan recognised the man's face well enough, despite it being disfigured by a latticework of scars. 'What the hell happened to you?' he exclaimed.

'You know perfectly well what happened.' Looking like an extra in a horror movie, Bob Biswas walked across the room and sat down in front of the desk. 'I imagine you're surprised to see me.'

'Surprised and delighted.' Durkan was appalled to notice that the man was wearing novelty socks. How could someone with Homer Simpson grinning over the top of his loafers expect to be taken seriously?

'You must have known I was coming.'

'It's always good to see you, Bob, although you might have made an appointment.'

'If I'd made an appointment, you'd be halfway to Brazil by now.'

'Hardly.' Durkan had been waiting for Mr Biswas for quite a little while. Payback can be a bitch, right enough.

If you decide to kill someone, you really should get the job done. In the case of Bob Biswas, Gerry Durkan had tried and failed.

Twice. Under the circumstances, it was hardly a surprise that the Indian gangster had turned up, looking for his revenge.

Durkan's eyes flicked to the top drawer of his desk. It had remained unlocked since the news of Balthazar Quant's death. The Beretta 9mm nestling inside should be more than sufficient to extricate him from any unpleasantness, assuming that his silver tongue couldn't do the job on its own.

Placing his hands on his knees, Biswas leaned forward. 'Not much of a business partner, are you, Gerry?'

Durkan knitted his eyebrows together, trying to look confused. 'What do you mean, Bob?'

'Well, first you steal my diamonds.'

'Good God.' The City Airport heist had been more than a year ago now. Durkan was proud of the robbery: it showed he still had the balls for that kind of thing. But it had not been a mere vanity project. The cash raised from the diamonds had helped see Macroom Castlebar Salle through a particularly vicious cash-flow squeeze. Indeed, if it hadn't been for Biswas's involuntary donation, the business might have gone under. 'Are you still going on about that?'

'I'm not the kind to forgive and forget.'

'You should try it.' Durkan's eyes sparkled with mischief. 'If I can forgive the Brits for the rape of my homeland over hundreds of years, what's a few stones?'

'You should never reward bad behaviour.'

'The police never did catch the people responsible, did they?' Durkan shook his head in dismay. 'Don't misunderstand me, Bob, I'm not being blasé about the whole thing. It was a shameful incident, truly shameful. And – from what I read in the newspapers – it was an extremely unsatisfactory investigation. You'd think with all the money spent on law enforcement in this country that, frankly, they'd do a much better job.'

'The whole fiasco has cost me a lot.' There was more than a hint of self-pity in Biswas's voice.

'Didn't the insurance cover it?'

'The excess was a killer,' Biswas admitted, through gritted teeth. 'And the bastards are already clawing much of the payout back through the increased premiums. It's a joke.'

'That's insurance companies for you.' Durkan edged the drawer open far enough to catch a reassuring glimpse of the loaded semi-automatic.

'Hands where I can see them, Gerry.'

Durkan raised both hands, in mock surrender. 'Anyway, I thought I heard you were getting out of the diamonds business.' According to the grapevine, Biswas's bookmaking operations were throwing off so much cash that the Indian no longer needed to bother with any of his ancillary activities.

'I like to keep my hand in. It's always good to stay diversified. And, besides, there are synergies.'

Durkan dropped his hands onto the table. 'I can see that.' Apart from anything else, diamonds were portable, discreet and difficult to trace. All in all, a very handy commodity to be able to utilise for money-laundering purposes. Forget the Silk Road, Agora and all that cryptocurrency nonsense. Try to do business on the so-called 'dark web' and the Americans would be all over you in a New York fucking minute. A small packet of diamonds, on the other hand, was far harder to track and intercept. Cyberspace was for the teenage geeks who never managed to get out of their bedrooms. Proper criminals knew that old school was best.

'What I don't understand is why you won't just admit that you were behind the robbery. These things happen – bygones and all that. But the basic lack of honesty – the lack of professional courtesy – that is what is so troubling.'

'I don't like to see you *troubled*, Bob, but the truth is, it wasn't me. You have plenty of enemies in this city – it could have been anyone.' Durkan flicked through a mental roll-call of his guest's enemies. It was an impressive list. 'Like your lady friend, for example.' Biswas had a soft spot for Elke Poosen, the London-domiciled head of a notorious Brussels crime family.

'Leave Elke out of this,' Biswas muttered. 'We have a very good relationship.'

'I hear she hasn't been around much recently.'

'She's still getting over the death of her husband,' Biswas told him. 'Spending quite a bit of time in Ibiza.'

'That must have been quite a shock.' The killer of Kevin Lamoot, Elke Poosen's late husband, had never been caught but Durkan had heard plenty of rumours about who might have been responsible.

'Yes.' Biswas stifled a cough.

'Thinking about it, that was another case where the police did a poor job.' Durkan's eyes flicked to the door. 'Is Emmanuel with you?'

'Manny!' Biswas waved a hand in the air. Seconds later, the massive henchman appeared in the doorway.

'Nice to see you, Manny,' Durkan lied. 'I trust you're well.'

The giant, hands clasped in front of his groin, said nothing.

Durkan turned back to Biswas. 'The British police like to think they're the best in the world but they're nothing special.'

'They caught you.'

'That was the army.'

'Big difference,' Biswas scoffed.

'Yes, there is. The point is that Kevin's death was yet another botched police investigation. There are so many of them, these days, no one even notices. So, you see, what happened to you isn't much of a surprise. For sure, it was nothing personal. You just have to shrug your shoulders and move on.'

'Justice is a lottery in this country,' Biswas agreed.

'Poor Elke, she lost her husband.'

'The man was an idiot.' Biswas briefly considered how he would feel if Arumina shuffled off this mortal coil. As with everything, there would be pros and cons. Being a widower, he decided, was something he would be able to take in his stride.

'I have no doubt that Elke'll recover, in time. She's a very strong woman.'

'And honest, too,' Biswas remarked pointedly.

Durkan gave a noncommittal response.

'I know she wouldn't steal from me.'

'And neither did I,' Durkan insisted. 'I had nothing to do with the airport job. I don't get involved in any of that rough-and-tumble, these days, I swear to God. There are easier ways to make money, believe me.'

'You swear to God?' A sickly smile crossed Biswas's face. 'I thought you were an atheist.'

'I am. A Catholic atheist.'

'Enough of this sophistry, Gerry. First you try to rob me. Then you send me a parcel bomb. And then – then you send a guy to shoot me. What kind of friend is that? I suppose you'll tell me I should be grateful you've only tried to kill me twice.'

Only twice, Durkan thought, so far.

'Thank God we're friends. I hate to think what you would have tried if we'd been enemies.'

'Bob—'

Biswas held up a hand. 'You know what the worst thing is? It's not the money. It's not the violence. It's the dishonesty, Gerry.' He tapped his breast with an index finger. 'If you're going to stab me, stab me in the front. Don't stab me in the back. Come on, we have standards.'

'We do,' Durkan agreed.

'We're grown-ups. We know the risks. Things happen in business. Bad things. But, like you said, it's never personal. You can't take it personally. I *don't* take it personally, even when someone tries to kill me. We play a big boys' game, with big boys' rules. You don't run away crying when things go off the rails.'

Durkan shifted in his seat. Get to the feckin' point, will ya?

'However, without honesty, it's difficult to maintain a professional operation. Impossible, in fact. You must have trust. That is simply essential.'

'Again, I have to repeat, not guilty as charged.'

The grin on Bob Biswas's ugly mug only grew wider. 'Gerry, you are a truly terrible liar.'

'If it had been me doing all these terrible things, I wouldn't try to bullshit my way out of it. Not for a second. It's just not my style.' Pausing for breath, Durkan sat back in his chair. If Bob Biswas wanted to argue the point, they could sit here all night. It was almost like being back in the IRA, enjoying a cosy little chat with his RUC chums in Castlereagh police station. Know your lines, keep a straight face and fuck the evidence.

'The guy you sent to kill me. He gave you up before Manny killed him.'

No, he didn't. Durkan held the gaze of his unwelcome guest. Don't try to bluff a bluffer, sunshine. 'Did you want something, Bob? I'm sorry not to be a better host but Security will be here in about . . .' ostentatiously, he glanced at the chunky Rolex clamped on his wrist '. . . thirty seconds to throw you out.'

'That Arab girl?' Biswas pushed out his lips. 'I'm afraid she won't be coming to your rescue any time soon.'

'She's Portuguese.' Sitting up in his seat, Durkan cursed Camila Steinbrecher. The woman looked good with a Glock in her hand, but he had always suspected that she was 'all talk and no trousers', as his old da liked to say. He was going to have to give some serious thought to his hiring procedures: the quality of people coming through the door simply wasn't high enough.

'Whatever,' Biswas said drily. 'I hope you provide health insurance.'

'We have full BUPA cover,' Durkan said stiffly. 'I look after my people.'

'Good. She's going to need it.'

'What do you want, Bob?' Buttocks tightening, Durkan forced himself not to look at Manny.

'The guy you sent to kill me – don't you want to know what happened to him?'

'I didn't send anyone to do anything,' Durkan repeated.

'Part of him ended up in a container going to Brazil.' Biswas turned to his goon. 'It was the head and the arms, wasn't it?'

'And his balls.' The monster smirked.

'Ah, yes, I forgot. Anyway, the rest of him ended up in Sweden.'

'What do you want?' Durkan repeated.

'Well, I was going to kill you—'

'Like you killed Balthazar?'

'That was just to get things warmed up. A demonstration of intent, something to help get you in the right frame of mind to die.'

Yes, yes, Durkan thought. And people say I'm the bullshitter.

'I like people to be able to see what's coming, give them time to contemplate their mortality. There's no benefit in making things too quick.'

'Bob,' Durkan chuckled, 'I've been ready to die since I was fourteen.' He felt himself begin to relax. It appeared that the only way this guy was going to kill him tonight was by boring him to death.

'Ah, yes. I almost forgot. Gerry Durkan, the hard man. The terrorist who tried to kill Maggie.'

'You were probably one of those guys who got a chub on for Mrs T. Am I right?'

Biswas gave an embarrassed grin. 'She was quite a woman, back in the day.'

Doesn't mean I ever wanted to fuck her. 'Those days are long gone.'

'No one can ever fully escape their past.'

'I don't know about that.'

'Well, *I* do. Anyway, it would be a shame for such a great fighter, a freedom fighter, the man who tried to blow up the blessed Margaret Thatcher no less, to end up shot behind his desk while playing on his computer. That would be such a poor ending to such a colourful life. It wouldn't look good in your obituary, would it?'

Durkan let his hand rest on the still-open desk drawer. 'So,' he sighed, 'let's write a different ending.'

'I want you to redeem yourself.' Getting to his feet, Biswas stuck a hand into his jacket pocket. Durkan stiffened, relaxing only when he saw Biswas pull out a photograph, rather than a weapon. 'I need you to help me recover something.' Biswas stepped forward and placed the picture on Durkan's desk.

Gerry Durkan looked at the tourist snap of the woman in front of the Eiffel Tower. 'What's this?'

'Other side,' Biswas grunted.

Durkan flipped over the photo and stared at the numbers on the back. 'A bank account?'

'Yes. I need you to empty it for me. Get me the money that's in this account – all of it, no skimming – and I'll call it quits.'

Durkan dropped the photo onto the desk. 'How much are we talking about?'

'Doesn't matter,' Biswas said. 'Just empty it. Make the money disappear before transferring the funds to my nominated account. Then we go our separate ways. This time for good.'

Durkan rubbed his chin, wondering how best to exploit his newly found leverage. 'And who does the account belong to?'

'That hardly matters either.'

'I wouldn't want to be taking money from a bunch of widows and orphans.' Durkan pouted.

'There are no widows and orphans, Gerry. And, if it makes you feel any better, the man who had the account is no longer with us. Stealing from the dead is hardly a crime, is it?'

'It's still illegal, of course.' Durkan picked up a pencil and scribbled down the account details on an orange Post-it note. 'And illegality is, as you know, definitely not my thing now.' When Biswas started to protest, he held up a hand. 'For you, however, I might be able to reach out to someone who knows about such things.' Getting out of his chair, he handed the picture back to Biswas. 'Give me forty-eight hours.'

TWENTY-TWO

Staring at the screen of his phone, Gerry Durkan emitted a satisfied cackle. Red Tassel had won its race by a short head, handing him a tidy profit. At least something had been retrieved from a miserable evening.

'Is something funny?' Propped up by a mound of pillows, Camila Steinbrecher carefully shifted her position in the bed in front of him.

'No.' Durkan looked around the private room on the fourth floor of the Cecil Wing of the Keays-Parkinson Memorial Hospital. The place was nothing spectacular, just a box with a TV bolted to the wall and a small window looking out onto an empty car park. But for this, along with a rather rudimentary room service and a random selection of glossy magazines, the insurance company was shelling out £860 a night. My premiums will go through the roof, he reflected dolefully, thinking back to Bob Biswas's comments about insurance companies. For all the difference it made, the cost might as well be coming straight out of his own pocket.

At least the room afforded them the opportunity to discuss MCS business. After Biswas and his goon had left the office, Durkan had downed a couple of large Scotches in an attempt to relax a little. Placing a hand on the frame at the bottom of the bed, he steadied himself, trying not to breathe on the patient.

The clearly chastened head of security gazed at her boss expectantly.

'Are they looking after you properly?' he asked.

'Yes, thank you,' she said primly. 'There was no reason for you to come over.'

'Yes, well, I just wanted to check you were okay.' Durkan now regretted having made the trip. He didn't expect people to bow and scrape in his presence, but a little gratitude went a long way. There was no need for any bad grace from Ms Steinbrecher. Apart from a bruised rib, a sprained wrist and a cut lip, she was essentially uninjured. Despite the gloom, it was clear that the woman's slightly equine good looks remained untouched. There was nothing that a steady intake of painkillers and a good night's sleep wouldn't take care of. Clearly, the man mountain Manny had gone easy on her, certainly compared to poor old Balthazar. Durkan was relieved that he didn't have another body on his hands. The last thing he needed was the police back at his door any time soon. MCS had always been run on the basis that it could withstand the occasional casual scrutiny of the authorities; this was the kind of 'light touch' regulation on which the long-term success of the City of London had been built. Anything beyond that and all bets were off.

Steinbrecher lifted a plastic beaker from the bedside table and drank some water. 'They're going to keep me in overnight for observation and then I can go home in the morning.' She returned the beaker to the table. 'All being well, I expect I'll be back into work the day after tomorrow.'

'No rush. Take your time.' Durkan wondered about handing Steinbrecher her P45. Even by his standards, though, it seemed a bit harsh to sack the woman while she was in her hospital bed.

Plus, she still had her uses.

Oblivious to her boss's thoughts, Steinbrecher broke the silence. 'I'll make a formal complaint to the police on my way home.'

'Eh?' He looked at her aghast.

'I'll go to the station at Canary Wharf,' she explained. 'You know who these people are, right? I want to press charges against them.'

Feeling himself start to sway, Durkan gripped the bedframe more tightly. 'No, no,' he stammered. 'I don't think there's any need for that.'

'But I want them arrested. And after what happened to Balthazar . . .' She let the thought trail off.

'I don't think the two things were connected.'

Steinbrecher raised a carefully plucked eyebrow.

'What happened to Balthazar was nothing to do with MCS,' he said, trying to sound casual. 'And what happened to you, well, that was just an overwrought client. Sometimes people get carried away. These things happen. Anyway, we've kissed and made up.'

She shot him a quizzical look.

'It's just an expression but, look, no police, okay? We don't need that kind of attention.'

Clearly unconvinced, Steinbrecher bit her upper lip.

'You've had to take one for the team,' he said soothingly. 'That's something I appreciate. It won't be forgotten. But it must be kept among ourselves. I'll deal with it – I have dealt with it. Now, we move on.' He paused. 'You will be properly rewarded, I promise you.'

'I think I need more painkillers.' Reaching behind her head, Steinbrecher pressed a green button on a small panel attached to the head of the bed to call for a nurse.

'My word, as they say, is my bond,' Durkan promised. 'And this is the best way of dealing with the issue, resolving the, erm, misunderstanding and moving on.'

'Whatever you think.'

That's right, whatever I think. Thank fuck we've got that sorted out. Sticking his free hand into his trouser pocket, Durkan pulled out a Post-it and handed it to her.

Steinbrecher squinted at his scribble. 'What's this?'

'It's the details of a bank account. Nothing fancy or complicated, just a regular retail depositor in the UK. I need one of our cyber-security guys to take a look at it.' Durkan mentioned the names of a couple of contractors MCS had used in the past. 'Their details are on the database. Can you see if either of them is available? Usual rates, usual billing arrangements.' That meant no invoices, payment via a paper bag containing cash. 'Needs to be done within the next thirty-six hours at the outside.' He wanted to give himself a bit of wiggle room, compared to the deadline he had agreed with Biswas. 'They just need to, erm, liquidate the account and route the proceeds to one of the Botswanan accounts, via Mauritius. Standard operating procedure.'

Steinbrecher's eyes grew wide. 'You want me to steal the money?'

'Not you,' Durkan said, irked by the woman's inability to execute the simplest request without the need for a debate. 'Use one of our sub-contractors.'

'That's not what I meant.'

'No one is *stealing* anything. These are simply funds that have been somewhat misplaced and need to be redirected to the right owners.'

Steinbrecher carefully folded the slip of paper into four, then into four again. 'Is this a service you are providing for the people who beat me up?'

'No. Completely different. Apart from anything else, I have told these guys that their behaviour was completely unacceptable. They have been banned as clients. For good.'

Steinbrecher gave the call button another stab.

'This other matter,' Durkan pointed at the piece of paper, which was still in her hand, 'is just an administrative issue, nothing illegal. Or unethical, for that matter.' He gestured towards her phone, sitting on the table by the bed. 'Just speak to one of the contractors. They'll know what to do. Nothing will come back to MCS.'

Muttering to herself, Steinbrecher gave the green button a third slap.

'It's a favour for another client and really quite urgent, so

let me know when it's done. We can talk again in the morning.'
Durkan turned slowly, shuffling towards the door. 'I hope you
have a good night's rest.'

TWENTY-THREE

The forty-sixth floor of Biffen Heights – a residential tower that housed thousands of Docklands worker ants – afforded sweeping views across the river. Standing in Balthazar Quant's tiny living room, Alison Roche watched the rain falling on Greenwich Park. The sergeant was in no mood to appreciate the view. The baby, David, had been up regularly in the night and Alex, citing an early work commitment, had excused himself from his share of the parental duties. By her own calculation, Roche had managed less than two hours' sleep. She downed the last of the cappuccino she had bought from a café downstairs. It would take a lot more caffeine for her to make it through the day.

'What are we looking for?' Standing in the doorway, WPC Ingrid Yates snapped on a pair of latex gloves.

'I don't know,' Roche admitted. 'Anything unusual, anything suspicious. Anything that might point to someone who might have wanted to smash Mr Quant's skull in.'

'That narrows it down, then,' the WPC said sarkily.

Don't give me attitude, girl. Roche made a mental note to give Inspector Carlyle, her erstwhile boss at Charing Cross, another call. The sooner Carlyle could help her escape from the hell of her east London posting the better. As far as Roche could determine, Limehouse was totally devoid of sympathetic colleagues, which made doing your job pretty much impossible.

WPC Yates was a case in point. A protégée of Detective

Inspector Jay Wrench, the petite blonde was the focus of much of the station's lurid gossip. Roche had barely been there an hour when two different people had told her the story of how the WPC had, allegedly, been caught giving Wrench a blow-job in the ladies' loos at the Prospect of Whitby, a favourite after-work drinking hole among officers. At least, Roche reflected, she herself wasn't going to be doing any after-work drinking for a while – for about the next eighteen years, give or take.

For her part, Yates, confident of her place in Wrench's affections, made no effort to kowtow to an interloper like Roche. Hands on hips, the WPC stood in the doorway, awaiting further instructions.

'Why don't you start in the bedroom?' Roche placed her coffee cup on the floor, then put on a pair of gloves. 'I'll start in here. Shouldn't take too long.'

'I hope not.' Yates sniffed. 'I've got to be somewhere in half an hour.'

Roche clenched her jaw. 'Shouldn't take too long,' she repeated mechanically. Now was not the time to pull rank. Her only concern was to get her old job back and leave this rabble behind as quickly as possible.

'Fine.'

Roche watched Yates skulk down the corridor. 'Right,' she muttered to herself, 'let's get on with it.'

After barely five minutes, the WPC reappeared in the living room to find Roche on her knees, with one hand stuck down the back of the sofa.

'Found anything?' the sergeant asked.

'No.' Yates sounded very happy about it. 'Other than an eclectic collection of porn and an unopened box of condoms, nothing of any interest at all.'

'Eclectic?'

'Yeah. Some straight stuff, some gay stuff, some weird stuff.'

'A broad range of interests.'

'Yeah.' Yates giggled. 'He has one magazine that's just naked men having sex with women wearing the hijab.'

Roche shrugged. Male peccadilloes had long since ceased to interest her much.

'*Burqa Babes.* Of course, it could be the same woman under different veils.'

Roche groaned.

'Maybe al-Qaeda took him out for crimes against the sister-hood.' Yates pulled off her gloves.

'I'm not sure women's rights are a priority for those guys,' Roche mumbled, more to herself than to her young colleague.

'Then again,' Yates added cheerily, 'they would have be-headed him, right? Stuck it on YouTube for everyone to watch.'

Jesus, Roche thought. Let's hope they never put you to work on community relations. The Met was spending millions on diversity awareness training yet you still had a kid like Yates who talked like that. It was just as well there was no one listen-ing to this conversation or they could both end up in all sorts of trouble.

'Anyway, I need to get going. Jay's waiting for me.' The WPC looked at Roche, as if defying the sergeant to veto the rendezvous.

Roche was too exhausted to argue. 'Off to the Prospect of Whitby?'

'No.' Yates blushed but didn't elaborate.

'I'll see you back at the station.'

'Erm, not for a while. I'm off for the next three days.' The message was clear: leave me alone.

Returning her attention to the sofa, Roche refused to give Yates the satisfaction of knowing how annoyed she was by Jay Wrench's rota arrangements. This was a bloody murder investi-gation, for God's sake, and the DI was fiddling the work roster so that his bimbo could bunk off for a quick shag on police time. Then again, even the worst kind of police work had to be prefer-able to shagging Jay Wrench.

'Enjoy.'

'I will. See ya.'

Roche listened to the flat's front door open and slam shut. 'I hope he gives you the clap,' she muttered angrily. Running her hand along the back of the sofa, she came up with several items. Dropping them onto the cushion, she inspected her haul: a 10p coin, a flyer for a local takeaway and two business cards. One of the cards was for Quant, the other for Nelly Ternan Escorts. The latter had a website address but no other contact details. Ignoring the other items, Roche dropped it into her jacket pocket.

'Maybe Mr Quant's range of interests wasn't that broad, after all,' she mused, struggling to her feet. In the end, it always came down to sex or money. Or sex and money. That was what Carlyle liked to say. Maybe, this time, the inspector would be right.

TWENTY-FOUR

Susan Phillips added just enough milk to her coffee to turn it the colour of Thames sludge. After some careful stirring with a tea-spoon, she took a tentative sip and signalled her approval. 'They do good coffee here.'

Carlyle looked around. 'It's a nice spot.' They were sitting at a table outside a café at the top end of Lamb's Conduit Street called Tutti's. On the corner of Great Ormond Street, it was about two minutes' walk from Holborn police station.

The pathologist had been stationed at Holborn for the last seventeen years, even longer than Carlyle had been working at Charing Cross. She shot him a wry smile over the top of her cup. 'Helen still trying to control your caffeine intake?'

'She's trying. And, to be fair, I'm not drinking as much as I used to.' Carlyle lifted his glass in mock salute. This morning he had plumped for a berry smoothie, one of the few things in this life that was supposed to be good for you and tasted nice. From the radio behind the counter, inside the café, he could make out David Bowie singing 'Kooks'. The song always made him think of when Alice had been born, a blissfully sunny day that would always exist in his memory as the high point of his entire life. It was a long time ago now, though.

The inspector sucked a mouthful of juice through his straw and watched a couple of doctors heading towards them, deep in conversation. Phillips carefully placed her cup back on the saucer. 'How's your dad?'

Carlyle watched the doctors disappear inside the cafe. 'Not good.' He tapped the screen of his phone, sitting on the table. 'I could get the call at any moment.'

Right on cue, the device started to ring. On the screen was a number he didn't recognise. The inspector made no effort to pick it up.

'Aren't you going to answer it?' asked the pathologist.

He shook his head. 'It's not Stine, the woman looking after him.'

Phillips reached forward and gave him a consoling pat on the arm. 'It must be a strain, waiting. Don't you wish you were down there with him?'

'To be honest, I'd rather be working. If – when – it happens, I can be down there in half an hour. As it is, the auld fella's completely out of the game. I sat with him for a while last night – he doesn't know you're there. I ended up reading the paper. If I was there on full-time death watch, I'd be sitting around, moping, drinking too much coffee and generally being a pain in the arse.' He gave her a weak smile. 'And going quietly round the bend at the same time.'

'Are you still using the stuff from Dominic Silver?' Apart from Helen, Phillips was the only person who knew about the illegal lengths to which the inspector had gone to get pain relief for his father. If she disapproved of his methods, at least she had the good grace to keep her thoughts to herself.

'There's no need – the NHS finally came through. He's on a drip.' Sucking the dregs of the smoothie from the glass, Carlyle made an unsophisticated rasping sound. 'All above board and legal.'

'That's good.'

'Better late than ever, I suppose.' Placing the glass on the table, he lifted his arms into the air, as if they were a pair of scales. 'It's some bureaucratic calculation: you don't get the drugs until things get so bad that one day you do get the drugs. It's a total pain, no pun intended, when all you want to do is die in peace.'

'I suppose that's why people end up going to clinics in Switzerland.'

'We couldn't afford that,' Carlyle admitted, 'so we went for the budget option. To be fair to Dom, he was very good about it. It's not really his thing, these days.'

'Yeah, I heard that his gallery on Cork Street was doing well. The man's certainly got an interesting CV.'

'You can say that again. Not many people go from being a cop to dealing drugs to selling Japanese watercolours. Good on him, though. People might look down their noses at him but he's a very decent bloke.' He was surprised by the vehemence in his voice.

'You two go back a long way.'

'We were at Hendon together, on the same training course. Dom's one of the few people from the Job, I've known longer than you.' A mail van roared through the junction, almost taking out a cyclist. 'When he said he was getting into the art business, I thought it was a joke, handy for a bit of money-laundering, you know. But, fair dos, it seems like he's making a proper fist of it. Then again, the prices he charges,' Carlyle shook his head, 'drugs would be a lot cheaper.'

Phillips said nothing.

'Anyway, speaking of career changes, what about you?'

'I just felt it was time to stop – you know?'

Carlyle didn't. 'What will you do now?' he asked, genuinely curious.

'I don't know. That's the fun of it all. I'm going to do some travelling, slow down a bit. Think about what I want to do next.'

'Sounds like a plan.' Carlyle scratched behind his ear. Truth be told, it didn't sound like much of a plan at all. He occasionally fantasised about retiring. Leaving aside the small matter of money, he knew he would struggle without the routine and discipline the Job imposed. Until he could find something to replace it, the idea of leaving was simply a non-starter.

'I was thinking about going back to university.'

'Oh?'

'Yes. There's a SOAS degree in conflict studies that I quite fancy doing.' She tapped the side of her head with an index finger. 'Something to keep the old brain ticking over.'

'Neat segue,' Carlyle suggested. 'I was going to ask you about the late Professor Grom.'

'I knew this wouldn't just be a social visit,' Phillips chided him. 'Not your style.'

'It was, kind of.' Carlyle gestured at her coffee cup. 'My chance to buy you a cup of coffee to celebrate your retirement.'

'You are too kind.'

He gave a small bow. 'I know.'

'You're coming to my leaving party, I hope?'

'Of course,' he lied enthusiastically. 'I'm looking forward to it. The, erm . . .'

'The Monkey in Orbit.'

'It's supposed be very good. Best new bar in Smithfield for ages.'

She raised a sceptical eyebrow.

'One of my sergeants told me all about it.'

'It would be nice to see you there.'

'Of course,' he said. 'Meantime, what about poor old Grom?'

Phillips toyed with her cup. 'You're not going to like this.'

'Not a heart attack?'

'It *was* a heart attack, but it looks like it was brought on by some kind of struggle. There were marks on his neck and bruising on his chest.'

'Great.' Carlyle began poking around the empty glass with his straw. 'So much for putting this one quickly to bed.'

'It was never going to be that straightforward,' Phillips responded. 'You were always going to have to investigate why someone stuffed him into a cupboard.' Pushing back her chair, Phillips got to her feet. 'I'll write up my report this afternoon and then I'm done.'

'Yes.' Jumping to his feet, Carlyle leaned over the table and

117

gave her an awkward hug. 'Good luck,' was all he could come up with.

'I expect to see you at my party,' Phillips said firmly.

'Of course.'

'And it won't be that long till I'm coming to yours.'

'I suppose not.' He shuddered at the thought.

'Anyway, good luck to you with this one, John. It's a rather messy and unsatisfactory case for me to be going out on.'

'It'll get sorted,' he vowed, 'one way or another.'

'Yes, I suppose it will. I'll see you later.'

'Yes.' Returning to his seat, he watched Phillips head back down the street, one of his peers, part of a small and dwindling band of friends, walking into the sunset. At this rate, he thought unhappily, I'm going to end up not knowing anyone on the Job at all.

TWENTY-FIVE

Calling the number on the escort-agency website, Roche was referred to a woman who introduced herself as the operations manager. With the business being run out of a 'virtual office' somewhere in cyberspace, the woman agreed to meet in the Golden Sun, a pub near Euston station.

'You're not Nelly Ternan?' Irritated at being unable to track down the agency to a physical address, the sergeant was further annoyed to find a composed and good-looking woman sitting opposite her.

'Nelly Ternan was the mistress of Charles Dickens.' Karen Jansen toyed with a large glass of Chablis. 'We were rather amused by the idea of calling the business after her.'

Roche opened a packet of salt and vinegar crisps and placed it in the middle of the table, inviting Jansen to help herself. 'And who's "we"?'

Jansen ignored the snack. 'Well, it was my idea. The owner was happy to go along with it.'

'And who is the owner?'

'Do we need to go into that?'

'Yes, under the circumstances, I think we do.'

'Your call,' Jansen conceded, not willing to argue the point. 'The guy's name is Vernon Holder. You might've heard of him.'

Sucking diet cola through a straw, Roche tried to think back to the various pimps she had come across during her time. Her mind remained stubbornly blank. The reality was that her pre-baby career was all a bit of a blur. She still had some considerable way to go to get properly back up to speed. 'Don't think so.'

'The police will know him,' Jansen said. 'I don't know if Vernon has a formal record but the kind of businesses he operates in, well, they inevitably attract the attention of the authorities.'

'And what about you? How long have you been working for Mr . . .'

'Holder.'

'Yeah. Mr Holder.'

Jansen scrutinised Roche carefully, unsure if the cop was as distracted as she seemed, or whether it was an act and she was just fishing. 'He took over the business I was working for, maybe seven or eight months ago.'

'And what do you do, exactly?'

'As the operations manager, I keep the show on the road on a day-to-day basis.'

'So, you know about all the clients?'

'That's right.'

'Including the ones that keel over?'

'Ah, yes, poor Professor Grom. I read about it online. Funny carry-on. How d'ya think the poor sod ended up in a cupboard?'

Roche looked at her blankly. 'Sorry?'

Jansen quickly backtracked. 'Forgive me, I was thinking about something else. I get my wires crossed sometimes.'

'Tell me about it,' Roche sympathised.

'Which client are you interested in?'

'A guy called Balthazar Quant.'

Jansen pursed her lips. 'The name doesn't ring any bells. Let me have a look at our database.' Taking a phone from her bag, she began tapping on her screen. 'See if I can find him.'

Roche looked on, impressed. 'You keep everything on there?'

'Great, isn't it? The wonders of modern technology. I have the whole office in my pocket.'

Roche considered the hundred thousand mobiles stolen in

London in the previous year. 'What happens if you lose the phone?'

'I have this killer app,' Jansen explained, not looking up, 'that wipes everything if it goes missing, or someone nicks it. Everything's backed up on the cloud and I can just get a new handset.'

Like most people, Roche had only the vaguest sense of what 'the cloud' was. 'Is that secure?'

'It is on the servers we use,' Jansen proclaimed. 'You can't cut costs when it comes to data protection.'

'No, I suppose not.'

'What we save on office costs, we spend on cybersecurity. Swings and roundabouts.'

Roche looked on, none the wiser.

'Anyway, O, P, Q. Here we go. Q is a good surname to search – we only have two Qs, including, bingo, a Mr B. Quant. Platinum Amex holder,' she gave a small grunt of approval, 'Docklands address.'

'I've got that.' Roche felt herself beginning ever so slightly to warm to the woman sitting opposite her. Apart from anything else, her attitude towards sharing information with the police was refreshingly relaxed.

Jansen dug deeper into her Excel spreadsheet. 'Looks like the gentleman was an occasional client. Outcalls. Three times in the last year, the last time just over two months ago. No complaints from any of the girls.' Reaching for her glass, she took a mouthful of wine. 'What's he done?'

'He's dead.'

'Dead?' Almost choking on her drink, Jansen coughed violently.

'Someone beat him to death,' Roche said, 'and stuffed him into a cement mixer.'

Getting the coughing under control, Jansen took another mouthful of wine. 'Bloody hell, they're falling like flies.'

'What do you mean?'

'Nothing,' Jansen said hastily. 'There's a lot of churn in this business, as you can imagine. I can see we're going to need another marketing push. Meantime, poor old Mr Quant can be removed from our database. No more special offers for him.'

Roche said nothing.

'When did this happen?' Jansen asked.

'Yesterday.'

'Bummer. Stuffed in a concrete mixer, eh?'

'It happened to be handy. For whoever killed him, that is.'

'I bet the media loved that. I wonder how I missed it.'

'It only made a paragraph at the bottom of page thirty-nine in the *Standard*,' Roche observed. She was very pleased that no other papers had reported the killing. Journalists were an added hassle that she could do without. 'Which of your girls met Quant last?' she asked. 'I need to have a word with her.'

'I won't have that on here.' Jansen gestured at the screen of her phone. 'But I can find out for you. She may still be working for us, she may not. Like I said, churn's a bitch.'

Struggling to empathise, Roche glanced at her watch. 'I need to get going.' Fishing a business card out of her bag, she dropped it on the table. 'You can get me on the mobile number.'

'Sure.' Jansen slipped the card into her jacket pocket.

'It's nothing heavy.' Roche tried to sound reassuring. 'I'm only interested in Quant. I'm not going to cause your girl any trouble.'

'Understood.' Jansen watched Roche get to her feet. 'I'll see if she's still on the books and let you know. Even if she's not, we might still have a mobile number or an email address, you never know.'

'Thanks.'

'No problem.'

Jansen tracked Roche as she walked out of the pub, turning her attention back to the phone as the cop disappeared from view. On the page of the spreadsheet, next to Quant's name, there was a series of dates. Next to each date there was a set of initials. Finishing the last of her wine, Jansen contemplated the last set of initials and sighed.

MR.

Melody Rainbow.

'Melody,' she groaned, 'you are such a total shit magnet.'

TWENTY-SIX

Back at Charing Cross, Carlyle was buttonholed by an energised Adam Palin.

'Looks like our dead professor liked a bit of a flutter,' the sergeant announced.

'Yes?' The deceased academic was turning out to be rather *too* interesting for Carlyle's liking.

'One of the neighbours called in last night, after we stuck a calling card through her letterbox.'

Jolly good, Carlyle thought morosely. In his experience, the only thing worse than useless members of the public were those who tried to be helpful. The latter always ended up wasting far more valuable police time than the former.

'I went round to have a chat with her at lunchtime,' Palin continued. 'Interesting woman, studying to be an architect. Made me a very nice cup of tea.'

Aha, the inspector thought. That explains the gleam in your eye. Carlyle wondered about the chances of a trainee architect being able to cure Palin of his unfortunate nun fixation. In theory, at least, the boy's chances of getting lucky had to be better if he wasn't facing competition from a Higher Being. 'She's not religious, is she?' he asked cheekily.

Palin's face darkened. 'What?'

'Nothing, sorry. What did this, er, lady . . .'

'Lucy. Lucy Briggs.'

Lucy? Carlyle conjured up an image of a wholesome smiling

Home Counties gal with a battered old Volvo and a Cocker Spaniel. Played hockey or, maybe, netball; at worst, an occasional Church of England member, which was essentially the same as being an atheist when you got down to it.

'What did Lucy have to say about the recently departed prof?'

'They used to have coffee now and again. I think she felt a bit sorry for him, being on his own and stuff.'

Carlyle thought back to what the cleaning lady had said about Professor Grom's lady visitors. He wondered if the old dog had ever tried it on with his neighbour.

'She said that he was very nice, polite. "A gentleman of the old school" was the phrase she used.'

Apparently not.

'And he sometimes looked after her dog when she went on holiday, which was a big help.'

'What kind of dog?' Carlyle felt impressed by his own prescience.

'A Labradoodle.'

Maybe not.

Palin misunderstood the dismay on his face. 'I think they're quite nice.'

'Eh?'

'Labradoodles.'

Not much of an animal lover at the best of times, Carlyle couldn't quite believe he was having this conversation. 'And what the hell is a Labra-whatnot?'

'A Labradoodle,' Palin explained, 'is a cross between a Labrador and a Poodle.'

'And that kind of thing is allowed?' Carlyle raised an eyebrow in disbelief. 'Isn't it messing with nature?'

'There's nothing illegal about cross-breeding, as far as I know. And it's big business. These animals can cost a lot of money. Elsie cost twelve hundred quid.'

'Elsie?'

'Lucy's Labradoodle. She's lovely.'

'Well, I'm glad we sorted that out.' It took a moment for the inspector to recall the original point of their conversation. 'What else did you find out about the hooker-loving, part-time dog-sitter?'

'The only thing that seemed like it might be important was the betting. Like I said, Grom was into it in a big way. He told Lucy he'd lost quite a bit over the years.'

The inspector tried to recall any evidence of a gambling habit from his visit to Grom's flat – betting slips, copies of the *Racing Post*, promotional flyers from different bookies – but nothing came to mind.

'He seemed quite relaxed about it, though, given that he didn't have any other uses for his money. It was an entertainment, rather than a money-making enterprise.'

'Just as well,' Carlyle observed.

'Have you spoken to the pathologist yet?'

'Yeah. Phillips says it was a heart attack, but it looks like it was brought on by someone roughing him up at the time. Perhaps they were trying to put the squeeze on him, get him to pay some gambling debts, and the guy just keeled over.'

'And they shoved him in the cupboard?'

'Why not? Maybe they had OCD. Didn't want to leave a mess.'

'Gambling debts are a reasonable motive for beating someone up,' Palin mused, 'or threatening them, at least.'

'I don't think Ladbrokes employ those methods,' Carlyle countered.

Palin stroked his chin theatrically. 'But what if Grom wasn't using a reputable bookie?'

The inspector knew a cue when he heard one. 'What makes you think that might be the case?'

Palin puffed out his chest and adopted a pose that said *inspired policeman in action*. 'Grom didn't have an account with any of the big bookmaking firms.'

'How do you know?' Carlyle asked, happy to play along for now.

'Lucy gave me his email. I tried to log on to half a dozen of the big websites but none of them recognised the address.'

Carlyle felt his technological knowledge fraying at the edges. 'Don't you need a password as well?'

'Only if the email is registered. I didn't even get that far. None of them had the address on their databases.'

The inspector scratched his head. This was the kind of information you usually needed a warrant and several weeks of chasing to acquire. The idea that Palin had managed to circumvent all the bureaucracy with just an email address didn't seem likely. 'But aren't there millions of different betting sites? Even if Grom wasn't registered with the big firms, he could still have been using some of the others. Serious punters have multiple accounts anyway – he could have been using loads of different sites. Or he could have walked into his local betting office and shoved a pile of borrowed cash into fixed-odds machines.'

'He wasn't that kind of gambler,' Palin said. 'Lucy told me he had a system.'

'They all have a system,' Carlyle replied archly. 'A system for losing money.'

'The professor spent a lot of time on data analysis. He didn't do things randomly.'

'A man with time on his hands.'

'Lucy said he liked to bet with some Belgian outfit. He'd been a punter of theirs for years, ever since he spent a couple of years on secondment, teaching at the University of Antwerp back in the mid-nineties.'

At the mention of a Belgian connection, Carlyle felt something flicker in the darker recesses of his brain. He tried to grasp it but it disappeared almost immediately. Why bet with a bookie in Belgium? It seemed a convoluted way of indulging a hobby. Then again, what the inspector knew about gambling you could write on the back of a postage stamp.

'Do we have a name for this Belgian outfit?'

'No,' Palin said. 'He told Lucy he used them because they gave him better odds and more credit.'

'Credit?'

'He was a long-standing and well-respected client. It seems he'd had some quite good years but, recently, had been on a bit of a bad run.'

Oh, aye? Carlyle thought. Here we go. 'How much are we talking about, losses-wise?'

'Dunno,' Palin admitted. 'Lucy seemed to think it was maybe tens of thousands but that was just a guess.'

'A decent wedge, then.' The inspector realised there was no way around it – he needed to take a closer look at the professor's affairs. 'Maybe I should go and have a word with your new friend, see if she can remember anything else.'

Palin didn't seem overly enamoured of the idea but kept any thoughts on the matter to himself. 'It's certainly a strange one.'

'That's what keeps us interested,' the inspector said loftily. 'Otherwise we'd never manage to get out of bed in the morning.'

'You wouldn't have thought he'd be the type, a quiet old guy like that.'

'A quiet old guy,' Carlyle repeated, 'who had a raging gambling habit and a thing for young female company. I won't be surprised if we find out he was on heroin, too.'

Palin frowned. 'There's no evidence of drug use.'

'It was a joke.'

'Oh.'

'Everyone has their vices. And, when you come to think about it, why not indulge them in your dotage? It's not like you can fuck up your whole life in the process, just a few crap years at the end when you're probably going to be stuck in an adult nappy anyway.' Carlyle wondered what he might get up to when – if – he reached that age. 'What did Grom like to bet on? Horses?'

'A bit of cricket, but mainly football. He seems to have come a cropper recently backing Man United.'

'What an idiot.' Carlyle shook his head in disgust. Everyone knew that Surrey's finest – who were always priced too short to start with – were on a long-overdue downward slide. 'Still, it gives us a clear line of enquiry. Have you got the keys to his flat?'

'Yup.' Palin patted his jacket pocket.

'Good. Let's go and take another look. And you can introduce me to your new pal, Lucy.'

Palin blushed slightly. 'She's not—'

'Whatever,' Carlyle teased, striding towards the door. 'Just remember, no asking her out until this case is closed.'

TWENTY-SEVEN

At Martin Grom's building, there was no sign of Lucy Briggs, the amiable neighbour, which meant no further opportunity to embarrass the hapless Palin. Instead, Carlyle had to make do with a quick rummage through the deceased's desk, before opening the mail that had arrived earlier in the day.

'Anything interesting?' the sergeant asked, emerging from a further investigation of the bedroom.

'Doesn't look like it.' Carlyle was flicking through an uninspiring selection of junk mail and utility bills. 'How about you?'

'Nothing much,' Palin admitted. 'He's got quite a collection of *National Geographic* magazines, but that seems to be about it.'

'Quite the polymath,' Carlyle mused.

'Huh?' Still wearing a pair of latex gloves, Palin helped himself to an apple from the fruit bowl on the kitchen counter and began rubbing it vigorously on his shirt.

'Never mind.'

Palin bit deep into the apple. 'He didn't teach maths,' he pointed out, through a mouthful. 'His subject was . . .' he tried to recall the old man's area of expertise '. . . something or other.'

Carlyle shook his head sadly. He was the first to admit that his own academic record was nothing to write home about, but these kids today? Some of them made him look like the Brain of bloody Britain. He looked on as Palin finished his snack and tossed the core into the sink.

'Would you do that at home?' the inspector asked.

'What?'

'Dump the core in the sink.'

'The cleaning lady will sort it out.'

'I doubt she'll be back. Put it in the rubbish.'

Palin glared at him, as if to say, *What difference does it make?* then pulled open a random selection of cupboard doors. Finally locating a bin, he carefully retrieved the core, picking up the stalk between his thumb and index finger, and dropped it into an orange plastic bag. 'Hold on a sec, what have we got here?' The sergeant came up with a scrap of paper that had been crumpled into a ball. Unfolding it with exaggerated care, he squinted at its contents, then read aloud, 'Passion Killer, twelve to one, Mysore fifteen thirty.'

'Mysore?'

'That's what it says.' Palin held up the slip for his boss to inspect.

'I thought you said Grom bet on football?'

'Maybe he fancied a change.'

'Mysore's in India. That's a bit exotic, wouldn't you say? What's wrong with British racing?'

'I suppose he had plenty of time on his hands to look for stuff beyond Haydock Park.'

Where was Haydock Park? The inspector had no idea. He pointed at the betting slip. 'How did we miss that first time around?'

'To be fair, we didn't know about the gambling thing when we were here before.'

'No, but still . . .' Carlyle checked himself before he launched into a rant. What was the point?

Palin placed the betting slip on the kitchen counter. 'I'll get it checked for prints.'

'Let's see if we can take a look at Grom's bank account, too,' Carlyle instructed. 'See if there's a money trail to these bookies.' Taking a step backwards, he flopped onto the sofa and closed his eyes, taking a moment to try to make some sense of the random bits of information they were collecting.

'Not a good time to go to sleep, boss.'

'I'm thinking,' Carlyle growled. 'You should try it sometime.' Opening his eyes, he asked, 'Who've you got tracking down the girls the professor used?'

Palin leaned against the fridge. 'Dombey.'

'Great.' PC Paul Dombey was one of the 'characters' at the station, a six-foot-three man-child from Bradford.

'He's contacting every escort agency within a three-mile radius.'

'That should take him the rest of the century, poor sod.' Realising that he was still holding the professor's junk mail, Carlyle dropped it onto the floor between his feet.

'Dombey's a good lad. He'll let us know if he comes up with anything.'

'I bet he will.' Leaning back on the sofa, the inspector allowed himself a stretch. A short power nap would be just the thing. On reflection, he should have left Palin at the station and come up here on his own. Stifling a yawn, he glanced at the bookcase off to his right. Once again, the empty picture frame on one of the shelves caught his eye, causing him to fret. Why would anyone display an empty frame? 'Did we ever find the photograph?'

'Sorry?'

The inspector pointed towards the frame. 'Did we ever find the photo that went in that frame?'

'Is it a big deal?' Palin's disinterested tone suggested that he didn't see the significance.

'That depends,' Carlyle deadpanned.

The boy took the bait. 'Depends on what?'

'Depends on whether it is or not.'

'Eh?'

'We won't know until we find it.'

'Well, we haven't found it,' Palin said dully.

'Okay,' Carlyle said wearily. 'Keep an eye out for it.'

'Sure.'

'In the meantime, let's get the frame bagged up and checked for prints, along with the betting slip.'

'Yeah?'

'Yeah.' Carlyle was not a big one for hunches, but he'd decided it was worth a punt. 'Maybe whoever stuck Grom in the cupboard removed the picture for some reason.'

'Maybe,' said Palin, doubtfully.

'We might as well check it out.' Carlyle got to his feet. 'See if you can track down the name of Grom's bookie. And let me know if Dombey turns up anything.'

'What about you?'

Carlyle thought about lying but, ultimately, couldn't be bothered. 'I need to go and see my dad.'

TWENTY-EIGHT

Melody Rainbow wasn't answering her phone. Still, Karen Jansen had a pretty good idea of where to find her. Worrying about the state of the agency, she headed into Covent Garden. If Nelly Ternan went tits up, so to speak, she would go home to Australia. After more than a decade in London, she had sufficient funds in the bank to make a fresh start.

Tsenpo House was a small block of ex-council flats located next to a Presbyterian church, down a grimy alley close to the Royal Opera House. It was the kind of place where the tarmac was invariably sticky underfoot and the smell of ammonia was to be expected. Despite that, the smallest studio apartment still sold for something around half a million pounds. Breathing through her mouth, Jansen walked up to the front door and pressed a button on the entryphone.

'It's not working, love.' Jansen looked round to see a hunched old woman in a dirty raincoat. 'You can press it all you like but you won't get a reply.'

U woan get a reply.

'Been bust for weeks.' The woman looked like a refugee from the Blitz. She was pulling a shopping bag on wheels and an unlit cigarette dangled from her lips. 'They're supposed to be sending someone to fix it, but I'll believe it when I see it. You know what it's like – everything takes for ever, these days.'

'Yeah.'

'At least we can still get in and out.' The woman keyed a code into a pad next to the entryphone. A buzzing noise signalled that the lock had released, allowing Jansen to push open the front door. 'Thanks, love. You'd think, with the service charges being what they are, they'd send someone round sharpish to fix it, but oh, no.'

Jansen gave a sympathetic cluck as she followed the woman inside.

'It's a joke, it really is.' The woman pointed a bony finger towards the heavens. 'And don't get me started on the roof. That's a right disgrace.'

While the woman waited for the lift, still complaining about the upkeep of her building, Jansen took the stairs. The climb to the third floor left her disappointingly out of breath and she took a moment for her heart rate to return to a less elevated level before ringing the doorbell to Flat 3F. The harsh electronic chirp caused her to grimace. After several moments, there was the sound of footsteps, followed by a chain being engaged. The door opened a couple of inches and a familiar shock of pink hair appeared in the crack.

'What do you want?'

'We need to have a chat, Melody.'

'I was asleep. You woke me up.'

Good God. One way or another, it seemed that the girl spent almost her whole life in bed. Jansen pushed gently at the door. 'Can I come in?'

'I suppose.' Melody reluctantly released the chain and took a step backwards. 'If you must.'

'Thank you.' Stepping inside the flat, Jansen watched the naked girl pad back down the hallway with an appraising eye. You need to start working on that arse, she determined.

'Let me put some clothes on.'

'Sure.'

Closing the front door, Jansen wandered into the kitchen and living-room area. The place was a mess of textbooks, magazines, fast-food packaging and beer bottles. Off to the left, Melody had ducked into the bedroom. Clearly, she wasn't alone. Through the open doorway, Jansen could see movement in the bed. After a moment, a tall, skinny young man slipped out from under the duvet, arched his back and stretched theatrically. Reaching the doorway, Jansen folded her arms as she contemplated his shameless erection. 'I'm guessing you must be Chris.'

Scratching his head, the guy gave her a cheeky grin.

Jansen turned to Melody, who was struggling into a pair of jeans. 'I thought you said you liked your men well-endowed.'

'Chris,' Melody giggled, 'put it away.'

The boy gave his balls a vigorous scratch, then shuffled off in the direction of the bathroom.

'Is he a mute?' Jansen asked.

'He takes time to get started.' Melody searched among a pile of clothes lying on a chair by the bed. 'His mouth anyway.'

'Bloody hell, how do you manage to lie in bed all day?'

'Weren't you young once?' Melody teased.

'The idea is you grow out of it,' Jansen pointed out, trying to ignore the sound of the urinating man next door. 'It's almost five in the afternoon.'

'Yeah, well.' Melody retrieved an off-white bra and slipped it on. 'We were going to go out for lunch then, well, you know . . . These things happen.' Grabbing a red T-shirt, she slipped it over her head. 'I'm starving.'

Jansen was momentarily distracted by the legend on Melody's chest: *You've read my T-shirt: that's quite enough social interaction for one day.* Quite good, she decided. 'I thought today was the day you were going to do your essay?'

Melody took a moment to recall the small matter of the Yarlung Dynasty. 'It's in hand,' she said finally.

'You've done it?'

'More or less.' Melody tried to shake her hair under control. 'Anyway, what are you doing here?'

'We need to talk.' Jansen gestured towards the bathroom. 'Without Lover-boy.'

'Okay,' Melody agreed. 'He's served his immediate purpose anyway. Let's go and get a drink.'

'I thought you were hungry?'

'Good point,' Melody nodded. 'Let's go and get something to eat . . . and a drink.'

Leaving Chris searching for his Calvins, they decamped to a nearby establishment called Telemann's, located in the basement of what had been, until recently, the headquarters of the BBC's World Service. Never a massive drinker, Jansen was rather nonplussed to find herself in her second bar of the afternoon. Sticking to a glass of Perrier water, she looked on as Melody simultaneously guzzled a pint of lager and shovelled a large slice of broccoli quiche into her mouth.

'Sex always makes me hungry, not to mention thirsty.'

'We need to talk about Professor Grom.'

Melody's face fell. 'He hasn't complained, has he? Just because I didn't want dinner.'

What was the girl prattling on about? 'Dinner?'

'He cooked dinner but I was too tired for any weird stuff. I just wanted to go to bed.'

'There was no complaint.'

Melody gulped down the last of her beer. 'What's the problem, then?'

'The problem is he's dead.'

'Dead?' Melody looked suitably shocked.

'Yep.' Jansen calmly sipped her water. 'And he's not the only one.'

Melody folded her arms under her breasts. 'What d'ya mean?'

'The police came to see me this afternoon. I thought it was about Grom but it turned out it was about another client, a guy called Balthazar Quant.'

Melody struggled to recall the name.

'A guy in the Docklands. According to our records you visited his place a couple of months ago.'

A dreamy look descended on Melody's face, like she was

trying to recall ancient times, shrouded in myth and mystery. 'Maybe that was before I had pink hair.'

Jansen stifled a curse. 'I don't think it really matters what colour your hair was at the time.'

Melody conceded the point with a shrug. 'What was the guy's name again?'

'Quant. Balthazar Quant. He had a flat in Biffen Heights.'

Melody gave a sheepish grin. 'No, I don't think I remember him.' The truth was that she only really remembered clients who were, for one reason or another, fairly hideous. If the guy was vaguely normal, she had flushed him from her memory by the time she was in the cab going home. 'What happened?'

'He died,' Jansen said blandly, not wanting to spook Melody with the details.

'If the police are interested, it must be serious.'

'A young guy dies,' Jansen ad-libbed, 'they always investigate. Matter of routine. The guy had one of our cards on him. That's why they came to talk to me. It was a nice policewoman. You need to have a word with her, too, but it'll be fine, don't worry.'

'But I don't remember the guy,' Melody protested.

'That's all the lady wants to know.'

'Can't you tell her?'

Jansen shook her head. 'She wants to hear it from the horse's mouth. It's just a matter of routine. It'll only take five minutes.'

'Vernon won't like it,' Melody ventured, invoking the higher authority of their boss.

'Vernon won't like it if you *don't* do it,' Jansen pointed out. 'The last thing Vernon needs right now is any problems with the police.'

'And what do I say about the professor?'

'You don't say anything about Grom,' Jansen said firmly. 'She's not interested in him. He was an old guy who keeled over from a heart attack. End of.'

'Urgh.' A look of disgust fell across Melody's face. 'Just as well it didn't happen when we were . . . you know.'

'I don't even want to think about it.' Jansen took a sip of her mineral water.

'It's not that uncommon, you know.'

'Hm.' Didn't it happen in a film once? Jansen failed to recall the movie in question.

'He was okay when I left,' Melody muttered. 'He'd gone swimming.'

'Don't worry about Grom.' Jansen reached into her bag and came up with Alison Roche's card. 'Just give the sergeant a call and tell her you don't remember Quant.' She handed over the card. 'Leave the professor out of it. Don't mention him at all.'

'Sure. I can do that.' Smiling, Melody shoved the card into the pocket of her jeans. 'No problem.'

Jansen smiled back, trying to ignore the sick feeling in her stomach.

TWENTY-NINE

Standing outside his father's flat, Carlyle fumbled with his key as the front door swung open. Taking a step backwards, the inspector found himself looking at a round, middle-aged man, holding a large case.

'You must be the son,' the man muttered, distinctly unimpressed. 'I'm Dr Scott, from the Dawes Road medical centre.' He did not offer to shake Carlyle's hand. 'I'm afraid you're too late.'

Carlyle looked at him blankly.

'Your father passed away an hour ago. My condolences.' The physician paused for a couple of seconds, in a seeming attempt to inject some professional sincerity into his words. 'We'll send someone around tomorrow to complete the necessary paperwork and collect the various bits and bobs.' He patted the bag with his free hand. 'I've taken the liberty of removing the pain relief that remained. It's better not to leave that kind of thing lying around.'

'Makes sense,' Carlyle mumbled.

'Anyway, my condolences,' the GP repeated. Slipping past Carlyle, he quickly disappeared down the stairs.

The inspector stood on the landing, listening to the retreating footsteps, followed by the sound of the entrance door to the building opening and closing. 'That's that, then.' He tried to think of something suitably momentous about his father, but his mind was resolutely blank.

Stine was sitting in the kitchen, staring at an empty cigarette packet. 'Just as well I remembered to pick up some more.'

Pulling a fresh packet from his pocket, Carlyle placed it on the table.

'Thanks.' Reaching forward, she expertly removed the cellophane wrapper, flicked open the packet and placed one of the smokes between her lips. 'Did you see the doctor on his way out?'

'Yeah.' Carlyle watched as she lit the cigarette and inhaled deeply, holding in the smoke for several seconds before blowing it towards the ceiling.

'Want one?'

'Nah. Not my thing. I've never smoked.'

She looked up at him, vaguely amused. 'Never?'

'I tried it once or twice as a kid, obviously. Never really liked it.'

'Good for you.'

'I've smoked maybe the equivalent of four or five cigarettes in my entire life.'

Stine watched the fog in front of her face slowly dissipate. 'Sorry, I should go outside.'

'It's fine. Don't worry about it.'

'I'm sorry about your father, John.'

'Thank you, but it's not like it's a bolt from the blue, is it? We knew it was coming.'

'I know, but still. It's always a blow.'

'Thank you for everything you did for him.'

'It was my pleasure.'

'I'm sorry I was late getting over here.'

Stine took another drag on her cigarette. 'Don't beat yourself up over it. He's basically been asleep the whole time.' She looked around for an ashtray, then tapped the end of her cigarette into the empty packet on the table. 'Have you told Helen?'

Carlyle shook his head. 'I should do that now.'

'Yes, I think so.'

'Okay.' Reaching for his phone, he headed out of the kitchen, in search of some fresh air.

Out on the balcony, he shivered against the cold. Lille Park was deserted: everyone had retreated inside for the night. Dialling his wife's number, he lifted the phone to his ear. Listening to it ring, he was wondering what to say if the call went to voicemail when Helen finally answered.

'Is this it?'

'Yeah. I'm down in Fulham now.'

'I'm very sorry, John.'

'It's fine. I'm fine. He didn't suffer.'

'Do you want me to come down?'

'No, there's nothing much to do right now.'

'I'll let the undertaker know.'

'Thanks.'

'Everything else can wait till tomorrow.'

'Yes. What about Alice?'

'She's at a friend's house at the moment. We can tell her when she gets back.'

'How will she take it?'

'She'll be fine.'

'I'm sure. Okay, I'll be home soon.' Ending the call, Carlyle gazed across the park. He knew he should look in on his father but the reluctance to do so was strong. His dawdling was rewarded when the phone vibrated in his hand. Hitting the receive button, he lifted the handset without checking the identity of the caller.

'Hello?'

'It's a miracle: Inspector Carlyle answers his phone.'

Delighted to hear a friendly voice, Carlyle's response was uncharacteristically cheery. 'How are you, sweetheart?'

'Don't "sweetheart" me, you dinosaur,' Alison Roche shot back. 'I've been trying to get hold of you for ages.'

'How are you? How's the family? When are you coming back to work?'

'I *am* back at work,' the sergeant explained. 'That's the problem. They've sent me to bloody Limehouse.'

'Limehouse? What's that all about?' He listened patiently

while she explained about DI Jay Wrench and the body dumped in the cement mixer. 'At least it sounds like you've caught an interesting one,' was his verdict.

'I need to get back to Charing Cross ASAP,' Roche said flatly. 'I've tried to get hold of Simpson, but she seems to have gone AWOL.'

'Tell me about it,' said Carlyle, with feeling. 'Tell you what, let's meet up for a drink and see what we can do to sort things out.' Turning round, he glanced in the direction of the kitchen. 'I could manage a quick one tonight, if you like.'

'You've got to be kidding,' Roche spluttered. 'I've got David to look after. And Alex is out.'

'How are things with Shaggy?' Carlyle smirked. He had unilaterally given Roche's boyfriend the less than flattering moniker on account of his similarity to the Scooby Doo cartoon character.

'Don't call him that,' she snapped.

'Sorry.'

'But things are fine. More than fine.'

'Good.'

'Alex is doing a great job, to be honest. If it wasn't for him, I don't think I'd have been able to make it back to work at all.'

'Glad to hear things are going well.' Carlyle meant it. Roche had endured more than her fair share of ups and downs – both personal and professional – over the years. She deserved a bit of stability and happiness.

'Things *are* going well.' Surprise mixed with delight in her voice. 'How are things with you guys?'

'Same old same old.' Enjoying the banality of their conversation, Carlyle was not about to start up a running commentary on the night's events. 'All good.'

'Say hi to Helen for me.'

'I will. I'm sure she'd like to see you and David soon. Alice would, as well.'

There was a pause. 'And what about you?'

'Me, too, obviously.'

143

Roche grunted something unintelligible. 'Get Helen to give me a call. Meantime, I think I'm going to pour myself a large glass of Malbec and see how much of it I can drink before the little so-and-so wakes up.'

'Enjoy.'

'I'll maybe pop into Charing Cross tomorrow. Are you around?'

'Give me a call.'

'Yeah, right. This is a one-in-a-thousand event, getting hold of you on the phone. Better I just turn up and take my chances.'

'Fair enough. Maybe see you tomorrow.'

'Maybe.' Ending the call, she left him standing in the cold, still reluctant to step inside. Pulling up the number for Charing Cross, he called the station. After what seemed like an eternity, someone picked up.

'Yeah?' a male voice demanded.

Jesus, Carlyle thought. And they say manners are dead. 'I'm looking for Adam Palin,' he said brusquely. 'Is he around?'

'Hold on a sec. Let me put you through.' There was the sound of an extension being dialled, then more ringing.

'Palin.' The sergeant sounded remarkably bright, given the late hour.

'Carlyle.'

'Oh, hi, Inspector. How's it going?'

'Fine. Look—'

'How's your dad doing?'

The question stopped him in his tracks. 'Er,' he stammered, 'he's, um, dead.'

There was a pause at the end of the line, then: 'Oh. I'm very sorry to hear that, sir. That's a real shame.'

'Thanks,' Carlyle said. 'It had been on the cards for a long time.'

'My condolences to you and your family.'

'Thank you. Look, I just wanted to check in. I'll probably be a bit scarce the next few days, sorting out stuff, so I thought I'd enquire whether there have been any further developments with Professor Grom.'

'Hold on.' There was a shuffling of papers before Palin began reading from his notes. 'The pathologist's report is in. Basically, he did have a heart attack, which may have been brought on by someone roughing him up.'

'Okay.' Carlyle declined to point out that he knew that already.

'Next,' said the sergeant briskly, 'I checked on Passion Killer, the horse on the betting slip. It finished seventh, so unfortunately for the professor, his last bet was a dud.'

'It would have been worse to win,' Carlyle mused, 'and not be around to collect the cash.'

'I suppose,' Palin agreed. 'I hope to take a peek at his bank accounts tomorrow.'

'You got a warrant?'

'No need,' Palin said. 'I found a username and password in the notebook we came across on the first visit to the flat.'

'Just make sure you don't do anything naughty on a police computer,' Carlyle instructed. 'Or on one of your own, for that matter.'

'No, of course not.'

'We don't want to come a cropper being caught hacking someone's bank account.' Despite his stern tone, the inspector was quite pleased with the boy's initiative. Maybe Palin would make a decent sidekick, after all. Then he remembered his conversation with Roche, who clearly wanted to return to the fold. Typical. You struggle along for months without a sergeant to call your own, then two plausible candidates turn up at once. Given the choice, which one should he go with? Cross that bridge when you get to it, sunshine, he told himself. There was no need to rush into any decision on that just now.

'And then there's the picture frame. We don't know what was in it but we did manage to lift four different prints.'

'Bloody hell, that was quick.' Genuinely impressed, Carlyle began to hope that the missing photograph wouldn't prove that important in the wider scheme of things. Either way, it was another tick in the box for young Master Palin.

'I've got a friend who works in the lab,' Palin said, obviously pleased with himself.

'One of the prints would be Grom's,' Carlyle speculated, 'and one would belong to the cleaner.'

'Correct.'

'Can you check the others out in the morning?'

'Already done it.'

Bloody hell, the boy was on fire. Bye-bye, Alison Roche. 'And?'

'We got a hit on one of the two unknowns.' Palin's voice bubbled with excitement.

Carlyle felt the familiar rush that came when an investigation took a jump forward. 'Name?'

'No name.'

'Ah.'

'But the print was a match to one found at a murder scene.' There was a pause while the sergeant consulted his notes. 'The victim was a guy called Kevin Lamoot.'

THIRTY

The cold was nibbling at Carlyle's frame. Rather than retreating inside, he embraced it. 'Kevin Lamoot? Are you sure?' He made Palin spell the surname.

'Did you know him?' the sergeant asked.

'I know the case,' the inspector muttered.

'Superintendent Maria Lockhead's in charge.'

'I know Maria. I'll give her a call.' A thought rumbled through Carlyle's brain. 'You haven't filed a report yet, have you?'

'I was going to do it tonight.'

'Leave it till tomorrow. If we drop something into the system that mentions the Lamoot case, we're going to get all sorts of people looking over our shoulder. God knows what we should make of finding this fingerprint. Let me speak to Maria first. It's better that she finds out from me.'

'Sure.' The sergeant seemed happy enough with that as a plan.

'Look, I need to get off. Sounds like you're on top of things, so just keep going.'

'Okay,' said Palin, uncertainly.

'Go where the information takes you,' Carlyle reassured him. 'Let me know if you find out anything interesting. Like I said, I'm probably going to be quite scarce the next few days, what with my dad and stuff, but you can get me on the mobile. Leave a message and I'll call you back.'

'Got it.'

'And, Adam?'

'Yes?'

'You're doing a good job, son. Keep it up.' Detecting his father's tone in his voice, he paused, took a breath. 'We'll speak later.'

'You were lucky to catch me.' Maria Lockhead dropped her kit bag onto the floor. 'I was just about to do my Zumba class.' She gestured across the road towards the neon sign indicating the entrance to a gym belonging to one of London's many fitness chains.

'Sorry to mess up your plans.' Carlyle placed a large cappuccino in front of the superintendent and took a sip of his Jameson's. Stine had looked nonplussed when he had scarpered from his dad's flat, citing a work 'emergency', but the death doula had kept her thoughts to herself. The reality was he couldn't get out of there fast enough. Helen had sent him a text saying the undertakers were on their way and he didn't want to be around to see his old man taken out of his home for the last time.

Lockhead, oblivious to her colleague's domestic dramas, took a mouthful of coffee and gave an appreciative sigh. 'Don't worry about it. It's harder and harder to find the motivation, these days. Exercise is so boring. There's got to be a point where you just say, "Fuck it," and let it all fall apart.'

'I reached that point about twenty years ago.' Pulling up a chair, Carlyle tried to recall the last time he had made it to the gym. Not in the last month at least. At least. 'But you're looking good.' He paused. 'If that's not an inappropriate comment.'

Lockhead laughed. 'Don't worry, Inspector. I'm not one of those snowflakes who can't take a compliment. I won't be reporting you to HR.'

'Glad to hear it.'

'Frankly, I need all the encouragement I can get. We're off to Ibiza next week, so I want to be ready for the beach.'

'All well with the family?'

148

'Very well, thank you. We're looking at secondary schools for Seb at the moment. It's hard to get it right, isn't it?'

'I know what you mean. Alice is starting to think about universities. She says she might want to try for Oxford.'

'Good for her. I went there.' She mentioned a college. 'I'd be happy to talk to her about it, if she wants.'

'That's very kind, thanks. I'll let her know.'

'Anyway, down to business.' Lockhead pushed away the coffee cup. 'What's so urgent that it comes between me and my Zumba?'

'Kevin Lamoot.'

Lockhead's face hardened. 'What about him?'

'His name has come up in an investigation.' The inspector explained about the fingerprint they'd recovered in Professor Grom's flat.

'And it's a match?'

'It's a match,' Carlyle confirmed. 'That's what I've been told.'

'So, there's a connection between the victims – they were both killed by the same guy?'

'Technically, my guy died of a heart attack, but it was probably brought on by being roughed up by the guy who killed your guy.'

'The guy who battered you.'

'Ye-es.' The inspector had omitted to mention to Sergeant Palin his personal interest in the Lamoot case: he had disturbed the killer in the act, who promptly smacked him across the head with a cooking pan. When he regained consciousness, Carlyle had been able to provide Lockhead with no useful information whatsoever. 'How long has the case been closed?'

'These things never get formally closed, you know that. But it ran into the sand after about two weeks. Pretty soon after that, the investigation consisted of me and a constable working on it in our spare time.'

'That must be very frustrating.'

'Do you have any idea what it's like?' Lockhead groaned.

'Last time I looked, there were only six open murder investigations in the whole of London.'

Seven, if you include Martin Grom. Carlyle would need to give careful consideration as to how best to classify the professor's death.

'Not that I'm obsessive or anything, but I do keep an eye on the stats.'

'You don't want to have one of those against your name for any length of time,' Carlyle observed.

'Definitely not,' Lockhead agreed. 'They can haunt you for ever. If you get the chance, make sure your guy goes down as natural causes.'

'I hadn't thought about that,' Carlyle lied, 'but good tip.'

'Of the other cases,' Lockhead continued, 'three are more than twenty-five years old.'

'The original investigators must be long since retired,' Carlyle mused, 'dead themselves, probably.'

She looked him in the eye. 'The fourth is a Ronnie Score case.'

'I hope it's tormenting the bastard in Hell.' Inspector Ronnie Score had been a bent cop who had tried to frame Carlyle for murder and ended up dead himself. 'Although, somehow, I doubt it.'

Lockhead moved swiftly on. 'One is brand new, only happened in the last few days.'

'The guy in the cement mixer.' Carlyle recalled reading about it in the *Evening Standard*.

'That's right. Odds on there'll be an arrest in the next few days, so I hear.'

'Yeah?'

'That's the gossip.'

'Which leaves Kevin Lamoot.'

'Which leaves *me* as the only current officer with an unsolved murder case of more than three months standing against my name. The only one in the whole of the sodding Met.' Lockhead's voice had risen to a level at which some of the nearby patrons were becoming interested in their conversation.

'It must be tough,' Carlyle empathised.

'It is tough. Why me, for God's sake?'

'Look,' the inspector leaned forward, keeping his voice low. 'I didn't come here to wind you up. I don't know if this new development is of much significance, but I wanted to tell you about it straight away.'

Lockhead composed herself. 'Thank you.'

'And, of course, if we make any progress that might help you find Lamoot's killer, I'll let you know first.'

'Okay.' She reached down for her kit bag. 'My class'll have started but I think I might slip in for the last half an hour.'

Good idea, Carlyle thought.

Sliding from her chair, she met his gaze. 'You realise something?'

'What?'

'Now we know that there were two people who were at both crime scenes – you and the killer.' Hoisting the bag over her shoulder, the superintendent headed for the door.

'I was only there after the event.'

'Yes, but still. And you were connected to Ronnie Score.'

'What can I say?' Carlyle shrugged. 'I'm just unlucky.'

THIRTY-ONE

The text from Camila Steinbrecher simply read: *Job done.* That's something, at least, Gerry Durkan reflected, pleasantly surprised that he had coverage in the subterranean cavern where he had been stuck for the last three hours. Sitting to his right, Rose Murray let out a disapproving cluck.

'Can't you leave that thing alone for a couple of hours?'

'You know what it's like,' Durkan grunted. 'Money never sleeps, work never stops.' Deleting the message, he dropped the phone into his jacket pocket. Looking up at all the tables squeezed into the basement of one of Park Lane's famous hotels, he stifled a burp. 'Remind me, what are we doing here?'

'You know precisely what we're doing here.' Rose put a hand on his arm and squeezed harder than was absolutely necessary.

Yes, to spend my damn money. Keeping his opinions to himself, Durkan tossed his napkin onto the table and reached for the glass of red wine in front of him.

'And I think you've had more than enough to drink already.'

'Very true.' Durkan drained his glass and winced. Invariably, the stuff they served at these charity dinners was terrible, but tonight's event had raised the bar in that regard. Through the fog of alcohol, he tried to remember what this one was for. AIDS? Global warming? Abused donkeys? An image of Rose on a donkey caused him to emit a drunken giggle.

'What's so funny?' Rose pushed away his hand as he reached for one of the wine bottles clustered in the centre of the table.

Most of the others on their table seemed to have buggered off to find more interesting people in the room to talk to. Even Delia, a last-minute replacement for the unfortunate Balthazar Quant, had drifted off. Out of the corner of his eye, Durkan saw his PA nearby, trying to chat up a worried-looking young man in a tux. Now there's someone who's had too much booze, he thought. Hundreds of conversations bounced off the ceiling, leaving them sitting in the middle of a sea of white noise. 'Why do we bother with this stuff? The noise is giving me a headache.' He glanced at his watch. 'And look at the time. I have an early start in the morning.'

'It's not that late,' Rose insisted.

'They didn't even serve the meal till almost ten,' Durkan reminded her. 'Not that it was worth waiting for.' The food at these events was even worse than the wine. 'We should have had a burger on the way over here. I'm starving.'

'You've been to enough of these things in your time to know what they're like. We're not here for the food.'

'Yeah, but I'm still hungry.'

Rose pointed at the plate of petits fours sitting on the table. 'Have a chocolate.'

Durkan stared at them without any enthusiasm. For all his vices, a sweet tooth was not one of them. 'Not exactly a balanced diet, is it?'

'Stop bloody moaning. We're here for a good cause.'

Yeah, but which one? Irritation mingled with defiance in his breast. 'There are no good causes, these days,' he ventured tendentiously. 'Everybody's on the make, one way or another.'

'That's your problem, Gerry,' Rose said drily. 'You gave up politics in the nineteen eighties.'

'Yeah, I was a slow learner. If I'd had any sense, I'd have given all that shit a wide berth from day one. As it was, I was a victim of circumstances, having had the misfortune to be born in a place where everyone fought the same battles over and over and no one ever learned anything.'

'In those days,' Rose corrected him, 'you wanted to stand up for your people, fight for justice.'

Spare me all that soppy undergraduate shite, Durkan thought angrily. Despite his irritation, though, there was something comforting in the latest rerun of a squabble that the pair of them had been having regularly for the last twenty-plus years.

'Nowadays, all you want to do is make money.'

'And all you want to do is spend it.'

Rose took a sip of her peppermint tea. 'That's what makes us a good team, don't you think?'

'A *great* team.' And, just as important, Rose was still a very good-looking woman. There was no doubt about it, he was a lucky man, albeit one with a nasty headache brewing. 'But things are winding up here. Surely we can make a polite exit.'

'For God's sake, Gerry,' Rose scolded him, 'we're just about to have the auction.' She pointed towards the MC for the evening, a vaguely famous comic, who was making his way to the stage. 'There's a couple of things I want to bid for.'

'Oh, feck.' Macroom Castlebar Salle had already dropped something like thirty K on buying the evening's table, and that was before you counted in all the additional bottles of rubbish wine he'd casually put on the company Amex. Depending on how much Rose splurged on the auction, the evening could easily end up costing him north of six figures. It was all tax-deductible, of course, but the reckless spending pained him.

'Don't be so *ungenerous*, Gerry.' Rose pointed at the catalogue lying on the table. 'This is your chance to give something back.'

'But I give a lot back, you know I do.' Durkan caught the eye of a pretty waitress and looked away. 'There was last month's fifty-grand donation to the Free Tibet campaign for a start.'

'Well, you can always do more.' Pushing back her chair, Rose stood up. 'I'm just going to nip to the Ladies before the auction gets going.'

Watching her disappear into the crowd, Durkan was

considering making a run for it when a meaty paw landed on his shoulder. Turning in his chair, he looked up. 'What the hell are you doing here?'

By way of reply, Emmanuel Bole bent down and shoved a hand under Durkan's arm, levering him to his feet.

'Hello? Hello, everyone.' From the platform, the MC tried to encourage people to return to their seats. 'We have some great items in tonight's auction, so let's get started.' No one responded to the invitation. Instead, the noise level rose further as people continued with their conversations.

'Hey.' Durkan looked around hopelessly for assistance. The monster's grip was so tight that the blood flow to his arm must have stopped. Gasping at the pain, he offered only the feeblest of protests as he was escorted away from the table, through the crowd, towards the exit.

THIRTY-TWO

Bob Biswas rocked on the balls of his feet as he watched the two men come through the swing doors. Under the kitchen's harsh strip lighting, his face looked worse than usual, even before you factored in the crazed grin.

'Your time's up, Gerry.'

'It's all sorted.' Durkan tried to sound relaxed while clenching his buttocks tightly. 'I just had confirmation. The money's been transferred.'

'All of it?'

'Of course.' Conscious of the man mountain at his back, Durkan took a cautious step forward, towards Manny's boss.

'Wrong answer.' Hopping up and down, Biswas jabbed a finger angrily in Durkan's face. 'What do you take me for? A fool?'

'It's done.' Durkan fumbled for his phone. 'I had a message.'

'Where's my damn money?' Biswas shrieked.

'The money's been transferred,' Durkan repeated, his voice beginning to crack.

Biswas recoiled at the smell of alcohol coming off the man's breath. 'You're drunk.'

'Well spotted.' Durkan jerked a thumb in the direction of the ballroom. 'You can't survive these charity events without getting pissed.' Feeling woozy, he had a sudden urge to empty the contents of his stomach over Biswas's shoes. Taking a couple of deep breaths, he waited for the moment to pass. Once he felt able to open his mouth again, he continued: 'The charity auction is just starting. Maybe you'd like to bid for an item or two.'

By way of reply, Manny gave him a firm smack across the back of his head.

'Ow,' Durkan complained. 'What the hell's that for? I told you, we made the bloody transfer.'

'Gerry,' Biswas said slowly, 'we know how much was in that account, down to the last penny. What you transferred is less than ten per cent of the total. Where's the rest of it?'

Durkan had a flashback to Camila Steinbrecher sitting in her hospital bed.

You want me to steal the money?

The Portuguese bitch had ripped him off.

The realisation was enough to sober him up in an instant. Got to play for a bit of time here, he told himself. Need to engage in a little damage limitation. Spreading his arms wide, he prepared to launch into preacher mode. 'Look, Bob—'

'No more bullshit.' Biswas's face twisted in fury. 'You think you're so bloody clever. You think you can rob me again? You think I'm the biggest fucking idiot on the entire planet?' Not waiting for an answer, the enraged bookie signalled to his henchman. A fierce blow to the back of his neck sent Durkan sinking to his knees.

'You don't scare me,' the Irishman wheezed. 'There's nothing you can do to me that the RUC and the Brits haven't already tried, many times over.'

'Fuck those pussies,' Biswas said quietly. 'They should have killed you years ago.'

'I'm not worth anything to anyone dead.'

'Maybe not.' Biswas sniffed. 'But you're not worth anything alive, either.' He paused for effect. 'You've done well to get this far – it's a miracle, really. Finally, however, you've reached the end of the road.'

Wiping his nose with the back of his hand, Durkan reached into his jacket pocket.

'Hands where I can see them, Gerry.'

'There's nothing to worry about.' Durkan slowly took out a small key and slid it across the floor in the direction of Biswas's beautifully polished brogues.

Biswas made no attempt to pick it up. 'What's that?'

'The key to my safety deposit box.' He mentioned the name of a private bank located a couple of blocks from the hotel. 'There's more than a million and a half in rings and cash in there.' He was giving away the family jewels, literally. Rose would have a fit but, then again, she wasn't the one staring death in the face. 'Take it.'

Reaching out a foot, Biswas dragged the key towards him. 'Maybe I will.'

'We will recover your *misdirected* money, as well,' Durkan said. 'The contents of the box can be a nice little bonus. It will offset the cost of the diamonds you lost before.'

'The diamonds you stole from me,' Biswas repeated.

Durkan tried his best to crack a smile. 'Do we have a deal?'

The answer came with a vicious kick to the ribs that sent him sprawling across the floor. His forehead resting on the cool tiles, Durkan tasted the blood in his mouth and wondered how Rose was getting on. He hoped she was enjoying spending what was left of his money in the room next door.

THIRTY-THREE

Carlyle stood in the kitchen drinking black coffee as he listened to the sounds of Alice getting ready for school. After a short while, she appeared in the doorway, a large backpack slung over one shoulder.

'Mum told me about Grandpa.' Stepping forward, she gave her father a hug. 'It's sad, isn't it?'

'Yes,' Carlyle agreed.

Breaking the embrace, Alice turned towards the door. 'But hardly a surprise.'

'No.' Her father's daughter, right enough.

'I mean,' she added, 'he had a decent innings.'

A decent innings? Had the girl been overdosing on Evelyn Waugh again? Her English teacher had a lot to answer for. Finishing his coffee, Carlyle placed the mug in the sink. 'Fancy getting some breakfast?'

'I can't. I've got double maths first up this morning with Mr Morrison – he's a right pain. I was just going to pick up a crois-sant or something on the way.'

Carlyle took the brush-off with good grace.

'Maybe you can take Mum out,' Alice suggested. 'That might be nice.'

'She's still in bed.'

'Take her breakfast in bed.'

'Hm.' He tried to give the impression of seriously considering the idea.

'Anyway, I've got to get going.' Alice gave him a quick peck on the cheek. 'I'll see you later.'

Carlyle listened to her bundle out of the flat, then recovered his jacket and headed off himself, confident in the knowledge that Helen would prefer not to be disturbed.

On the way to the station, he stopped at a new café off Long Acre and sampled their macchiato. Inevitably, the caffeine, mixing with the residual effects of the previous night's Jameson's, left him feeling both skittish and jaded. Reaching Charing Cross, he ascended to the third floor and parked himself behind his desk.

'Time to prioritise.'

He was about halfway through his to-do list when he caught a glimpse of Palin heading towards him. The sergeant had an excited look on his face, like a five-year-old arriving at a birthday party.

Oh, God, Carlyle thought wearily. What's he got now?

'I thought you were going to be out,' the sergeant said, standing to attention by the desk.

'I am out,' the inspector said firmly, 'unless I tell you otherwise.'

'I checked Professor Grom's bank account.' Palin couldn't contain himself any longer.

Carlyle looked round the room. There was a surprisingly good turnout for the early hour. Sitting back in his chair, he indicated for Palin to keep the volume down.

'It's been cleaned out,' Palin whispered. 'Someone went in last night and transferred all the cash.'

Carlyle pushed out his lips. 'How much are we talking about?'

The sergeant hopped from foot to foot, as if he was about to wet himself. 'Almost a quarter of a million.'

Carlyle shot upright. 'Pounds?'

'Yeah.'

'How the hell does a retired academic have that much cash sitting in a bank account?'

'He doesn't any longer.'

'Where did the money go?'

'No idea,' the sergeant admitted. 'I've got something that looks like an account where the money went to, but I'm no expert on these things.'

'No.' The inspector flicked through his mental Rolodex, trying to think of someone he could go to on this. There was one obvious name. 'You covered your tracks,' he lowered his voice to a whisper, 'when you hacked the account?'

'Yes.' Palin beamed. 'I used an internet café in Waterloo.'

'Do those places still exist?'

'For the benefit of criminals,' Palin confirmed, 'and cops. I paid cash. And, as a bonus, there was no CCTV.'

'Good lad. Give me the details and I'll take it from here.'

Palin pulled a folded sheet of A4 from the back pocket of his jeans and handed it over. 'This is a screen grab.'

'Fine.' Carlyle unfolded the piece of paper and looked at the columns of numbers.

'What do you think?'

'I think it looks like a bank account.' Suddenly energized, Carlyle jumped up from his seat. 'But I'm no expert either.'

'Two hundred and fifty grand,' Palin said dreamily. 'It's a motive for killing him, though, isn't it?'

'It sure is,' Carlyle agreed. 'But we'll get to the bottom of it, don't worry.'

'What shall I do next?'

Keen to keep the youngster busy, Carlyle thought about it for a moment. 'See if you can find out more about Grom's time in Belgium. What was he doing there? Did he pick up any bad habits other than gambling?'

It was a vague mandate, but Palin seemed happy enough with his allotted task. This boy never complains, the inspector mused. I really should snap him up. Given the continued absence of Commander Simpson, however, that was easier said than done. 'And why don't you have another word with the cleaning lady?

Be a bit circumspect but see if she knew anything about the money.'

Palin raised an eyebrow. 'You think she was in on it?'

'You never know,' the inspector told him. 'You just never know.'

THIRTY-FOUR

Detective Inspector Diana Cooper wondered what to make of the carefully constructed scene in front of her.

'Funny business, isn't it?' Appearing at her shoulder, her sergeant, a professional Cornishman called Ian King, munched happily on a ham sandwich.

The detective inspector looked on in dismay. 'Don't mess up the crime scene.'

'Course not.' King shoved the last of the bread into his maw and stalked off, muttering something that sounded suspiciously like 'Bitch.'

Ignoring him, Cooper addressed the pathologist, Gabriel Herbert, on secondment to the Victoria police station from somewhere in the provinces. 'Did he drown?'

Arms folded, Herbert contemplated the man standing in front of them, bent over the stove. 'Too early to say.'

'But he's got his head in a pot of soup,' Cooper said.

Herbert was at least prepared to be definitive on one point. 'It's carrot and coriander.'

'Is that relevant?' Cooper asked crossly.

'It might be.' The pathologist refused to come off the fence. 'Not for me to say.'

Cooper pressed on: 'Have we got an ID yet?'

'Not as far as I know.'

'His name is Gerald Durkan.' Cooper and Herbert turned to face a tired-looking redhead walking towards them in a pair of faded jeans and a leather jacket. Cooper thought she looked like one of those unfeasibly cool French cops from the BBC4 show that her husband liked to watch. Herbert was clearly impressed, if the tongue hanging out of his mouth was anything to go by.

The new arrival flashed an ID. 'I'm Alison Roche, currently working out of Limehouse.'

'Diana Cooper,' the DI grunted.

The pathologist waved a latex-gloved hand. 'Gabriel Herbert.'

Cooper gestured towards the body. 'You know this guy?'

'Mr Durkan was involved in an ongoing investigation of ours,' Roche explained. 'His wife reported him missing a couple of hours ago. They were at a charity event in the hotel ballroom last night.'

Cooper was distracted by the reappearance of Sergeant King who was now happily munching a pastry. All that bloody man ever does is eat. Not for the first time she fantasised about having King reassigned to some distant outpost of the Met empire, leaving her free to choose a new sidekick.

'And the partner, she didn't know her other half was missing until this morning?'

'According to her, she went home alone, took a sleeping pill and went to bed. Got up this morning, found he hadn't been home, couldn't get hold of him and freaked out. We took the call and here I am.'

'This is *my* investigation.'

'No one's suggesting otherwise,' Roche said coolly. 'I just wanted to compare notes.'

Cooper looked around for King, but the sergeant had disappeared again. Probably gone hunting for more food. 'Okay,' she said finally. 'Let's start with Mr . . .'

'Durkan. Gerry Durkan.

'Let's start with Mr Durkan. Who is he?'

It was a beautiful morning with clear blue skies and a bracing nip in the air. As he made his way around Durfee Gardens,

Carlyle was feeling good about his home city until his nostrils were assaulted by a most appalling odour. He looked around, and the source of the smell quickly became apparent: a tramp was asleep on a wooden bench, with a flattened-out cardboard box for a mattress. Holding his breath, Carlyle scuttled past, looking for number 47C. After a couple of false starts, he found a small nameplate at the top of a flight of stairs leading down into a dirty-looking basement: Carew Forensic Services.

'Can I help you?'

The inspector turned to face a young blonde woman hiding behind a pair of outsized spectacles. In one hand, she grasped a small cup of coffee. In the other was a copy of the *Financial Times*. Over her shoulder, a canvas bag advertised a health-food store.

Carlyle took a step away from the stairs. 'I was looking for Dudley. Is he around?'

The woman looked at him suspiciously. 'Are you a client?'

'I'm a cop.' He reached for his ID but she waved it away.

'What's he done now?' Her tone suggested amusement, rather than concern.

'Nothing, as far as I know.'

'Thank God for that.'

'Inspector John Carlyle.' Extending a hand, he realised she was in no position to shake it so he shoved it into his trouser pocket. 'I've known Dudley for a long time. I just want to ask him about something.'

'Well, if you know Dudley,' the girl chuckled, 'you'd know that he's not an early starter.' Skipping down the stairs, she carefully placed the coffee cup and the paper on the ground, then pulled a set of keys from her bag. 'I wouldn't expect him to put in an appearance for another hour, at least.' Unlocking the door, she turned to the inspector. 'Feel free to come in, though.'

Carlyle waited patiently while she recovered her things, pushed open the door and disarmed the alarm. Then he followed her inside to a large, shabby room containing two desks and enough computer equipment to run a small country. The girl tossed the FT onto one of the desks and dropped her bag on the floor. 'I'm Gloria.' She smiled. 'Dudley's daughter.'

'Nice to meet you.'

'Please, take a seat.' She gestured towards a battered leather sofa lined up against the back wall.

'Thanks.' The inspector slipped between the desks and sat down.

'So,' the girl eyed him over her coffee cup, 'how do you know my dad?'

'We've worked together a few times over the years.'

'Did you ever arrest him?'

Yes. 'No.' The inspector shifted uneasily in his seat. He had come to ask a favour of the man, not embarrass him in front of his kid. 'We kind of got to know each other professionally, as it were, when our paths crossed. That kind of thing.'

'You don't need to be polite.' The girl laughed. 'I know all about what Dad's got up to over the years.'

'You do?'

'He liked to duck and dive when he was younger.'

'That's one way of putting it.'

'What did you nick him for?' She giggled. 'The timeshares or the VAT fraud?'

The timeshares? Carlyle knew nothing about that. 'The alleged VAT fraud.' He felt protective of Dudley in the face of his daughter's questions. 'As I recall, there might have been an arrest, but he was never formally charged with anything.'

'He did a deal, right?'

'He helped us out with a couple of things,' Carlyle said evasively. 'It's always good to have a forensic accountant on your side.'

'Especially a bent one.'

'Something like that.' Carlyle looked at his watch. 'Maybe I should get going. You could ask Dudley to give me a bell.'

Sitting down at her desk, Gloria fired up her iMac. 'What is it you were after? Maybe I can help.' She shot him a knowing look. 'I am my father's daughter, after all.'

Carlyle thought about it. 'This is strictly confidential . . .'

She pushed away his concerns with the words, 'Everything we do is confidential, Inspector.'

'Right.'

'We have a lot of surprisingly big clients. They come to us because we can find things out and we can keep our mouths shut.'

Us. She looked barely out of her teens, but she seemed an integral part of the family business.

'Okay. Well, I'm trying to find out what happened to some money that vanished from a dead man's bank account.' He walked her through the story of Professor Martin Grom and his missing cash.

'Not an unusual story,' was Gloria's verdict. 'Happens far more often than people like to think.'

'I can imagine,' Carlyle lied. He was resolutely old school when it came to cybercrime. Hacking into a bank with a computer just didn't seem as serious as waving a sawn-off shotgun in a terrified teller's face.

'And the police don't want to check this out themselves?'

'There might be an issue about how we came by the information,' Carlyle conceded.

'You mean you hacked his account?' Gloria squeaked with delight.

'We're not looking to generate any evidence that will stand up in court,' was as far as the inspector would go on a first date.

'Just as well.'

'We know the money has disappeared – but where is it now?' Getting to his feet, the inspector pulled a scrap of paper from his pocket and stepped over to the desk. 'That is what we've got.'

Unfolding the paper, Gloria studied the screen grab of Martin Grom's account. 'We have some really good AML software and spyware.'

Carlyle looked at her blankly.

167

'Anti-money-laundering and surveillance software,' Gloria explained. Dropping the piece of paper onto the desk, she began tapping her keyboard. 'State-of-the-art stuff sold by a Swedish company. The Swedes really are the best at this type of thing. Expensive, though. I read somewhere that the Met can't afford to buy any licences.'

Typical, Carlyle thought.

'You can use it to remotely access computers, log keystrokes, take screenshots and listen in to conversations. Pretty much everything, really. So, you've come to the right place. Let me run a few searches and see what we can come up with.'

'Great.'

'It'll take a few hours.'

'No problem.'

'And I'll be able to give you an idea of the cost.'

'Cost?' Carlyle didn't like the sound of that.

'Or do you have some kind of arrangement with Dudley?'

I bloody hope so. The inspector dropped a business card on the desk before turning for the door. 'Give me a call when you've had the chance to take a look. I'll speak to your dad about the money.'

'Fair enough.' Hitting some more keys, she didn't say goodbye.

THIRTY-FIVE

Looking round the flat, there was little to suggest that Alexander's death doula had ever existed. In the kitchen, the inspector found a simple note on the table, black ink on a small sheet of thick ivory paper: *Thank you for letting me join your family for this time.*

Carlyle stared at the message for several moments. Nice handwriting, he thought. But no contact details. The woman had moved on.

Next to the note, Stine had left her set of keys, along with a business card for the undertaker, a local firm called Harris & Miller. Carlyle called the number. After a little to-ing and fro-ing, he ended up speaking to Mr Miller, who issued pro-forma condolences and assured him that everything was in order.

'Your father is in our chapel of rest. We're just waiting for confirmation from the second doctor,' the undertaker explained, 'and then we can arrange the time of the cremation. I expect we'll be looking at next week now.'

'Second doctor?'

'There needs to be two doctors involved,' Miller said gently. 'They changed the rules after that doctor killed a number of his patients.'

'Yes, of course.' Carlyle immediately remembered the notorious physician's name. 'Harold Shipman.'

'That's him. One of the reasons he got away with what he did for so long was because he was signing off all the death certificates himself. Now you have to have a second doctor's signature.'

'Hm.' Carlyle thought about all the drugs his father had taken in recent months, prescribed and otherwise. Deciding that was unlikely to be a problem, he realised that he hadn't yet spoken to Dominic Silver about Alexander's death. Dom and his wife Eva would want to come to the funeral. Apart from the Carlyle family, they would probably be the only ones there.

'It's just a matter of routine,' Miller observed, 'but it can delay things a bit. There's no point in taking a slot at the crematorium until the paperwork is done. We'll need to get the death certificate and sort out all the other bits and pieces before we can confirm a time.'

After Miller ended the call, Carlyle rummaged around in various kitchen drawers until he found a serviceable pencil. Taking a seat, he pulled Stine's note towards him, flipped it over and began making a list of all the people who would need to know about his father's death: council tax, pension, utilities, bank accounts, telephone.

What else?

Library card.

TV licence.

He gave it a few more moments but nothing else came to mind. At some point, he would have to clear the flat. It would be a chore and a half, but it was hardly an immediate priority. He decided it could wait for a couple of weeks at least.

Feeling on top of the situation, he rang Helen. When the call went to voicemail he didn't leave a message.

What to do now?

Feeling a vague sense of abandonment, he stared vacantly out of the window. After a while, the phone started vibrating across the table. Happy that Helen was paying attention to her missed calls for once, he hit receive.

'Hello, sweetheart.'

'Hello, yourself,' Roche replied.

'Sorry.' Carlyle groaned. 'I thought you were the missus.'

'And here's me thinking you were pleased to have me back,' the sergeant quipped. 'We were going to meet up, remember?'

'Of course,' he lied. In the background, over the hum of traffic, he could make out the warning sound of a van reversing. 'Now's quite good, actually. Where are you?'

'I'm at the Trinity on Park Lane.'

Carlyle let out a murmur of approval. 'Very nice.'

'Not in the basement it isn't,' Roche observed. 'Tell me, what do you know about a guy called Gerald Durkan?'

'Not much,' Carlyle admitted. 'I met him once but never really got a good read on the man. Why do you ask?'

'Because someone drowned him in a pot of soup last night.'

'What?' Carlyle had a flashback to Kevin Lamoot, drowned in a vat of stew in the kitchen of his restaurant, a place called Kaplan's.

'The pathologist thinks Durkan might have been dead before his head went into the pot,' Roche advised, 'but it's a pretty distinctive MO, don't you think?'

'Gimme forty-five minutes,' the inspector growled. 'I'll be right there.'

THIRTY-SIX

'Who's in charge of the investigation?'

'A DI called Cooper.'

'Diana Cooper?'

'Yeah. Seemed a bit uptight.'

Carlyle made a noncommittal gesture. He knew the name but didn't have a view on her one way or another.

'I think she was worried that I wanted to nick her case,' Roche speculated. 'And the press didn't help.'

'Gerry Durkan comes a cropper, you're going to have the media take an interest.'

'I suppose.'

'Live by the sword, die by the soup.' Carlyle gestured past the police tape towards the stoves lined up at the far end of the empty kitchen. 'They found him over there?' The body had been removed and, other than the tape, there was remarkably little to suggest this was an active crime scene.

'Yeah. It was weird, just as if it had been posed.' Roche yawned. 'It was like a bit of performance art or something.'

'You got here quick.' Carlyle wondered if he was being too hasty in plumping for Palin over Roche in his search for a sergeant.

'We took the call from Durkan's partner just as the details of this were coming in. It wasn't all that hard to put the two things together.'

'No, but still . . .' Taking a step away from Roche, the

inspector put his hands on his hips and imagined Gerry Durkan's last moments on this earth. Poor bugger, he thought. You managed to survive the British Army, MI5, MI6, the RUC, UVF, UDA and fuck knows what else, only to end up murdered on the rubber-chicken circuit in the basement of a nine-hundred-quid-a-night hotel. Who says that God doesn't have a sense of humour? The obit writers were going to have lots of fun with this one. 'It's a sad end for one of the IRA's finest, to be sure.'

Leaving the hotel, they carefully crossed the six-lane racetrack that was Park Lane before heading through an open gate into Hyde Park. Glancing in the direction of Marble Arch, Carlyle gritted his teeth. Several years earlier, he had been caught up in the shooting of a couple of police officers near Speakers' Corner. Since then he had avoided the area, only returning once or twice.

Heading away from the scene of that particular disaster, he led Roche towards the Serpentine. The park was largely empty, save for the odd tourist or jogger. Closing his eyes, Carlyle tried to imagine keeping the city at arm's length, if only for a short while.

'How's the family doing?'

Opening his eyes, Carlyle blinked twice. 'My father died.' He watched a woman, twenty yards off to his left, throw a ball for a dog of some description to chase. 'Cancer.'

'Oh.' Roche stopped in her tracks. 'I'm very sorry to hear that, John.'

She lifted a hand towards his shoulder, but the inspector kept on walking. 'It had been on the cards for some time.'

Catching up, she took his arm. 'When did it happen?'

'Yesterday.'

'Yesterday?' Shocked, she brought them both to a halt.

'Last night,' he admitted.

'What are you doing here, then?' Disengaging, she took a step backwards, the better to inspect this strange creature.

'Everything's in hand,' he mumbled. 'It's not like there's a lot to do. The old fella sorted it all out in advance. To be honest, I was quite impressed. It was a good effort on his part.'

'I'm not talking about paperwork. Losing a parent is a big deal.'

'Happens to us all.'

'Everybody needs some time and space when something like this happens. The grieving process and all that.'

'I've already had quite a lot of time to come to terms with it.' He felt like a complete berk discussing his dad with Roche who, frankly, had more than enough problems of her own to deal with. Why hadn't he just kept his big mouth shut? 'He was ill for quite a long time. Work is busy and, there's something comforting in the routine, I suppose.'

'I can understand that. Business as usual. There's a lot to be said for it. The watershed moments in your life can be really tiresome.'

'Tell me about it.'

They continued in silence until they reached a rather decrepit café sitting at the edge of the boating lake.

'Fancy a coffee?' Roche asked.

'Nah.'

She shot him a funny look. 'Are you ill?'

'Just trying to cut down,' he reassured her. Out of the corner of his eye, the inspector saw a couple on roller skates give up a bench by the water's edge and wobble off in the direction of Holland Park. Skipping over to the seat, he gestured for Roche to join him.

The sergeant gestured at the murky water as she sat down. 'Looks disgusting.'

'It's the middle of London,' Carlyle said. 'What do you expect? It's nice here, though. You should bring David.'

Roche made a disapproving noise. 'Too far away.'

Suit yourself, Carlyle thought, vaguely narked that no one ever seemed willing to take his advice.

'There's a small park at the end of our road. We go there quite a lot.'

'Hm.'

After a while, she asked, 'What about me coming back to work at Charing Cross?'

'You'll have to speak to Simpson,' said Carlyle, passing the buck.

'But where the hell is she? It's like she's disappeared off the face of the planet.'

'Tell me about it.' Carlyle felt conflicted about Commander Simpson's absence. Although he was perfectly content to be operating without supervision, it was sometimes rather disconcerting. Apart from anything else, he knew that, sooner or later, he would need Simpson to bail him out of whatever mess he managed to land himself in next.

Probably sooner.

'Well?' Roche demanded. 'I can't sit in Limehouse waiting to see if Simpson makes it back from the dead. It's driving me round the bend. The people there are truly appalling. Plus, the commute is a nightmare.'

'All right,' Carlyle said reluctantly. 'I'll see what I can do. In the meantime, let's try to tie up all these loose ends.' He talked her through the Kevin Lamoot killing and the connection with the fingerprint found in Professor Grom's flat.

'You got smacked in the face with a pan?' Roche sniggered.

'Yes.' The inspector gingerly touched his nose. 'Fortunately, my youthful good looks haven't suffered any significant long-term damage.'

Roche guffawed some more. 'And you think you were ambushed by the guy who killed both Gerry Durkan *and* Balthazar Quant?'

'Maybe. That's rather speculative at this stage.'

'But there's a connection,' Roche persisted.

'Looks to be, yes.'

'Durkan was a crook and so was Lamoot.'

'That's one way of putting it. For sure, they were both colourful characters.'

'What I don't understand is where a retired professor fits into all this.'

'Absolutely no idea.' Carlyle watched a small dog wander up to the water's edge and take a drink. Rather you than me, pal, he thought. 'Other than the fact that he had a gambling habit and a lot of cash in the bank, which has gone missing.'

'Maybe there's no connection between any of them,' Roche mused, 'except they were killed by the same man.'

'Maybe. Although, technically Grom had a heart attack.'

'The CPS would go after the guy who stuffed him in the cupboard for manslaughter.'

'Possibly. You never know with the CPS.' Rising from the bench, he looked down at Roche. 'What are you going to do now?'

'Go home and put my feet up.'

He gave her a sideways look.

'Only joking. I've got to speak to a couple of people about Mr Quant. In fact, there might be a connection there with Grom, too.'

'Oh?'

Roche explained how Karen Jansen had let slip that Grom, like Quant, had been a client of Nelly Ternan Escort Agency.

'Shit. I need to get to Palin on that.'

'Let me speak to Jansen again first – woman to woman – and then see where we get to.'

Carlyle agreed that was a sensible approach.

'I'd better check in with DI Cooper as well.'

'Good.' The inspector was beginning to remember just how efficient Roche could be. 'Meantime, I'll bring Superintendent Lockhead into the loop and make a few more enquiries. You never know, if we clear this, everyone gets a win.'

THIRTY-SEVEN

With various gloomy thoughts floating through his head, Carlyle reached his destination on autopilot. Turning into Gertrude Street, he belatedly considered the possibility that Elke Lamoot might have sold up since the death of her husband. For all Carlyle knew, the widow had taken her family and gone home to Belgium. Or maybe she had relocated to some other gilded enclave, like Monaco or Manhattan.

There was only one way to find out.

Set back from the street, the house was as he remembered it: well-kept but lacking in warmth. Skipping up a small flight of steps, he stood at the front door, stared at the CCTV camera above his head and pressed the bell. To his surprise, there was an almost immediate response. The sound of footsteps on a wooden floor was followed by the door clicking open. Smiling, Carlyle looked down at the familiar face of a tiny, walnut-faced woman.

'Marjorie Peterson.'

The woman ran a hand through her fragile hair, which was dyed a shade of sky blue. It was a rather different look from the last time the inspector had stood in front of her when she had been flaunting a bright red barnet.

'Yes?' The woman feigned ignorance, but he had caught an initial spark of recognition in her eyes; she remembered him well enough.

'Inspector John Carlyle.' He offered a business card. Taking it, the woman didn't look at the details before stuffing it into the pocket of her cardigan.

'I was looking for Mrs Lamoot.'

'She uses her maiden name, these days.'

'Ms Poosen,' Carlyle corrected himself.

'She's not—'

Before the lie could be fully articulated, Carlyle registered movement behind Peterson in the hallway.

'Who is it, Marjorie?'

A moment later, the inspector found himself looking at the woman herself. Or, rather, he was looking at an approximation of the woman he remembered. It seemed that Elke Poosen had responded to her husband's death by going in for a form of extreme makeover. Utilising knowledge absorbed from too much exposure to the kind of junk TV shows beloved by Alice and Helen, Carlyle counted off the different procedures: fashionable haircut – check; platinum blonde dye – check; Botox; collagen implants; liposuction.

I suppose it's not only men who have midlife crises, the inspector thought smugly. Dressed in a pair of oxblood red leather trousers and a pearl blouse, with a face that seemed as frozen as a turkey on Christmas Eve, she looked like a rock chick who had been caught up in a bad car crash some years previously. He tried to stop his jaw dropping too far.

If she was less than delighted to find a policeman standing on her doorstep, at least Elke Poosen didn't try to pretend that she didn't know who he was. 'Can I help you, Inspector?' she asked curtly.

'I wondered,' he coughed, 'if I might be able to talk with you.' He glanced at the housekeeper. 'In private.'

Poosen considered his request for several seconds. 'We can talk in the study.' Turning, she retreated down the hallway.

Pulling the door fully open, the housekeeper invited him to step inside. 'Take your shoes off.'

'Sorry?'

'The floors.' Peterson pointed at the wooden boards. 'They mark very easily. Take off your shoes.'

Reluctantly, the inspector obliged, hoping she didn't catch a glimpse of the embarrassingly large hole in the sole of one of his socks.

Muttering something that couldn't quite be deemed approval, the housekeeper pointed to a door leading off the hallway. 'Second on the right.'

'Thank you.' Walking towards it, the inspector paused at a series of framed black-and-white photographs of rock stars hanging on the walls on either side. One he recognised immediately: Pennie Smith's famous image of Paul Simonon smashing his bass on stage in New York in 1979, the cover image for the *London Calling* album, widely considered the greatest rock 'n' roll photograph of all time. The inspector had once seen a copy of the picture, signed by the photographer, for sale in a gallery in Piccadilly. Venturing inside, he had made the fatal mistake of enquiring after the price. The shop assistant, correctly sizing him up as a time-waster, delivered the answer in a devastatingly deadpan style. 'Five thousand two hundred pounds.' There was a pause. 'Plus VAT.'

His cheeks red, the inspector made the calculation of the final price. Six grand? For a photo?

'That's for the smaller print,' the assistant confirmed. 'We have larger sizes at eight thousand four hundred, and eleven thousand one hundred.'

Ah. Trying not to knock anything over, the inspector had backed towards the exit as quickly as possible. 'Thanks,' he'd stammered. 'I'll have a think about it.'

'Second on the right.' Marjorie appeared at his shoulder but refrained from giving him a shove down the corridor.

Chastened by the flashback, the inspector ducked into the study, to be confronted by a view of a surprisingly large, beautifully manicured garden.

Lifestyles of the rich and infamous, he thought dolefully.

Elke Poosen gestured towards a pair of matching green

179

leather sofas, which sat in the middle of the room, either side of a glass coffee-table. 'Please, take a seat.'

'Thank you.' Carlyle lowered himself onto the nearest sofa, glancing at the massive book on the table.

The James Bond Archives.

Hm. Carlyle felt neither shaken nor stirred.

'So, Inspector, you wanted to talk to me?' Poosen took up a carefully composed position by the side of a closed-off fireplace, which was memorable for the complete absence of photographs on the mantelpiece.

'It's about your husband.' This should have been DI Lockhead's conversation, but Carlyle wanted to see how Poosen would react to the news. 'There's been a development in the investigation.'

'After all this time?'

The inspector fancied he identified something in her eyes. What was it? A flicker of hope? Concern? Dismay?

'A case like this,' he went on, 'is never closed, obviously. We never stopped looking for the killer.'

'No,' Poosen said coolly, 'but, still, it has been quite a while now. And you have made so little progress.' She made it sound like a casual observation, rather than a criticism. 'There has been nothing for months. I have always tried to be realistic.'

'That's a very sensible attitude. However, we discovered a connection between Mr Lamoot's death and another, erm, incident, something that happened in the last couple of days.'

An eyebrow shot up. 'What incident? What connection?'

'I can't go into any detail at this stage. It's an ongoing investigation.'

'Of course.'

'However, I wanted to keep you fully informed.'

'Thank you.'

'Following this latest development, I'm reasonably confident that we will be looking at some kind of breakthrough in your husband's case in the near future.'

The widow didn't respond.

'Against that background,' Carlyle continued calmly, 'I was wondering if you might have had any *further* thoughts about who could have wanted to kill your husband.'

A look of irritation crossed Poosen's face. 'If I *had* had any further thoughts, I might have mentioned them before now, don't you think?'

'Yes, indeed.' Carlyle spread his hands, reasonableness personified. 'But I just wanted to check.'

'It always seemed to me to be a senseless and random attack. Kevin was a very popular and amiable man. He had no enemies that I knew of. None whatsoever.'

'No.' Carlyle let his gaze drift towards the colours of the garden. Now was not the time to call her on such a blatant lie.

'It is hugely disappointing and hurtful that, even after all this time, no arrests have been made.'

Don't over-egg it. The inspector returned his attention to the widow. 'Hopefully that will change.'

'Hopefully.'

'When there is more to report, we will be in touch. Are you going to be in London for the foreseeable future?'

'That's the current plan. The children are in school and I respect the timetable. We might go away for half-term, but I am not one of those parents who think you should be able to yank your child out of the classroom whenever you feel like it.'

'Me neither.' Carlyle was amused to discover a small patch of common ground with this dangerous woman.

'Apart from anything else, what kind of signal does that give to the children? These days, people feel they don't have to abide by any rules and regulations at all. Everything can be done on a whim. The egotism of it all is outrageous. There is no discipline, no self-control. It's a truly terrible state of affairs.'

Carlyle said he thought she was talking a lot of sense.

'School timetables exist for a reason. When you have to turn up, you have to turn up. Children must understand the importance of this. Ninety per cent of success in this life is just a question of being present. You can't do that if you're on holiday.' Poosen checked herself. 'Anyway, even if we go away in the holidays, we won't venture far.' She thought about it for a moment. 'Italy, maybe. Just a short break.'

Carlyle, whose idea of travel was a trip to Brighton, grunted an indistinct acknowledgement.

'Wherever we are, you can always get hold of me via Marjorie. And I think you have my mobile number. It hasn't changed.' She paused, allowing Carlyle to take his cue to leave. 'Thank you for coming, Inspector.' Poosen made no effort to move from the fireplace as he left the room. 'I will await news of any developments with great interest.'

You're certainly a cool customer, Carlyle thought. Ducking down the hallway, keen to avoid another brush with the housekeeper, he walked briskly past Paul Simonon smashing his guitar, put his shoes back on and let himself out.

THIRTY-EIGHT

Reaching the King's Road, Carlyle slipped into a convenience store in search of sustenance. A minute later, he was back on the pavement, taking a healthy bite out of a king-sized Mars Bar, savouring the sugar rush. Empty calories, he thought, you can't beat them.

A shock of blonde hair on the far side of the road caused him to do a double-take. The woman with a phone clamped to her ear, heading in the direction of the Saatchi Gallery, looked distinctly like Elke Poosen. Acting on impulse, the inspector slipped between the slow-moving traffic and fell in five yards behind the woman who, courtesy of her leather trousers, he had now positively identified as the Belgian widow.

Passing the advertising hoardings proclaiming the gallery's current exhibition, Poosen arrived in a small pedestrianised square. Selecting one of the empty tables outside the gallery's café, she took a seat. Ducking into the first door he came to, the inspector observed her from behind the window display of a shop that appeared to be selling surfing gear. Picking up a menu, Poosen scanned it, still talking on the phone. From the expression, such as it was, on her plastic face, it didn't appear to be a happy conversation.

'Can I help you, sir?'

Keeping one eye on his target, Carlyle half turned to address a pleasant-looking young shop assistant. She was wearing a T-shirt that prominently displayed the store's name. According to a tag pinned above the logo, she was called Jen. He waved her away. 'I'm fine, thanks.'

Confronted by truculence, the girl upped the politeness quota in her voice. 'Are you looking for anything in particular today?'

Fuck off.

Behind the girl, a uniformed security guard hovered in the background. The guy looked to be in his sixties, about five foot five, thin as a stick and almost totally bald, apart from a few strands of silver hair stuck randomly to his skull. A great deterrent to would-be thieves, Carlyle thought. 'Look,' he pulled out his warrant card and held it up for Jen to inspect, 'I just need to stand here for a little while, okay?'

'You're a cop?' Jen giggled nervously.

Tell the world, why don't you? Carlyle thought. But, other than the three of them, the place appeared to be empty.

'I thought you might be a shoplifter.'

Carlyle looked at a selection of Hawaiian shirts. 'I don't think this is my type of gear.'

'Wouldn't stop you trying to nick it,' the girl said. Looking past him, she let her gaze drift across the square towards the scattering of patrons sitting outside the café. 'Who are you spying on?'

'I'm not spying on anyone. I just need to stand here for a bit.'

The security guard appeared at Jen's shoulder. According to his name badge, he was Rob.

Maybe they get three letters each, the inspector mused.

The security guard beckoned Carlyle forward. 'Come with me?'

WTF? Didn't you see my badge, idiot? Carlyle was about to lose his rag when the man pointed towards some stairs behind the counter. 'If it's going to take a while, I can set you up in the storeroom up there. It'll be more comfortable and you'll get a better view, too.'

Somewhat chastened, Carlyle followed him to the back of the shop and climbed the stairs. On the first floor, he stepped into a cramped room full of cardboard boxes of different sizes.

'Here you go.' Rob manoeuvred one of the boxes into a position in front of a window giving a view over the square. 'Take a seat.'

Making himself comfortable, Carlyle looked down on Elke Poosen, still sitting at her table. She had finished her call and was giving her order to a waitress.

'Are you from the Chelsea station?' Rob asked.

'Eh?' Carlyle kept his gaze on the scene outside. 'No. I work out of Charing Cross.' He stuck out a hand. 'Inspector John Carlyle.'

'Robert Butler. Rob.'

'Thanks for setting me up here, Rob. It's a big help.'

'Always happy to help the police. Can I offer you a cup of coffee? It's only instant but it's not bad.'

'Why not?'

'I was in the army for twenty-two years. The original idea was to do five, learn a trade. But you know how it is.'

'Yeah.' Carlyle stifled a yawn. Robert Butler had taken him through his entire life story, twice, in less time than it had taken Elke Poosen to finish her pot of tea. The woman had been sitting outside the café for almost half an hour. She hadn't made another call. No one had turned up to meet her. If his surroundings hadn't been relatively comfortable, the inspector would have buggered off long since.

'When you get out, a lot of guys don't know what to do with themselves.'

'No.'

'I knew I needed to get a job, or I might find myself in real trouble. Too much interest in the drink, you see?'

'Hm.'

'And the horses.'

Hardly an original story, the inspector reflected.

Rob gestured at his uniform. 'This isn't much, but it keeps me occupied.'

Not occupied enough.

'Don't you have some work to do?' The inspector's question was answered almost immediately. From downstairs came the pulsing beep of an alarm, followed by the sound of Jen shouting.

'Rob! We've got a runner.'

'Shit.' The old fella darted from the door.

From his improvised seat, Carlyle watched a boy in a green parka emerge from the shop entrance and run in the direction of the King's Road. A few seconds later, Rob appeared, chasing after the lad.

'Not a bad turn of speed, for an old guy,' Carlyle murmured appreciatively. As the guard disappeared, he moved his attention back to Poosen. 'Here we go,' he muttered. 'Things really are warming up now.'

THIRTY-NINE

Elke Poosen looked on as a teenage shoplifter steamed out of the store across from where she was sitting, setting off the alarm in the process. The garish surf shorts in the boy's hand were familiar. Poosen had bought a pair for her son a few weeks earlier. She recalled that the price had been ridiculous, bordering on criminal.

A few seconds later, a superannuated security guard came chasing after the kid. Red in the face, the man looked set for a heart attack. You're never going to catch him, Elke thought, as she watched the youth disappear down the King's Road.

A shadow fell across the table. 'What's all the excitement?' Bob Biswas pulled out a chair and sat down. 'Some kid almost ran straight into me.'

'You took your time,' Poosen observed tartly. She had vowed not to let her sometime business partner rile her but, already, her resolve was fraying. Biswas annoyed her in a way that few other people managed, apart from her late husband. The late husband had been taken care of. Biswas's time, Poosen realised, was rapidly approaching.

'I'm sorry,' Biswas replied evenly. 'I got here as quickly as I could.' He unbuttoned his red jacket, revealing a canary yellow polo shirt underneath. 'I got caught up with some other business.' The waitress appeared to take their order as the shop alarm mercifully fell silent. Poosen briskly ordered more tea while Biswas asked for a double espresso.

'What's so important we need to discuss it face to face?'

Poosen watched the waitress disappear inside the café. 'I've just had a visit from the police. The same cop as last time. A shabby little man called Carlyle.'

'The cop Manny smacked in the face with the pan?' Biswas giggled. 'I told him he should have hit the guy harder.'

'Manny might want to think about lying low for a while. Is he in London?'

Biswas shook his head. 'Antwerp.'

'Good. He should stay out of London for the foreseeable future.'

Biswas agreed that was a sensible idea. 'What did the cop say?'

'He said there's been some kind of development in the investigation into Kevin's death.'

The waitress reappeared with commendable speed. They sat in silence while she put their drinks on the table.

'After all this time?' Biswas lifted his demitasse and downed the coffee in a single gulp. 'What development?'

'He didn't go into any details,' Poosen poured her tea, 'other than to say they had found a connection with another case.'

'What other case?'

'Funnily enough, I was going to ask you that very question, Bob. What's Manny been up to?'

Biswas feigned insouciance. 'Nothing much. Things have been pretty quiet recently.'

Poosen regarded him with scepticism. 'The policeman gave me the impression that they were on to something. He said he'd be back.'

Reaching forward, Biswas offered her a reassuring pat on the arm. Poosen shied away, almost knocking over her teapot. 'Don't worry,' he said gently, ignoring the snub, 'the cops always say that. The reality is that they're clueless. I'm sure he's just rattling your cage.'

'Yes, but why now? The timing is not helpful. I could do without the attention.'

'Why?' Biswas tried not to sound too curious. 'Got anything interesting happening?'

'The usual,' Poosen said blandly. 'Bits and pieces. You know what it's like, always something going on. Apart from anything else, we're still trying to complete the sale of Kaplan's.'

'Poor old Kevin.'

'Trying to shift a restaurant in this market is a total nightmare.'

'It always was a bit of a vanity project, wasn't it?'

'That's why I'm prepared to take a big loss to get rid of it. We have a couple of potential buyers lined up and I don't want them scared off by the police investigation starting up again.'

'Look, don't worry about it.' Pushing back his chair, Biswas got to his feet. Fishing a twenty-pound note out of his trouser pocket, he placed it under his saucer. 'I'll make a few enquiries, see what I can find out. In the meantime, just go about your normal business. Don't worry, the police have nothing, I'm sure of it. This will all blow over fairly quickly.'

Her eyes narrowed. 'What are you up to, Bob?'

'Like you, bits and pieces. It's all very boring, these days.' Biswas buttoned up his jacket. 'The only reason I happen to be in London is to visit my art dealer. I'm off to Cork Street now, as it happens.' He glanced at his watch. 'I'm supposed to be there in half an hour.'

'I'd take the tube,' Poosen advised, 'or you'll never make it. The traffic's so bad, it could take you more than half an hour just to get round Sloane Square. I hardly ever bother with taxis, these days. You never get anywhere.'

'Good tip.' An idea popped into his head. 'By the way, have you ever heard of an artist called Ting Sasse?'

Poosen made a face. 'No, I don't think so. Why do you ask?'

'He's going to be the next big thing.' Biswas beamed. 'Think Damien Hirst meets, erm, Jackson Pollock.'

Poosen raised her eyes to the heavens. 'The cops are circling and you're trying to sell me a painting?'

Biswas shifted in his seat. 'No . . . Well, actually, yes. There's this series called *Death Smiles*, about the Four Horsemen of the Apocalypse. Amazing. And a great investment. Over the last four years, the price of the artist's work has more than doubled. I can get you a great deal on one, if you want.'

Poosen rolled her eyes. 'Spare me the sales pitch, Bob. I didn't call you so that we could talk about art.'

'No,' Biswas agreed, 'but it would be nice to do some business together. We haven't done anything for a while. Not since Kevin's unfortunate demise.'

'Leave my late unlamented husband out of this. I'm always happy to do business but it has to be the right kind, in the right way, at the right time.' She paused. 'With people I can trust.'

'You can trust me.'

Sadly not. It wasn't exactly an epiphany, but Poosen suddenly realised that Bob Biswas needed to be dealt with as a matter of urgency.

Oblivious to her dark thoughts, Biswas ran a hand across his jaw. 'There's maybe something else brewing I could interest you in.'

Poosen sat back in her chair and folded her arms. 'This isn't another of your great ideas, is it? Like the pigeon scam?'

'No, no.' Biswas didn't like to be reminded about his unsuccessful attempts to make a killing betting on pigeon racing by doping some of the birds.

'Maybe we should wait until the police have retreated into the background a little before we try anything new.'

'But that's the beauty of this. It just fell into my lap. A collection of wonderful items in need of a home.'

'We're not talking paintings again, are we?'

'No, no.' Biswas leaned across the table and lowered his voice. 'Jewellery. Top-end stuff.'

'I'm not a fence, Bob.'

'No, but you are a *collector*. This, also, would be a fine investment.'

Poosen thought about it. Keeping the man close meant it would be easier to take care of him. 'What've you got?'

'I can show you. Gimme a couple of hours.'

'All right. Just give me a call.'

From his vantage point above the surf shop, Carlyle used his phone to take a couple of pictures of Elke Poosen and the man in the red jacket. The distance was too great – and the picture quality too poor – for them to be much more than an aide-memoire. Still, snapping away made him feel like he was achieving something.

After a while, Robert Butler reappeared, looking hot and bothered.

'Catch him?'

The security guard shook his head. 'The little bugger was too fast for me,' he wheezed. 'I lost him somewhere down the King's Road.' He sucked more oxygen into his lungs. 'I'm not quite as fit as I was in my army days.'

'We're all getting older,' Carlyle commiserated. 'I hope the shop doesn't take it from your wages.'

'Don't give 'em any ideas.' Butler slumped onto a box of T-shirts. 'After tax, I'd have to work for two days to buy a pair of those damn shorts. It's crazy.'

'It's crazy,' Carlyle agreed. As the man's colour slowly returned to something approaching normal, the inspector had an idea. He pointed across the square. 'How do you fancy going across the road for a coffee? Sit at the table next to my woman. See if you can eavesdrop on their conversation.'

Butler pushed himself into a sitting position and wiped a bead of sweat from his brow. 'Sure, why not?'

Carlyle fished a handful of change out of his pocket and handed it over. 'Courtesy of the Metropolitan Police.'

'Thanks.' Struggling to his feet, Butler pocketed the cash and stepped over to a line of coats hanging from a rack attached to the wall. 'I'm due for my break anyway.' Grabbing his jacket, he lumbered down the stairs. Carlyle watched as he wandered across the square and sat at a table next to Elke

Poosen and her companion. Taking out his phone, Butler began tapping the screen, just another digital zombie, oblivious to the world around him. A waitress appeared to take his order, just as the man in the red jacket got out of his chair.

'No,' Carlyle hissed, 'not yet, you bugger.' Jumping to his feet, the inspector watched the man exchange a few more words with Poosen, then head out of the square. What to do now? Carlyle skipped down the stairs, signalled his thanks to the assistant and left the shop.

Using a couple of obese American tourists as cover, he exited the square without attracting Poosen's attention and made his way back onto the King's Road. The traffic was in familiar gridlock. Carlyle winced as he inhaled a noxious mixture of exhaust fumes from a hundred different vehicles. Walking beside this shit, he reflected morbidly, is probably the equivalent of smoking a couple of packets of cigarettes each day. Hovering on the kerb, he caught sight of the man in the red jacket making his way past the Peter Jones department store on the far side of the road, heading for the Underground station at Sloane Square.

'I love a man who uses public transport.' Carlyle jogged towards the station, picking up a copy of the *Standard*, then tapping his way through the gates and heading down to the platform. The man went east on the District Line to South Kensington, then jumped on the northbound Piccadilly Line. Three stops to Green Park gave Carlyle plenty of time to catch up on his current affairs. Reappearing above ground, he was up to speed with what was going on in the world. Dropping the newspaper into a bin, he watched his target turn into Dover Street. Seemingly oblivious to the inspector's attention, the man headed north at a brisk pace, as if he were late for an appointment. Hands in pockets, Carlyle ambled behind, doing a little window shopping as he went about his business. After turning down Stafford Street, the man slipped round the back of the Royal Academy. Moments later, Carlyle found himself in the familiar environs of Cork Street.

'Bloody hell.' Stopping in his tracks, the inspector watched the man duck into Molby-Nicol – Dominic Silver's gallery.

FORTY

Molby-Nicol was exhibiting an artist called Ting Sasse in a newly opened show entitled *Death Smiles*. Looking through the window, Carlyle saw the man in the red jacket talking to the receptionist. After a moment, a door opened inside and the familiar figure of Dominic Silver made an appearance. Carlyle quickly retreated to the other side of the street and watched the two men disappear into the office at the back of the gallery.

Pondering his next move, he tried calling Maria Lockhead. When the superintendent's voicemail kicked in, he left a message asking her to return his call, hanging up just as his target reappeared in the gallery. The man said something to the receptionist as he headed for the door.

That was quick. Shrinking back in the doorway, Carlyle pretended to play with his phone as the man emerged onto the street and hailed a black cab.

To follow or not to follow?

Letting him go, the inspector crossed the road and stepped inside the gallery.

'Can I help you?' Doubtless a graduate of the Courtauld or Central St Martins, the receptionist was very pretty and equally self-aware.

'I'm looking for Dom, erm, Mr Silver.'

The woman tapped at the keyboard on the desk, then consulted her computer screen. 'Do you have an appointment?'

194

Carlyle shot a glance towards the office. 'Just tell him John Carlyle is here.'

The woman followed his gaze but stayed in her seat. 'I think he might be on a call.'

'It's a business matter,' Carlyle said firmly, keeping hold of the smile. 'He knows who I am and it's rather important.'

The woman shot him a look to suggest that she was in no position to judge the veracity of either statement. 'One minute, please.' Getting to her feet, she moved briskly to the back of the gallery. Knocking on the door of the office, she waited for a response before slipping inside. Ten seconds later, she reappeared, holding the door open. 'Please.'

'Thank you.' Carlyle ducked past her and stepped into the inner sanctum. The room was cramped rather than cosy, with barely enough space to accommodate two chairs on either side of a rather battered Regency desk. The back wall was lined with floor-to-ceiling bookshelves, filled with different catalogues and reference books. The other walls were decorated with posters of previous exhibitions held at the gallery.

Dom had his feet on the desk, a glossy magazine open on his lap. 'Long time no see.'

'I was just passing.' Taking a seat, Carlyle gestured towards the magazine. 'Your receptionist said you were on a call.'

'Lucy's still learning the ropes.' He lowered his feet and sat back in his chair. 'She didn't know who you were.'

'I didn't tell her I'm a cop.'

'Very diplomatic.'

The inspector gave a small bow. 'I try.'

'We don't want to spook her. This is only her second week. I hope she stays for a while – Eva's getting fed up at having to cover every time another receptionist gets bored or distracted and packs it in.'

'Distracted?'

'Normally a euphemism for getting picked up by one of the clients. You know what these posh girls are like.'

Not really, Carlyle thought sadly. 'How's the family?'

'Fine, fine. Everyone off doing their own thing, as usual. Eva and I are bouncing around in that big house all on our own most of the time. Now that the kids are all growing up, we don't know what to do with ourselves.' His face grew serious. 'What about you? What's the latest on Alexander?'

'He died.' Carlyle stared at his hands. 'Yesterday.'

'I'm sorry, man.' Getting to his feet, Dom retrieved a half-full bottle of single malt from one of the bookshelves. Pulling a couple of shot glasses from a desk drawer, he filled them both almost to the rim. Handing one to Carlyle, he lifted the other in toast.

'To Alexander.' Tipping back his head, he tossed the whisky down his throat.

'Alexander.' Carlyle did the same, not raising any objections when Dom refilled their glasses.

'He was a good man.' He returned to his chair and took a careful sip from his refreshed glass.

'Yes.' Feeling the warm embrace of the spirit, Carlyle cradled his carefully.

'When's the funeral?'

Carlyle realised he didn't have a clue. 'TBC,' he blustered. 'Probably next week.'

'Eva and I will be there, of course.'

'Thank you.'

'Send me the details. And, of course, if there's anything we can do in the meantime, you must let me know.'

'It's all in hand.' Carlyle ran his tongue around his mouth before taking another sip of the Scotch. It was excellent, and he knew he would have to exercise self-control to call a halt after the second glass. 'The auld fella turned out to have been very organised about it. Just about everything was dealt with while he still had his faculties. The undertaker was sorted and paid for. I think Alexander would've signed his own death certificate in advance if he could.'

'Good for him.' Dom looked at Carlyle. 'We're not going to have any problems, are we?'

'With the death certificate?' Carlyle shook his head. 'No. It's just a formality. Anyway, the drugs in his system when he died were all NHS-prescribed.'

'The Health Service got there in the end, huh?'

'The bitter end.' Carlyle cleared his throat. 'It was just as well we could sort him out with some drugs in the interim. It was the only thing I was really able to do to help him.' Suddenly choked, he fell silent.

'That was my last-ever drugs deal,' Dom mused.

'Until *I* need some,' Carlyle joked, quickly recovering his composure.

'You and me both. But that won't be for a while yet.'

'Here's hoping.' Now it was Carlyle's turn to raise a toast.

'Here's hoping.' Emptying his glass, Dom reached for the bottle.

'Two's plenty.' Carlyle raised a hand. 'I'm good.'

'Are you sure?' Dom half filled his own glass and pointed the neck of the bottle towards his guest.

'Yeah. Apart from anything else, I'm on duty.'

'You're working?' Dom screwed the cap back on the bottle. 'Seriously? Doesn't the Met do compassionate leave? I would have thought they'd let you have the rest of the year off. At least.'

'Better just to get on with things,' Carlyle said. 'No point in moping about.'

'That's the Calvinist in you talking.'

'That's why I'm here. The guy who was with you a minute ago. Red jacket.'

'Bob Biswas?'

Carlyle pulled out his phone. 'How do you spell that?' Dom obliged and the inspector carefully typed the name into the device. 'Who is he?'

'A client. Been coming here for a couple of years now. Fairly eclectic taste. Doesn't have much of a clue about art, but knows what he likes. He's a regular buyer, though, which is the main thing. Spends money. Not a time-waster.'

'Time-waster'. He made the word sound like 'serial-killer'.

'Know anything else about him?' Carlyle asked.

'Not really.' Dom pushed out his lower lip. 'He's a businessman.'

'That narrows it down.'

'His face,' he reflected, 'suggests a man who's seen a bit of action, of one sort or another.' Carlyle shrugged; he hadn't got close enough to notice the guy's mug. 'Looks like he's suffered some burn injuries somewhere down the line. Maybe took some shrapnel.'

The inspector tried to think how this additional nugget might fit into the story he was trying to piece together. 'Any idea what happened?'

'Funnily enough, I didn't ask. It's not usually a good idea to ask customers why they're so ugly – doesn't help seal the deal, know what I mean?'

'Fair point.' Carlyle moved quickly on. 'What else?'

'I can show you his account. He normally picks things up when he's in London but we'll have a billing address, maybe a shipping address too.'

'That would be handy.'

'Sure. Give me a sec.' Dom disappeared into the gallery. Feeling pleasantly intoxicated, Carlyle closed his eyes. He had so many things to do but hiding out in this little bolt-hole for a while seemed a very attractive proposition.

I close my eyes and the world falls dead. Where was that from? Struggling to recall the long-forgotten poem, he felt himself peacefully drifting off.

'Wakey, wakey. Now is no time to be sleeping on the job.'

The inspector reluctantly opened his eyes.

I blink and the world is reborn.

'Here you go.' Dom dropped a couple of sheets of A4 paper

into his lap. 'That's everything we have on your guy, his buying record and a shipping address.'

Blinking, Carlyle scanned the data in front of him. 'He's based in Antwerp?' His mind flicked to the Grom case. Hadn't the dead professor taught at the University of Antwerp for a while? He had a sense of fragments of information moving around in his head. They weren't quite coming together, not yet anyway.

'My clientele is international,' Dom said airily. 'I have quite a few Benelux clients. Why are you interested in him?'

'I'm not sure,' Carlyle admitted, 'but he's certainly a person of interest, let's put it that way.'

He folded up the sheets of paper and was about to shove them into his pocket when Dom stuck out a hand. 'Sorry, you can't take that with you.'

'Seriously?' The inspector shot his friend a pained look. 'C'mon.'

'Client confidentiality.'

Carlyle unfolded the papers, not happy about it.

'I'm doing you a big enough favour as it is.'

He didn't say 'again' but Carlyle got the point. Their relationship was becoming dangerously one-sided. Now that Dom had successfully reinvented himself as a legitimate businessman, he had much less need for police protection than had been the case back in his drug-running days.

'You can make some notes.'

'Thanks.' Like a weary schoolboy, the inspector began laboriously typing the address into his phone.

'I can't let anyone have a printout of this kind of thing,' said Dom, looking on, 'even you. These high-net-worth individuals, well, they all have some skeleton or other in their cupboard. If they thought the police could just walk in and see their details, they'd sue my arse off.'

'All right, all right,' Carlyle said gruffly. Handing back the papers, he pointed to a line that had been redacted near the top. 'It would be handy to have his full bank account details.' He could see another trip to Durfee Gardens appearing on the horizon. Hopefully, the late-rising hacker Dudley Carew had made it into the office by now.

'Bloody hell,' Dom complained, 'you don't want much, do you?'

'It's an important investigation.'

'OK.' He disappeared again. This time he came back with the relevant details scribbled in pen on a large yellow Post-it. 'To save your thumbs.' He handed it over. 'Burn after reading.'

'Will do. Thanks.' Carlyle shoved it into his pocket. Getting to his feet, he gave Dom a friendly pat on the arm. 'Thanks for all this. And the Alexander stuff as well. It's been a great help and I really appreciate it.'

'No problem.' Dom shepherded him back into the gallery. 'Working for you, I somehow seem to end up doing far more police work than I ever did when I was in uniform.'

'Life is full of ironies,' Carlyle agreed. Waving at one of the larger pictures hanging on the wall, he asked, 'Is Biswas buying any of this stuff?'

'He bought one piece.'

'Which one?'

'It's gone. He took it the other day. Bob can be quite impulsive. He fell in love with it in an instant and insisted he had to take it immediately. A day later, he'd changed his mind and wanted me to buy it back from him.'

'And what did you say?'

'I told him we don't give refunds.'

'Even for a good client?'

'Especially for a good client. These guys, if they think they can mess you about, you'll never end up selling anything. Some galleries will take things back for their best clients but I made a conscious decision at the start not to do that. People don't respect you if you give them their money back. A sale's a sale. No refunds.'

'Richard Branson, eat your heart out.' Carlyle strolled

towards the exit. The receptionist, carefully writing a note in her desk diary, didn't look up.

'I'm not sure he would be flattered by the comparison.' Reaching for the door, Dom pulled it open. 'Keep me posted about the funeral.'

'Will do.'

'Best to Helen and Alice.'

'And to your lot.' Shoving his hands deep into his pockets, Carlyle slipped through the door and headed down the street.

FORTY-ONE

Still profoundly irritated by the art dealer's oh-so-polite refusal to take back *Death Smiles IV*, Bob Biswas was deep in thought as the taxi slowed almost to a halt.

'Is this it?' the driver asked.

Biswas glanced at the dirty stucco terrace. 'Yes, thank you.' He pointed to a spot further up the road. 'Just stop behind the van. Drop me there.'

'Sure.'

Biswas clocked the outrageous sum on the meter and did a double-take. What a bloody scam. No wonder most people used Uber these days.

Waiting for the doors to unlock, he struggled out of the cab onto one of the depressing residential streets that criss-crossed the no man's land behind Victoria railway station. Retrieving his wallet, he handed over two twenty-pound notes, holding up a hand when the driver began making change.

'Cheers,' said the cabbie, pleased at the tip. 'Wanna receipt?'

'It's fine.' Biswas watched the cab pull away, then started down a cobbled alleyway that led away from the street until it hit a brick wall that blocked off access to a railway culvert. On each side stood a dozen single-vehicle garages that had been built in the early 1970s. The twenty-four were part of a portfolio of more than eight hundred properties that Biswas had built up across the city over the last few years. He had another hundred-plus in Antwerp and was looking to expand into Brussels. His interest

202

had been stimulated after he'd read a story in the *Financial Times* about a businessman dubbed 'king of the lock-ups'. Garages were easy to acquire and required little maintenance, yet offered decent yields and good cash-flow. And they could be pressed into service for matters other than parking a car.

Approaching the far end of the alley, Biswas could make out the constant rumble of rolling stock coming from the train lines. The final garage to his left boasted a set of ancient, decaying wooden doors, painted red, one of which was starting to come off its hinges. The paint was flaking badly and had disappeared altogether in several places. Stepping up to a key-pad lock he punched in the code.

Ducking inside, the smell – reminiscent of an open toilet in Mumbai's Dharavi slum – caused him to gag. Breathing through his mouth, Biswas waited for his eyes to adjust to the gloom. By the back wall, Manny sat on a bench, casually eating an apple.

'Why haven't you got the light on?'

The henchman pointed to the narrow glass window above the garage door. 'I didn't want anyone to think we were in here.'

'Pffff.' Biswas scanned the room. 'Where's the switch?'

'Behind you.' Getting to his feet, Manny pointed to a spot somewhere past his boss's left ear.

Biswas turned and flicked it on. The sudden illumination brought a whimper from the middle of the room. He looked at the woman, bound, gagged and tied to a chair, with a mixture of dismay and disgust. Beside her, a man sat slumped forward, his face covered with blood. Biswas stepped in front of the man, pulling his head up by the hair and staring into his lifeless eyes.

'Did you get what we need?'

'Yeah.' Manny took a final bite from his apple and tossed the core into a large bin in the corner. 'The money's finally been transferred to the right place.' He gestured towards the stiff. 'It was the last thing he did before he died.'

'Good.' Biswas released his grip, letting the man's head drop. Wiping his hand on his trousers, he turned his attention to the woman, who was looking at him in wide-eyed horror.

'Camila.' Biswas glanced at Manny. 'It is Camila, right?'

Manny nodded.

'What did you do, Camila?' Reaching forward, he pulled the gag down under her chin.

'It was Mr Durkan,' Camila Steinbrecher stammered. 'He told me what to do with the money.'

'Who is this guy, then?' Biswas pointed at the stiff. 'Just some random hacker you hired to steal my money?'

Steinbrecher stared at the floor. 'It was Mr Durkan's idea,' she repeated.

'Durkan, before he died, blamed you,' Biswas told her.

'The dead guy said the same,' Manny added. 'She's the mastermind of the whole thing.'

'That's something you'd never call Gerry,' Biswas scoffed. 'He's no one's idea of a mastermind.'

'He's no one's idea of anything, now,' Manny observed.

'Very good point, Emmanuel.' Biswas chuckled. 'Another job well done.'

The bruiser shrugged. 'Just another day in the office, boss.'

Their love-in was interrupted by Steinbrecher's sobbing. 'I only did what I was told,' she wailed.

'Camila, Camila.' Extending an arm, Biswas ran a hand across her scalp, feeling a frisson of excitement in his chest as she tried to shy away from him. That, ultimately, was what he was here for: he wanted to taste the woman's existential terror as she faced the enormity of her mistake in trying to take on Bob Biswas. It was the total experience – not least the stench of death – that he craved. That was what life was all about, these days, wasn't it? Experiences.

He brought his face down until it was so close he could inhale the woman's stale breath. 'We know *exactly* what happened,' he whispered. 'Who did what. When they did it. Why they did it. We just know these things.'

'I can get the money back.'

'We've already got the money back.' Biswas took a step backwards. 'I'm not here because of the money. The money's not the point any longer.'

The woman fought for breath. 'I only wanted to go home.'

Biswas looked at Manny. What was she talking about?

'I only wanted to go back.'

'Back where?' Biswas asked gently. 'Where is home?'

'Lisboa.' Steinbrecher gulped down some air. 'Portugal.'

'Lisbon?' Biswas scratched his chin. 'I've never been there. They say it's very pretty.'

'It is.' Tears rolled down the woman's cheeks.

'Well,' Biswas said brightly, as if talking to an unhappy child, 'I tell you what. I promise you, when this is all done, we will send you back there.'

In an urn.

He gently put the gag back in its place. 'Maybe I'll go there myself. God knows, I could do with a holiday.'

Steinbrecher started squealing. In response, Biswas pulled the gag tight, choking off the words in her throat. Turning to Manny, his tone became glacial. 'Once this is done, I need you to do one more thing, here in London.' Explaining the errand, he looked for any signs of confusion in his associate's face. For an ex-soldier, Manny occasionally struggled to follow orders as precisely as his boss would wish. 'Does that make sense?'

'Sure, boss.' Manny pointed to a scooter lined up against the far wall. 'I can be there in an hour. It won't take a minute to finish up here. I can come back and tidy up later.'

Ignoring the woman's renewed screams, Biswas agreed that was a reasonable plan. 'After that, you'd better lie low for a while. Head back to Belgium. Or, even better, Mumbai.'

'Yes, boss.'

'Before you go, though,' Biswas instructed, 'make sure you get this place cleaned from top to bottom. We've got someone renting it from the start of next month and I need to get the bloody doors fixed first.'

FORTY-TWO

'It's raining, then?' Dudley Carew looked on, amused, as the inspector stood in the middle of his office, dripping onto the carpet.

'I got bloody soaked,' Carlyle complained.

From behind her computer, Gloria giggled.

'Help yourself to some coffee.' Dudley indicated a pot sitting on a hotplate in the corner.

'Thanks.' Carlyle padded across the room and filled a polystyrene cup with a liquid the consistency of tar sand. Taking a cautious sip, he felt an immediate jolt. 'Wow.'

'We accept no responsibility for the consequences of drinking that stuff.' Gloria raised her own cup. 'That's why I go to Starbucks.'

Carlyle took another mouthful. 'I like it.'

'At your own risk.' Gloria beckoned him over. 'Let me show you what I've got.'

Stepping round the desk, Carlyle saw she was working at two computer screens simultaneously. Each one was divided into quarters, which were filled with different charts and data.

'Bloody hell, how do you keep track of all that?'

'She's a very talented girl,' Dudley said proudly.

Gloria blushed slightly. 'It's just a question of being organised, methodical and focused.'

'You'd make a good cop,' Carlyle mused.

'Over my dead body,' Dudley proclaimed.

'That's what my old man said,' Carlyle responded, 'and look at me now.'

'My point exactly.'

'Dad,' Gloria said, exasperated, 'go back to your crossword.'

He muttered something under his breath, then settled down.

'Now we've sorted that out,' Gloria pointed at the top right-hand corner of the nearest screen, 'this is what we should be looking at.'

Carlyle squinted at a sea of numbers. 'What's it showing me?'

'There was a succession of withdrawals from Grom's account early yesterday morning. Someone emptied the whole thing.'

After he was killed, Carlyle thought. 'Where did the money go?'

'All over the place. So far, I've tracked a couple of payments back to an account in Botswana but this is a big job. It's going to cost money.'

Carlyle's heart sank. Then she quoted him a number and it nearly exploded.

'And that's the friends and family rate,' Dudley chimed in, 'before you ask.'

Knowing there was no way the Met would ever sanction such expenditure, the inspector changed tack. 'Can you tell me anything about this?' Pulling the Post-it from his pocket, he handed it to Gloria. 'It's the bank account of a guy called Bob Biswas.'

'That's still going to cost,' Dudley said.

'Okay, okay. Let me see what I can squeeze out of the budget.' Everyone knew that was an empty promise. Carlyle moved to reclaim the Post-it.

'Hold on a sec.' Gloria began hitting her keyboard. 'Bob Biswas.' Carlyle watched a succession of pages pop up on the screens. At least one was familiar – a restricted Europol database – but he kept his mouth shut. Gloria's eyes flitted from one screen to the next. 'Indian born. Belgian national. Fined for tax evasion four years ago. Main businesses listed as diamond trading. There's also a bookmaking operation.'

'Anything about his face?'

'Pardon?'

'He's disfigured – burns or something.'

Gloria flicked through a succession of pages. 'Not that I can see on first glance.' Pulling up a memo of some sort from the Europol database, she leaned forward in her chair. 'But this looks quite interesting.'

'What?'

She tapped the screen with a biro. 'The known associates of Mr Biswas include one Gerald Durkan.'

'The recently deceased Gerry Durkan,' Carlyle pointed out. The inspector recalled a visit to Durkan's Docklands offices in relation to an earlier investigation. He had bumped into a couple of Indian guys in the lift. Had one of them been Bob Biswas?

'May he rot in Hell,' Dudley interjected. 'Dirty Fenian bastard.'

Gloria ignored her father's nuanced political commentary. 'Also,' she continued, 'Biswas is connected to an interesting guy called Emmanuel Bole.'

'How do you spell the surname?' Carlyle asked.

'Manny Bole. B-O-L-E.' She copied the name onto the Post-it. 'Served in the Indian Special Forces before going private and turning up in Europe as a "security consultant". He was arrested three years ago in connection with the murder of a small-time criminal in Brussels but the charges were dropped and someone else went down for it.'

'That's your lot,' Dudley interjected gruffly. 'If you want anything else for free, go to a public library – if you can find one that's still open.'

'Fair enough.' The inspector understood where Dudley was coming from: everyone needed to make a living. He pointed at the screens. 'How are you able to access all of this stuff?'

Looking more than a little pleased with herself, Gloria tapped her nose with a forefinger. 'Trust me, you *really* don't want to know.'

'Gloria is a whizz-kid,' Dudley said proudly. 'She has a double-first from Oxford, and a post-grad degree from MIT.'

What's she doing stuck here, then? Carlyle wondered uncharitably.

The girl blushed. 'Dad, please.'

'Doesn't know the first thing about making a living, though,' Dudley teased.

'You've made your point, *Father*.' Gloria scribbled down Biswas's bank details, then handed Carlyle back the Post-it, along with a business card. 'Don't worry about Mr Grumpy over there,' she said, sotto voce. 'I'll see what else we can find out.' The inspector looked at the card: *Carew & Daughter, Forensic Investigations*.

'We're always keen to go above and beyond when it comes to helping the forces of law and order,' Dudley said sarcastically.

'Glad to hear it.' Carlyle headed for the door.

'By the way,' Dudley added, 'do you still work for Carole Simpson? How's she doing, these days?'

Good questions, Carlyle reflected. Wondering how Dudley knew the commander, he restricted himself to a bland 'Fine.'

'She's a good woman. Give her my best.'

'I will,' he promised. 'If I can ever bloody find her.'

FORTY-THREE

White Knight Essays – *meh*. WKE had charged £1625.44 for an essay on the Yarlung Dynasty and what had she got?

B minus.

A bloody B minus.

At this rate, the university wouldn't let her complete the year. If WKE had an ounce of self-respect, they would have returned the fee. However, the website made it very clear: *No refunds*.

Irritated beyond belief, Melody Rainbow vowed she would write her own essays from now on. Tapping on the screen of her phone, she googled *Buddhism and the Tibetan tradition*.

'Shall we get started?' asked Alison Roche.

Melody didn't look up.

'This is just an informal chat,' the sergeant persevered. 'Nothing is being recorded and I won't mention your name to anyone. I'm not looking to get you into any sort of trouble.'

'She's perfectly capable of doing that herself,' quipped Karen Jansen.

'But I'm not in any trouble, am I?' Melody scowled at the screen.

'Tell me about Professor Martin Grom,' said Roche.

So much for keeping her mouth shut. Melody's scowl deepened. 'I thought this was about the other guy.'

'Balthazar Quant,' Jansen reminded her.

'Yeah, him.'

'You're connected to both men,' Roche said patiently, 'and we're investigating both fatalities.'

'But I thought the professor was just a heart attack.' Melody sniffed.

'That doesn't explain how he ended up in the cupboard,' Roche said.

'Well, I didn't do it.'

'Is there a connection,' Jansen asked, sounding a bit too interested, 'between the two deaths?'

'Melody is the only connection,' Roche admitted, 'as far as we know.'

'As far as you know,' the girl muttered, still glued to her phone. 'You don't seem to know a lot, do you?'

'We have no current reason to believe that there's a wider connection,' Roche conceded, 'but it's certainly an unusual coincidence.'

'Yes,' Jansen agreed.

'Let's start with the professor.' Roche patiently returned to the matter in hand. 'Did you notice anything strange that night? Anything that was unusual or unexpected?'

Melody finally looked up from the screen. 'It was the first time I had ever been to his place,' she said quietly. 'He seemed a perfectly nice old man. He cooked dinner. We talked a little – about his wife, mainly – but I was really tired. We went to bed. Didn't take long. He didn't get very hard but then, he was old.'

Jansen shot her a look that said: *Keep to the point.*

'After we did it, I went to sleep. I slept like a log. When I got up in the morning, there was no sign of him. When the cleaning lady turned up, she said he must've gone out.'

'It was the cleaner who found the body.'

'That must have been after I left. I bumped into her on the way out and she said that he usually went swimming. We assumed that's what he'd done. I got my stuff and went. That was it. I had no idea that he was in the cupboard.' Melody impersonated shivering. 'How creepy is that?'

Roche scribbled a few notes on the pad in front of her. 'And Balthazar Quant?'

'That was a while ago. I tried to think back when Karen mentioned it but I don't really remember much.' Melody gave an apologetic shrug. 'The men all just kind of merge into one big mass, you know? They don't really stand out as individuals. They're just guys.'

'Yeah.' Not for the first time, Roche started to wonder why she had bothered coming back to work at all.

'I remember thinking he had a funny name. His apartment was cool, though. Spent a lot of time moaning about his boss. And he was pissed off with Camila. She was a new girl at work.'

That's quite a lot for someone who doesn't remember anything. Roche kept scribbling.

'Camila with one *l*.' Melody giggled. 'That's what he kept saying. I think the spelling annoyed him for some reason.'

Roche looked up from her pad.

Warming to her theme, Melody added, 'He said he was having to pay for her salary out of his bonus. He kept complaining about it. But that's men for you, isn't it? Always moaning about something.'

Roche mumbled something noncommittal. Running through the list of people at Gerry Durkan's firm, Macroom Castlebar Salle, who had been interviewed about Quant and his boss, she didn't recall any 'Camila with one *l*', or even with two. That was another loose end she would have to check. She gave a weary sigh. Another visit to MCS's Docklands offices beckoned.

'I mentioned the gender pay gap,' Melody smirked, 'and he nearly had a fit. I thought he might throw me out but he'd already paid.'

'We always take payment in advance,' Jansen confirmed. 'Makes life a lot easier.'

'I can imagine.' Roche looked at Melody. 'Anything else?'

'I don't think so.' Melody returned to her online search. 'Was that any use?'

'You never know. Thank you for your time.' Getting to her feet, Roche handed Melody a card. 'If you remember anything at all that might be useful, give me a call.'

'Sure.' Melody shoved the card into the pocket of her jeans.

Roche gave Karen Jansen a friendly nod. 'Thanks for arranging this meeting. I'll let you know if I need anything else.'

'No problem.'

Roche made her way outside and disappeared into the throng.

'She looks knackered,' Melody mused.

'She's got a young kid.' Busy texting Victor – *they've got nothing* – Jansen focused on her phone. 'I don't suppose she's getting much sleep.'

'Do you think that's the end of it?'

'For us? Sure.' Jansen hit send and the message disappeared into the ether. 'What else can we tell her?' Dropping the phone back into her bag, she retrieved a slip of paper and handed it to Melody.

'What's this?'

'It's your gig for tonight. An Indian bloke.'

Melody scrunched up her face.

'Indians are notoriously polite,' Jansen added. 'And they come quickly.'

'They do?'

'In double-quick time,' Jansen promised. 'They're not as porn-addicted as we are in the West. No edging for them.'

Melody's response was less than enthusiastic.

'The guy's a repeat client. Early thirties. I've never had any complaints about him.'

'But I've got an essay to write,' Melody whined.

'Don't give me that crap again,' Jansen said firmly. 'Just get your skinny arse over there and get the job done.'

FORTY-FOUR

Carlyle contemplated Adam Palin with dismay. 'What do you mean, you haven't been able to find the professor's cleaning lady?'

'The woman goes from job to job,' the sergeant offered weakly. 'She's non-stop. Every time I try to catch up with her, she's moved on somewhere else. She does a minimum of three jobs a day, every day.' He shook his head in wonder. 'She really does work hard.'

'Good to know that someone does.' The inspector idly wondered if Niza Curkoli might be able to fit in one more client: Helen was regularly complaining that the flat was a mess, which was her way of telling him he wasn't pulling his weight when it came to domestic chores. He wondered how much the cleaner would cost. 'Have you thought of calling her mobile?'

'She never answers,' said Palin, rather defensively, Carlyle thought. 'I even went to her house to find her.'

'And?'

'I met the daughter, who just confirmed that the mother works all the time. She didn't know when she'd be back.'

Two hours a week should be enough, the inspector mused, given the size of the flat. Maybe three. Despite Helen's annoyance, he didn't think the place was particularly messy. And he could promise that no dead bodies would be falling out of cupboards.

'Seven days a week.'

Three, max.

'She's quite cute, though.'

'Huh?' Carlyle was thrown by Palin's random change of tack. 'Who's cute?'

'The daughter. Hana.' A dreamy look descended on Palin's face. 'She's studying urban development at Queen Mary's.'

Is there any girl in London you don't fancy? the inspector wondered. 'For God's sake,' he muttered, 'this is the Met, not a dating agency.'

'Just saying.'

'Anyway, what happened to Professor Grom's neighbour?' Carlyle remembered that he still hadn't spoken to the trainee architect. 'I thought you quite liked the look of her?'

'You told me to leave her alone,' Palin reminded him, 'until the investigation is concluded.'

'You have to leave everyone alone until the investigation is concluded,' Carlyle stressed, 'or we're never going to put this thing to bed, so to speak.'

Poor Palin adopted the expression of a five-year-old who had just dropped his ice cream on the pavement.

'Only joking.' The inspector felt vaguely ashamed of himself for teasing the lad. Trying to date and do his job at the same time must be hell.

Palin said nothing.

'Okay, so we still haven't caught up with the cleaner, but what have we got?'

The conversation was interrupted by Carlyle's phone bursting into life. No number came up on the screen but he took it anyway.

'Yeah?'

'Inspector? It's Rob Butler.'

It took Carlyle a moment to recall the security guard from the surf shop. 'Oh, hi.' He shifted uncomfortably in his seat.

'Sorry to take so long to report in, but I didn't have your number and by all accounts you're a very hard man to track down.'

'People tell me that all the time,' the inspector admitted. 'But you're not still sitting in that café, are you?'

'No, no,' Butler assured him. 'The woman stayed for about another hour after you left. In the end, she took another phone call, then got up and left.'

'Did you hear what she was saying?' Carlyle asked hopefully.

'No.'

'Ah.'

'So, I followed her.'

Oh, shit. Carlyle was now facing the consequences of breaking one of the most basic rules of policing: never deploy a civilian in the field.

'So,' he asked nervously, 'where are you now?'

'I'm sitting in a pub called Demon Days.' Butler gave him the name of a street in Notting Hill. 'She's in a house across the road.'

'What about the shop?' the inspector asked. 'Won't they be missing you?'

'I'm sure they'll understand, when you explain it to them.'

I'm sure they won't. Carlyle worried that the bloke had been sacked already and didn't know it. 'Sit tight,' he commanded. 'I'll be right there.'

'What if the woman comes out in the meantime? Shall I keep after her?'

'No. Just sit tight. I'll take it from here.'

'Okay.' Butler sounded a little disappointed but didn't protest.

'Gimme twenty minutes,' Carlyle said brusquely, ending the call.

'Who was that?' Palin asked.

'Erm, an informant.'

'A tip?'

'Maybe.' The inspector jumped to his feet. 'Anyway, I've got to go.'

'Want me to come too?' Palin asked eagerly.

'No, I need to handle this myself.' The last thing the inspector wanted was Palin finding out about his unorthodox helper. If something happened to Butler, he could be in real trouble. 'Why don't you, erm . . .' he fumbled in his pocket '. . . why don't you check out this guy?' He handed Palin the Post-it that Gloria Carew had written on and started jogging towards the stairs.

Palin stared at the scribble. 'Emmanuel Bole. Who's he?'

'Long story,' the inspector shouted over his shoulder, 'but we need to do a full search on him. Check all the usual international databases and anything else you can think off. We need to track this guy down as a matter of urgency.'

'What about the cleaning lady?'

'Leave her for the moment – and park the daughter, too.' Approaching the stairs, Carlyle nearly collided with a member of the civilian administrative staff carrying a large box of photocopier paper. Swerving past the glowering woman, he hovered on the top step. 'And if you can find any fingerprints for Mr Bole, check them against the ones we found in Martin Grom's flat.'

FORTY-FIVE

Dropping her bag onto the sofa, Elke Poosen looked around the spacious living room. 'This is your London bolt-hole?' The address was a few steps down from her own neighbourhood, but not too shabby.

'It does the job,' Manny Bole conceded.

Poosen eyed the ex-soldier thoughtfully. The man mountain had snuffed the life out of her useless husband. Might she have occasion to make use of his skills again? It was a possibility. 'This is where Bob stays when he's in London?'

Manny thought about it for a moment. 'Not really.'

Not really? Poosen considered the neutral décor and the lack of any personal touches, photographs and the like. Just another empty London home.

'I've used it a few times but Bob likes to stay in a hotel when he's in London. His preference is the Imperial Court.'

Poosen gave a nod of approval. 'Nice.'

'He bought this place recently to add to his London property portfolio. It's being rented out.' Manny paused. 'If you know anyone looking for somewhere, we can do them a good deal. Cut out the realtor.'

I'm not an estate agent, Poosen thought tartly. 'Interesting time to be getting into residential property,' she mused.

'It makes a change from garages.' Manny smirked.

Poosen stifled a yawn. Biswas had bored her silly talking about his lock-ups. It sounded like the dullest business in the world. That was the thing about men: they got excited about the strangest things. 'I haven't got too long. The kids should be home from school already. I don't like leaving them with the housekeeper.'

Manny's reaction suggested that childcare wasn't the kind of problem he was particularly familiar with. He gestured over his shoulder with a thumb that was almost as thick as her wrist. 'The stuff's in the kitchen.'

She invited him to lead the way. 'Show me.'

A large modern kitchen had been built out into the garden at the back of the house. Opening a set of French windows, Poosen stepped out onto a concrete patio. The garden was small and drab, overlooked by the back of the house on the next street along. Conscious of Manny busying himself behind her, she waved in the direction of a group of desiccated rose bushes. 'This could do with some attention,' she said. 'I can recommend a good gardener, if you'd like.'

Manny replied with a grunt that suggested he couldn't care less.

'He's not that expensive,' Poosen continued. 'And a nice garden will help you rent the place out.'

'I'll mention it to Bob,' Manny promised. 'Now, come and look at these.'

Stepping back inside, Poosen looked at the booty he had placed on the kitchen table and gasped. The surface was completely covered with a selection of gold and jewellery, interspersed with large bundles of cash – dollars, euros and sterling.

'Like it?'

'There are certainly some interesting pieces here.' Poosen was no great expert but she knew quality when she saw it. Picking up a gold and diamond necklace, she resisted the temptation to try it on. Along with a couple of other necklaces there had to be at least two dozen rings, half a dozen watches, a couple of ruby-encrusted brooches and various other bits and pieces.

'How much?' Manny asked.

Poosen did a rough calculation in her head: wholesale prices, minus seventy per cent because the stuff was obviously stolen, minus her cut. It was still a sizeable sum. 'Too early to say.' She kept her expression blank. 'I'll have to get an expert opinion. Where did all this come from?'

'It was a windfall.' A crooked grin creased Manny's face. 'We came across it along the way.'

'And the owner?'

'The *former* owner no longer needs the goods.'

'Good, good.'

Manny caught her looking at the gold Rolex on his thick wrist. 'Bob said I could have it.'

'Very nice.' Not wanting to argue about it, Poosen quickly began thinking through the logistics of disposing of the remaining inventory. She would take a couple of the pieces for herself. The rest she would spread around friends and family in London and Brussels, generating a bit of *argent de poche* in the process. 'Bob wants me to launder the cash and sell the rest?'

'Yes. Transfer the final amount to the usual bank account.'

'Fine.' Elke began looking round the kitchen for a pen and some paper. 'First, we'd better make a list.'

It took the best part of an hour to make a full inventory of Biswas's 'windfall'. Manny struggled with his allotted task of counting the cash. In the end, he took a guess, shoving a thick wad of fifty-pound notes into his jeans for good measure. Keen to get home, Poosen ignored the blatant thieving. She knew she could always make the final numbers add up with a bit of reverse engineering. She handed the list to her big helper. 'Does that look okay to you?'

Manny scanned the list but she could see that his brain was not processing the information. 'Yep,' he said finally.

'Good.'

'Take this off.' Manny picked a rather vulgar diamond ring

221

from the pile and shoved it into his trouser pocket, along with another wodge of notes. 'Bob won't mind.'

'Fair enough.' Poosen wasn't going to argue with a man who could snap her neck like a twig. Taking a fresh sheet of paper, she carefully copied out the amended list and handed it over. 'This one's for Bob.'

Folding it, Manny asked, 'How long will it take to sort all this stuff out?'

Two weeks. 'A month. Tell Bob I'll have a better estimate of the receipts for him in a week, ten days maximum.'

Manny began clearing the table.

Poosen watched, dismayed, as he tossed everything into a plastic shopping bag. 'Don't you have anything better than that?'

'Does it matter?'

'I suppose not.' At least the bag was from Harvey Nichols, sturdy enough not to break, despite the weight of the contents. 'I'll be in touch. Are you guys staying in London?'

Manny shook his head. 'I'm going home.'

Belgium or India? She didn't ask.

'Bob's staying around, though, I think.'

Bag in hand, Poosen started down the hallway. 'Either way, I'll be in touch.'

FORTY-SIX

Demon Days was a nondescript bar, located at one end of a residential street, not far from the Westway. By the time Carlyle arrived, the place was filling with an equally nondescript after-work crowd. Rob Butler sat by the window, nursing a half-pint of lager. As the inspector approached, the security guard gestured towards the row of stucco-fronted houses on the far side of the road. 'She's still in there. It's been well over an hour now.'

Carlyle squinted through the dirty lenses of his glasses. 'Which one?'

'Number forty-two. The one with the dark green door and the Vespa parked outside.'

A thought popped into the inspector's head. 'How did you manage to follow her here?'

Smiling, Butler reached into his trouser pocket and pulled out a travel card. 'She got the bus.' He waved the card at Carlyle. 'I just jumped on it too.' He pointed down the street. 'There's a stop just along there.'

Elke Poosen used public transport. Who'd have thought it? Carlyle pulled up a chair and sat down. 'Well done. Good thinking.'

Butler beamed. It was clear the old geezer was enjoying himself royally. The inspector wondered how he was going to get rid of him.

'She got off at the stop down the road,' Butler explained, 'went up to the house and rang the bell. Someone answered the door and she went inside. That's when I came over here and gave you a call. She's been in there ever since.'

'Well done,' Carlyle repeated. He gestured towards the man's glass. 'Want another?'

By the time the inspector made it back from the bar, Butler's glass was almost empty. Carlyle placed the replacement lager in front of him, along with a couple of bags of crisps. 'Salt and vinegar and cheese and onion.'

'Thanks.' Butler finished his existing drink, eyeing Carlyle's glass. 'I thought you weren't supposed to drink on duty?'

Carlyle sat down. 'I'm not actually on duty at the moment. This is unpaid overtime.' He lifted his glass. 'Cheers.'

'Cheers.' Butler lifted the fresh beer to his mouth, pausing before he took a drink. 'Look,' he whispered, 'she's coming out.'

Carlyle looked across the road in time to see Elke Poosen close the front door and step onto the pavement. As well as the bag hanging from her shoulder, she was carrying a heavy-looking plastic carrier bag. Sticking her free hand in the air, she hailed a taxi that was barrelling down the road.

'No public transport this time.' Carlyle fumbled for his phone.

'She didn't have that plastic bag when she went in.' Butler began gulping down his beer. 'Want me to keep on her?'

The side of the cab bore the livery of one of the big taxi firms. 'Can you make out the registration of that cab?'

Getting out of his seat, Butler read off the number as the vehicle pulled up to the kerb.

The inspector quickly typed it into his phone.

After telling the driver where she wanted to go, Elke pulled open the back door and jumped inside.

Butler remained standing. 'What d'ya reckon?'

'Let her go. I'll check with the taxi firm later and find out where he took her. She's probably heading home, anyway.'

The security guard slowly lowered himself back into his seat. 'What do we do now?' He looked at the inspector expectantly.

'I think that's it,' Carlyle said gently. 'You've been a massive help, but I think I can take it from here.' Fishing a business card from his pocket, he handed it to Butler. 'If there's a problem back at the shop, with you taking off like that, get them to call me.'

'All right.' Butler got slowly to his feet.

Standing up, Carlyle shook his hand. 'And thank you.' Watching the security guard leave, the inspector decided he deserved another whiskey. By the time he had returned from the bar, the table had been colonised by a group of students. The cheeky buggers had even helped themselves to his crisps. Profoundly irritated, he stood morosely in a spot by the window that offered him an unrestricted view of the house Elke Poosen had just left. Placing his glass on the sill, he returned to his phone. Pulling up Google, he typed in the address – 42 Rossiter Gardens – and hit search.

Near the top of the list of results was an entry for a local estate agent. The inspector dialled the number, listened to it ring for what seemed an eternity before the call was answered and a young male voice announced, 'Rentals.'

'Ah, yes,' Carlyle said pleasantly. 'I wanted to make an enquiry about the house you have for rent – the place on Rossiter Street.'

'Which one?'

The man sounded less than happy at being caught so late in the day. There was the sound of voices in the background and the inspector wondered if the office phone had been diverted to the man's mobile. 'Number forty-two,' Carlyle said.

'Eh? That's only just become available. I didn't think we had the board up yet.'

Carlyle realised he shouldn't have known the house number, which wasn't listed on the website. 'Erm, it must have just gone up,' he fibbed. 'I walked past it a minute ago. I was wondering if I could take a look at it.'

In the background, a girl shouted, 'Hey, Ollie, get off the phone.'

'Just a sec,' the agent snapped in response to her. 'Why don't you call back tomorrow?' he asked Carlyle. 'We can make an appointment and I can get your details and—'

'C'mon, Ollie. I want a drink.'

'Can we do it tonight?'

'We haven't got the keys,' the man lied unconvincingly. 'It's a new instruction. No one's seen it yet. The owners only want us showing it at certain times anyway.'

'But—'

'Sorry.' Ollie had established his story and he was sticking to it. 'Why don't you call back tomorrow? We'll get you booked in to see Rossiter Street and maybe look at a few other things as well. I've got a lovely penthouse round the corner for the same rent. Higher-spec finish and great views.' The inspector tried to give it one last push but the agent cut right across him: 'Gimme a call in the morning. Speak then. Bye.' The line went dead.

Finishing his whiskey, Carlyle wondered about Elke Poosen. Was she thinking of renting the place? That didn't seem to make a lot of sense given that she already had a much nicer gaff in Chelsea. And, anyway, Ollie had told him the place had yet to be shown to anyone. The phone began to vibrate on the windowsill. Picking it up, he squinted at the screen.

Palin.

Carlyle headed for the relative quiet of the street. 'Yes?'

'We've done it,' the sergeant squealed.

'Done what?' Carlyle demanded.

'We've only gone and cracked it,' the sergeant burbled. 'I got a match.'

FORTY-SEVEN

'I got a match.' Palin sounded positively giddy. 'Emmanuel Bole's prints were in the Europol database. They're a match to the ones we found at both crime scenes. We've got him. We've *got* him.'

'Don't get too carried away,' Carlyle counselled. 'We still have to find the bugger.'

'Yes, but it's progress, isn't it?'

'Most definitely,' the inspector agreed. 'Well done.'

'I've already tagged him as a suspect on the system.'

Carlyle thought it through: Bole was an associate of Bob Biswas; Biswas knew Elke Poosen; Poosen was up to something. Something that involved Emmanuel Bole? What were the chances of Bole being in London right now? Not very high, he decided. 'Have you checked with Border Security?'

'Bole arrived at City Airport two days before Professor Grom died.' Palin's excitement ratcheted up a notch. 'As far as we know, he's still here.'

'Hm.' So Bole was in the frame for stuffing Grom, dead or alive, into the cupboard, as well as killing Gerry Durkan and Kevin Lamoot. And, last but not least, the vicious assault on himself. When it came to boosting the crime-solving figures, the man was a lottery win on legs. Don't get too excited just yet, Carlyle told himself. He made a mental note to check Bole's movements around the time of the Lamoot killing. Superintendent Lockhead needed to be brought up to speed. And DI Cooper. Not to mention

Alison Roche. His to-do list just kept getting longer and longer. Feeling the effects of the whiskey in his system, Carlyle tried to shake the fuzzy euphoria from his brain.

'What do you want me to do next?'

Wearied by Palin's relentless enthusiasm, Carlyle checked his watch. 'Write up a full report of where we've got to and then I think you should call it a night.'

'Are you sure?' The dismay in Palin's voice was clear.

'We've –' he quickly corrected himself '– you've made a lot of progress. Let's review where we are in the morning. I need to bring the world and his wife up to speed with developments and then we need to see what we can do to flush out Mr Bole.'

Palin reluctantly agreed to the inspector's suggestion.

'I'll see you tomorrow.'

'Right.' Palin was about to hang up, then clearly remembered something else: 'Commander Simpson was looking for you.'

Carlyle scratched his forehead. 'Simpson's back?'

'Yeah. I saw her in the station earlier on.'

'Is she still there now?'

'I don't think so.'

'Okay. I'll give her a call.' Finishing the conversation, Carlyle stared at his shoes. He felt decidedly ambivalent about the commander's reappearance. Over the years, Simpson had developed into a friend and ally, of sorts. On the other hand, being liberated from the dead hand of management supervision had been a blessing.

Still contemplating the pros and cons of her apparent return, he headed for a nearby bus stop and checked out the buses that would help him return to Chelsea to see Elke Poosen. An electronic board informed him that a 452 was due in just one minute. Waiting patiently, he caught sight of a girl with pink hair walking up the opposite side of the street. Not a good look, Carlyle decided, glancing away before she could catch him staring. Once again, he hoped that Alice would never do anything like that.

* * *

Some creep was staring at her from the bus stop across the road. Bowing her head, Melody Rainbow lengthened her stride and headed up the road, out of his line of sight. Finding number forty-two, she paused on the pavement, in no hurry to go in. As a bus rumbled up to the stop, she caught the eye of a young boy who was watching the world go by from the lower deck. The boy gave her a sheepish smile. Melody smiled back, keeping her eyes on the bus until it pulled away.

Inside the house, she sat primly on the sofa while the man sorted a drink. Jansen had said he was big, but that had turned out to be something of an understatement. Even in his bare feet, the guy had to be approaching seven feet tall. Melody shifted uncomfortably in her seat while she considered the implications, pro rata.

On the plus side, the giant seemed friendly enough. On first impression, he appeared calm, considerate and not, as far as she could tell, drugged up to the eyeballs. That pretty much put him in the top quartile of clients, straight off the bat.

He handed her a large glass of white wine.

'Thank you, Mr—'

'Call me Manny.' He had a surprisingly sing-song voice for such a large man, almost as if he was putting it on.

'Manny.'

'Emmanuel is rather formal, don't you think?' Arms folded, he stood in front of her, as if impatient to get on with the evening's business.

'Maybe.' With his crotch at eye level, Melody dropped her gaze to the floor. Looking at his feet, she saw his toenails were painted a delicate shade of blue. What kind of man painted his toenails? She gulped down the wine. After three or four glasses, that would not be an issue. Neither would anything else.

'Is it all right?' Manny asked solicitously.

'Very nice, yes.' Melody gestured towards the open bottle on the coffee-table. 'Are you not having one?'

'I don't drink. Alcohol is not one of my vices.'

Melody stuck out her bottom lip. 'No?'

'No.'

'So,' she giggled, draining her glass and reaching for the bottle, 'tell me, what *are* your vices?'

FORTY-EIGHT

Finishing her third glass of wine, Melody realised that her memory of their conversation up to that point had been miraculously erased. She pointed to the empty bottle. 'You wouldn't have another of those in the fridge,' she asked, slurring her words ever so slightly, 'would you?'

'Sure.' Having ensconced himself in an armchair by the window, Manny made to get up.

'It's okay.' Melody struggled to her feet. 'I can get it. I need to go to the loo anyway.' Careful not to walk into the coffee-table, she wandered into the hallway.

'Bathroom's on the left.'

'What a nice man,' Melody muttered to herself, as she found the door and slipped inside.

Waiting for the girl to do her business, Manny pulled out his phone. Inevitably, there was a message from the boss.

All good?

Laboriously, he typed in a reply.

All good.

After he had finished with the girl, he would go back to the garage, dispose of the bodies and clean the place up. Then, his work in London complete, he would take a flight to Mumbai out of Heathrow.

From the hallway came the sounds of the toilet flushing, followed by the girl heading into the kitchen. She seemed pleasant enough. The pink hair was a nice touch, something memorable. If she wanted to get totally drunk before they headed upstairs that was fine by him. Switching off his phone before he could receive another message, he placed it on the arm of the chair and contemplated exactly what he might do to her.

In the kitchen, Melody looked around. Where was the fridge? Opening the door of the nearest cupboard, she found herself looking at a selection of mugs. The neighbouring cupboard revealed some plates.

And the third . . .

Melody's eyes widened. 'Wow.' Sitting on the shelf, right in front of her, was a large pink diamond ring, on top of a bundle of crisp fifty-pound notes.

'Wow, oh, wow, oh, wow,' she whispered to herself. For a couple of moments, she was frozen to the spot. Then, instinctively, she thrust out a hand and grabbed the rock.

'What are you doing?'

'Erm, nothing. I couldn't find the fridge.' Closing the door, Melody shoved the ring into her mouth.

'On your left.' Manny crossed the room in two massive strides. Placing a meaty paw on her shoulder, he spun her around. 'What the hell are you playing at, girl?'

'Nothing.' Gagging, she couldn't swallow the ring.

'Are you stealing from me?' Taking her face in his hand, he pinched her cheeks firmly between his thumb and forefinger. 'Open your mouth.'

'Ow, gerroff.' Pulling away, Melody tilted her head back and spat the ring onto the floor. As Manny scrabbled to recover it, she darted back down the hallway. Ducking into the living room, she grabbed her bag and turned to leave, only to find the giant blocking the way.

Shit. Melody slipped a hand into her bag, coming up with a small pink tube three inches tall and an inch in diameter.

'Get out of the way,' she demanded, in a trembling voice.

Manny looked at the small canister in her hand and grinned. 'I'm going to break your neck.'

'Sod you.' The adrenalin flooding her body gave Melody an unexpected feeling of invincibility, not to mention sobriety. 'You might be big but you're just another crappy punter.' Lifting her arm, she took two steps forward and fired the pepper spray directly into Manny's eyes. Girlish screams filled the room. Dropping the ring, he began clawing at his face with both hands.

Melody delivered a further blast for good measure. 'You need water,' she advised, 'to rinse out your eyes.' As he retreated to the kitchen, she dropped to one knee, grabbed the ring and tossed it inside her bag, along with the spray.

But what about that crisp pile of fifties? How many more essays would they pay for? Feeling invincible, Melody grabbed the wine bottle by the neck and marched back towards the kitchen.

FORTY-NINE

'The guy has nail polish on his toes.'

'Yeah.'

'Nice shade of blue,' Alison Roche mused. 'I wonder what it's called?'

'Dunno.'

'How many times did you hit him?'

'Three or four.' Arms folded, Melody watched impassively as the heavily sedated Manny was taken out of the house, towards a waiting ambulance.

'They reckon he's got a fractured skull.'

'It was self-defence.' Melody glanced at the bag at her feet. Safely stashed in the bottom was the ring, along with around five thousand in cash. She allowed herself the smallest of smiles. 'I thought he was going to kill me.'

Roche grunted. It was a reasonable assumption.

'I hit him as hard as I could.'

I would have done the same, the sergeant reflected.

'And then I called you.'

'Sensible.' She had taken the call just after David had gone down. Alex was at home so she'd been able to rush across London to take control of the investigation before Melody could be whisked off to a police station to be processed. Under the circumstances, Roche was confident that she could save the girl from a night in the cells.

'I don't suppose I should ask you where you got the pepper spray from.'

'I bought it online.' Again, Melody showed no sign of any embarrassment or remorse. 'You should always be prepared to protect yourself,' she observed matter-of-factly. 'It's the first time I've ever had to use it and, I have to say, it worked a treat.'

'It's illegal,' Roche reminded her.

Melody shot her a look that said, *Who gives a shit?* 'Would you rather be legal and *dead*,' she demanded, 'or illegal and still alive?'

'Fair point,' Roche conceded. She found herself warming to the girl with the pink hair. At least the kid knew how to look after herself.

Melody gestured towards the canister, sitting on the kitchen table. 'It gives you more than twenty shots from a distance of up to ten feet. It certainly stopped that bastard in his tracks. You should get one.'

Maybe I will, Roche thought. Maybe I will.

Why can't people put their fucking rubbish into a bin? Kicking a succession of takeaway wrappers into the gutter, Carlyle walked east along Betterton Street, heading towards Drury Lane. It had been a long day and he was both tired and pissed off. With grim predictability, Elke Poosen had not been home, rendering his detour back to Chelsea a waste of time. Now he would have to go back tomorrow to quiz her on her relationship with Bob Biswas. On the bus, heading towards Covent Garden, he had tried to catch up on his various outstanding calls. First, he tried Carew Forensic Services, only for Gloria Carew's number to go straight to voicemail. There was more success with Maria Lockhead, who was delighted by the news of a breakthrough in the Lamoot investigation.

The superintendent listened patiently as Carlyle explained about the match to Emmanuel Bole's fingerprints. 'He's our man, then?' she asked brightly.

'It's looking likely.' Carlyle was always reluctant to jump to conclusions but now was no time to rain on Lockhead's parade.

If he could help her erase the stigma of being responsible for an outstanding murder case, he would be more than happy to do so. He promised to keep her abreast of any updates before moving on.

Third on his list was Detective Inspector Diana Cooper, the officer in charge of the Gerry Durkan investigation. Cooper's response to his news was considerably cooler than Lockhead's. 'None of this is much good if you can't find the guy,' she pointed out gracelessly.

If *I* can't find the guy? What happened to *we*? 'It's progress,' Carlyle offered lamely.

'We'll see.' The DI sniffed. 'Send me the report and I'll take a look at it in the morning.'

'My pleasure,' Carlyle said tartly, but Cooper had already hung up on him. He tried Alison Roche; when the call went to voicemail, he didn't leave a message.

Getting off the bus at Cambridge Circus, the inspector ducked through Seven Dials, picking up a bag of chips from the fish-and-chip shop on Endell Street, a block from Winter Garden House, where the Carlyle family had their small flat. Crossing Drury Lane, he shoved the last of the chips into his mouth and dropped the wrapping paper into a bin on the corner of Macklin Street. Hovering on the kerb, he tried Roche's number for a second time. The sergeant answered immediately.

'Sorry to interrupt your family time,' he started.

'It's okay.' Roche sounded all business. 'I'm not at home.'

'Having a night out?' he asked. 'Shaggy holding the baby, so to speak?'

'I've told you,' Roche snapped, 'don't call him that. But, yes, as it happens, Alex *is* looking after things at home. I had to head out to deal with a problem with a witness in the Balthazar Quant case. Long story.'

'Hm.' Carlyle couldn't muster any interest. From the pub across the road came a loud collective groan, followed by a series of colourful curses. The inspector recalled that Arsenal were playing this evening; it sounded like London's perennial underachievers were at it again.

'Anyway,' Roche continued, 'what can I do for you?'

'We've got a break on the Gerry Durkan killing.' Carlyle yawned. For the umpteenth time that evening, he explained about Emmanuel Bole's fingerprints. Once he had finished, there was a long pause. 'Hello? Are you still there?'

'Emmanuel Bole?' Roche said quietly. 'Manny Bole? The guy with the painted toenails?'

'What?' Carlyle looked up at the windows of his flat. The lights were on. He wanted to go inside and be embraced by his loving family.

'You'd better get over here,' Roche counselled, 'right away.'

FIFTY

Sitting on the sofa, flicking through a glossy magazine, Melody Rainbow looked as relaxed as if she was waiting for a haircut. Her hairdresser, Carlyle thought, should be shot. Happily, the girl showed no sign of recognising him as the gawker from the bus stop across the road. The inspector didn't want to have to explain to Roche that he had been staking out this very house earlier in the evening, only to bugger off just before things had got interesting. To properly cover his tracks, he'd need to have a word with Rob Butler, too. Slipping the security guard a few quid, Carlyle would tell him to keep his mouth firmly shut about their little adventure. After all, it was a highly confidential police operation and it needed to stay that way.

As the last of the forensics technicians departed the crime scene, Carlyle led Roche into the kitchen. In the fridge, he found a couple of Cokes. Cracking one open, he offered the other to the sergeant.

'No, thanks. I'm trying to cut back on the fizzy drinks.'

'Suit yourself.' Taking a long drink, Carlyle stifled a burp.

'Now you've seen her,' Roche asked, 'what do you think?'

'Melody Rainbow. Crazy name, crazy girl.'

'At least she knows how to look after herself.'

'I'm sure her parents would be very proud.' Carlyle took another slug of Coke. 'Paying her way through university as an escort. Hired by three men, two of whom end up dead.

The third – the suspected killer of the first two – has his head smashed in with a wine bottle. That's a hell of a track record.'

'She's a clear link between Quant, Grom and Bole,' was how Roche preferred to put it.

'Where is he, by the way?'

'Bole? They took him to A & E at St Mary's. The uniforms with him are under strict instruction to transport him back to Paddington Green as soon as the doctors allow it.'

'When will that be?'

'Dunno yet. The guy's got some serious injuries.' Roche gestured back in the direction of the living room. 'Melody gave him a hell of a battering. Got him with the pepper spray, then repeatedly cracked him over the head with the wine bottle. She hit him so hard, I'm surprised she didn't smash it.'

'Do you believe the self-defence thing?'

Roche pushed out her lips. 'It seems credible enough, even before you think that the guy is the prime suspect in multiple murders.' Stifling a yawn, she rubbed her face. 'He hires her for the night, then decides to get violent. Perfectly plausible.'

'Perfectly,' Carlyle agreed.

'Put it another way, I can't imagine that Mr Bole is going to be pressing assault charges.'

'No.'

'And even the CPS might have the sense to leave this one alone.'

'We can but hope.' An idle thought passed through Carlyle's brain. 'How much did the guy pay her?'

'Why do you ask?'

'No particular reason.' Finishing his drink, he crumpled the can in his fist. 'I was just wondering how much Professor Grom had paid for the privilege of making her a meal. Which she didn't eat.'

'I think the professor paid her for more than sharing a meal,' Roche pointed out.

Yeah, the dirty old bugger. Carlyle began opening cupboards, searching in vain for a bin.

'Anyway,' Roche continued, 'I don't know what the agency was charging. I can find out.'

'Not a big deal.' Squashing the can flat, Carlyle shoved it into the pocket of his jacket, vowing to get rid of it on his way home.

Roche perched on the edge of the kitchen table. 'I asked her if the guy had paid her, and you know what she said?'

'What?'

'She just narrowed her eyes and snapped, "No refunds".' Roche chuckled. 'You look at the pink hair and the small frame and you don't imagine she could have such a steely core.'

'You need it in her line of work,' Carlyle reflected. 'What are you going to do with her?'

'I've got someone coming to pick her up. Not that I think she needs looking after, more to keep an eye on her and make sure she turns up at the station tomorrow to give her statement.' She looked at the inspector. 'I've told her to come to Charing Cross.'

'Fine.'

'It saves me having to schlep all the way out to Limehouse.'

'Sensible.'

'And it gets me away from that total berk Wrench.'

'I might sit in.'

'That would be good.'

'It's a date, then.' Looking at Roche, Carlyle realised he had reached a decision about his preferred sidekick. Now that Simpson had reappeared, he would lobby to have Roche restored to her rightful place in Charing Cross. Young Palin had his merits but Roche was a grown-up. And she would put up with his idiosyncrasies.

Roche caught him looking at her. 'What?'

'Nothing,' Carlyle replied, rather embarrassed. 'Let's get these cases wrapped up and then we can get you back to Charing Cross full-time. Simpson has finally resurfaced, so I'll have a word and get it sorted.'

'Great,' Roche said, adding: 'What's she been up to?'

'No idea,' Carlyle admitted.

'Maybe she's been ill.'

'Maybe.' Whatever the reason for his boss's disappearance, the inspector hadn't heard it.

'Have you seen her?'

'No. But sources tell me she's been at the station.'

Roche grinned. 'Reliable sources?'

'As reliable as you're ever going to get in a uniform.'

'You could give her a call,' Roche nudged. 'Get it sorted out right now.'

'I could try.' Retrieving his mobile, Carlyle found Simpson's number and hit call. The phone rang five times before the commander picked up.

'I'll call you back,' she said brusquely, not waiting for a response before hanging up.

Nonplussed, Carlyle dropped the phone back into his pocket.

'Happy to hear from you, then?' Roche said.

The inspector scratched behind his ear. 'She says she'll call back later.'

'Hm.'

'I don't think she realises we're about to hand her a number of big wins on a plate,' Carlyle mused. 'Help her come back with a bang.'

'Three murders – that's a hell of a bang.'

Kevin Lamoot, Balthazar Quant, Gerry Durkan. Sadly, none would go down as wins against his name. 'Three and a half,' Carlyle suggested, 'depending where you put Grom.'

'And to think the guy responsible for all that carnage was brought down by a girl with pink hair.'

'You must have missed all this excitement when you were away, huh?'

'The Job has its moments,' Roche conceded. 'Just so long as I don't have to spend the rest of my career in bloody Limehouse.'

'Don't worry,' Carlyle repeated. 'I *will* get it sorted.'

'Thanks.' The sergeant was about to say something more when they were interrupted by the sound of the doorbell. 'That'll be Melody's minder.' Pushing herself off the table, she headed out of the kitchen.

Carlyle listened to the sound of the door opening, followed by female voices. After a few moments, Roche led the new arrival into the living room. Switching off the kitchen lights, the inspector went to join them.

Melody was still reading her magazine. Her 'minder' stood in front of the fireplace, tapping the screen of her phone. The woman was, Carlyle guessed, somewhere in her mid-thirties. A statuesque brunette with a deep tan that was in no way fake, she was a very attractive woman, by anyone's standards. In a pair of jeans and a red blouse, under an elegantly cut leather jacket, she radiated a sense of sophisticated cool.

Roche quickly made the introductions. 'Inspector, this is Karen Jansen.'

The woman finished fiddling with her phone and looked up. 'Nice to meet you, Inspector, at last.' She flashed a set of perfect white teeth that had probably cost more than the inspector earned in six months.

'You too,' Carlyle offered, making no effort to come closer.

Roche eyed the pair of them suspiciously. 'You two know each other?'

'Our paths have crossed,' Carlyle muttered.

Conscious of his discomfort, Jansen gave an amused smirk. 'I'm a friend of Christina O'Brien. We worked at Everton's together, back in the day.'

The inspector watched Roche's brain try to turn the snippets of information into something approaching a coherent whole.

Christina O'Brien.

Former stripper at a club called Everton's.

Widow of former Metropolitan Police Sergeant Umar Sligo,

242

sometime sidekick of one Inspector J. Carlyle, who was shot to death alongside one of his girlfriends.

The sergeant started to say something, then stopped. A couple of seconds later, she tried again. 'So—'

'It's a long story.' The inspector turned to Jansen. 'You're still in the same business, I take it?'

'Under new management,' was all Jansen offered in reply.

'Maybe we should have a chat about that.'

'Maybe we should. Now is not really the time, though, is it?' Jansen reached into her pocket and retrieved a business card. Flipping it over, she showed Carlyle the number scribbled on the back, then handed it over. 'Maybe we can grab a drink sometime.'

Carlyle shoved the card into his pocket. 'I'll call you.'

'Fine.' Jansen gestured for Melody to stand up. 'Let's get going.'

The girl immediately jumped to her feet. 'I'm hungry.'

'You're always hungry.' Taking the girl's magazine, Jansen carefully returned it to the rack by the end of the sofa. 'Let's see what we can get down the road.'

'Okay.' Slinging her bag over her arm, Melody slipped past the inspector and down the hallway.

Jansen started after her. 'I'll bring her down to the station in the morning to make her statement,' she promised Roche, 'as agreed.'

'Thanks.' The sergeant still looked less than happy with the way the conversation had gone. 'What was that all about?' she asked, after the two women had left.

'Like I said, it's a long story.'

Roche gestured round the room. 'Relevant to this?'

'I don't think so.' Carlyle glanced at his watch. 'Look, we both need to get home. I'll give you chapter and verse another time.'

Roche was too tired to argue. 'I'll give you a text when I've dropped David at the nursery. You can buy me breakfast before Melody turns up.'

'Deal.'

'Right.' The sergeant ushered him towards the door. 'Let's get out of here.'

FIFTY-ONE

His dream saw him walking through the kitchen of Kaplan's, Kevin Lamoot's restaurant, before being smacked in the face with a kitchen pan. Then he would get up and do it all again from the beginning. It was like he was repeatedly playing the same video game, unable to get past the first level. After one final knockout, the inspector shook himself awake. Rolling over, he squinted at the clock-radio on the table by his side of the bed.

05:13.

Pushing himself out of bed, he padded into the bathroom. After a quick shower and a shave, he dressed, grabbed a pair of shoes and his North Face jacket, then slipped quietly out of the front door.

The first westbound Central Line train of the morning took him to Lancaster Gate. Heading towards Paddington station, he ducked into a twenty-four-hour café, waiting in a short queue to buy a takeaway coffee and an egg roll.

By the time he reached St Mary's Hospital, breakfast was a dim memory. A sleepy receptionist at the front desk peered at his ID, and revealed that Emmanuel Bole was being held in a private room in the Templeton Wing. She pointed down the corridor. 'You'll find the lifts at the far end. Third floor.'

Upstairs, Carlyle found a young constable asleep in a chair. Striding forward, the inspector emitted a loud cough and thrust his ID in front of the boy's face. 'Everything okay?'

The constable blinked a couple of times, then squinted at the warrant card. 'All good, sir,' he stammered. 'No problems to report.'

'Good.' Carlyle peered through a porthole window in the door. The prisoner appeared to be sleeping soundly in his bed. Even lying down it was clear that Emmanuel Bole was a massive bloke. Was this the man who had knocked him out cold? It seemed so. He turned back to the constable. 'What's your name?'

For a second, the officer seemed stumped by the question. Then his brain kicked into gear: 'Whiting, sir. Barney Whiting.'

Barney? When did the Met start recruiting Barneys? 'Well, Barney,' Carlyle asked, 'where are the others?' He jerked a thumb towards the door. 'I thought Sergeant Roche had put three uniforms on the big guy.'

The constable stared at his boots. 'They've gone off duty,' he admitted. 'There was an issue with the overtime.'

'Great.' Carlyle had heard it all before. Even in the most serious of cases, it was harder and harder to get approval for overtime payments.

Yawning, Whiting struggled to his feet. 'I was supposed to be off myself,' he looked at his watch, 'more than an hour ago.'

'I'll see what I can do about sorting out a replacement,' Carlyle lied. 'Why don't you nip down to the café and grab some breakfast? I need to have a word with Mr Bole here.'

Whiting stole a glace through the porthole. 'He's asleep. They sedated him.'

'I'll wake him up gently.'

'You're the boss.' Whiting started down the corridor. 'Just be aware, the guy's not handcuffed to the bed. The doctor wouldn't allow it on account of his injuries.'

'Don't worry.' Carlyle chuckled. 'I can look after myself. He's not gonna cause me any problems.'

'Wakey, wakey.' Flicking on the overhead light, Carlyle stepped into the room. 'Rise and shine, you bastard.' Giving the bed-frame a firm kick, he waited for a response.

After a moment, Bole groaned and his eyes fluttered open. Lifting an arm, he shielded his face from the glare of the strip lighting.

Carlyle gave the bed another kick. 'Do you know who I am?'

Bole said nothing but the malicious grin spreading across his face gave the inspector his answer.

'What do you want?' Struggling into a seated position, Bole wiped the sleep from his eyes.

'I need you to explain a few things for me.' Carlyle pulled up a chair and sat down. 'Like what happened to Martin Grom, for a start.'

'He was an old man.' Bole yawned. 'I think he had a heart attack. I didn't do anything to him.'

'Why did you stick him in the cupboard?'

The giant looked genuinely surprised at the question. 'I was just being tidy. And he was dead, you know, so what did it matter?'

That's all I need, Carlyle thought sourly, a giant killer with OCD.

Bole pushed back the duvet, slowly swinging his legs over the side of the bed. 'I need to use the toilet.' He scratched himself vigorously through a pair of black boxer trunks.

Carlyle glanced towards the en-suite in the corner. 'Leave the door open.'

Planting both feet on the floor, Bole reached under the bed, coming up with an oval stainless-steel bowl. 'I could use the bedpan, if you prefer.'

The inspector gestured towards the bathroom. 'Get on with it.'

As Bole headed for the bathroom, Carlyle took out his phone and pulled up Roche's number. Was it too early to call the sergeant? Would she be busy getting little David ready for nursery? Putting his concerns to one side, he made the call.

Roche answered as the toilet flushed next door.

'Alison, I was thinking—'

Realising that Bole had returned, the inspector got to his feet. Something in the giant's hand glinted under the lighting as it flashed in front of Carlyle's face. There was a hollow thud, then nothing.

FIFTY-TWO

Coming around, it took the inspector several moments to realise that he had been installed in the bed recently vacated by
Emmanuel Bole.

I hope they changed the bloody sheets.

A monster headache raged inside his skull and he felt like he
wanted to vomit. Taking a series of shallow, regular breaths, he
waited for the feeling to pass and squinted at the figure standing
at the bottom of the bed.

'What happened?'

'The giant brained you with the bedpan.' Roche sniggered.

'Glad you think it's funny.'

'Look on the bright side, at least it was empty.' The inspector
slid off the bed and staggered into the toilet. When he reappeared, she pointed to a can of Diet Coke, sitting on the bedside
table next to a packet of extra-strong painkillers. 'Have some of
that. It should help.'

Muttering to himself, Carlyle popped a couple of the pills and
washed them down with the Coke.

'It happened again,' Roche pointed out, somewhat gratuitously.

'Yeah.' Carlyle cautiously felt the bump on his temple. At
least it had been just a glancing blow.

'Don't worry,' said Roche, sarcastically, 'your good looks are
intact.'

'Not an unimportant consideration.'

'What the hell were you playing at?' the sergeant demanded.

'We were supposed to meet at Charing Cross. Instead, you wander over here for a bedside chat with a multiple-murderer.'

'Multiple-murder *suspect*,' Carlyle corrected her.

'With a multiple-murderer,' Roche repeated, 'who casually smacks you on the head, gets dressed and walks out of here, without anyone trying to stop him.'

'There was nothing casual about it,' Carlyle argued. 'Anyway, it wasn't my fault that the uniforms had been sent home, was it?'

'Whiting said you told him to go and get some breakfast.'

The inspector reluctantly admitted the truth. 'It wasn't his fault.'

'Oh, I know whose fault it was.'

'I thought I could handle it.'

'Well, you were certainly wrong on that one.'

'Yes.' Being confronted with the consequences of his own incompetence, Carlyle contemplated retreating into the bathroom. Instead he said, 'I couldn't sleep. I came over to see what Bole could tell me about Grom and the others.'

'And now he's in the wind,' Roche huffed, 'and we're back to square one.'

Carlyle tried to look suitably sheepish.

'I need to get over to Charing Cross,' Roche sighed, 'to conduct the Melody Rainbow interview. I'm sure she'll be very impressed that we've managed to lose Bole in double-quick time.'

'Is there anything I can do?'

Roche's expression hardened. 'I think you've done more than enough for one day already.'

All right, all right, Carlyle thought petulantly. I know I've fucked up. Let's move on, shall we? It dawned on him that his latest run-in with the bedpan-wielding giant would already be the talk of police stations across Central London. He would have to put up with having the piss taken – no pun intended – for weeks, if not months, to come. The grim realisation made his headache throb even more violently.

'Anyway, the doctors want you to stay here for a while, just to make sure there's no lasting damage.'

Sounds good to me, Carlyle thought.

'Do you want me to ring Helen to tell her what's happened? Or Simpson?'

Good God, no. 'It's okay,' he said hastily. 'I'll give them both a call. Later.'

'Suit yourself.' Roche started for the door, then stopped. 'By the way,' she said, the smirk returning to her face, 'before he knocked you out, did Bole tell you anything interesting?'

'Not really.' Carlyle groaned. 'Let me know how you get on with Melody. I'll be back as quickly as possible.'

'You just take it easy.' Roche pointed under the bed. 'And, remember, the bedpan's there if you need it.'

FIFTY-THREE

He was woken by his phone vibrating across the bedside table. 'Were you asleep?' Gloria Carew asked anxiously. 'I haven't woken you up, have I?'

'No, no,' Carlyle muttered groggily. 'I was just, er . . .' Unable to come up with a credible fib, he quickly changed tack: 'What can I do for you?'

'I've been doing some more digging,' Gloria explained, 'and I think I've come up with something interesting – a trading company called M and A Services.'

Carlyle stared up at the ceiling. 'Never heard of it.'

'It belongs to Bob Biswas. So far, I've come up with more than two dozen different businesses that are linked to him in some way or other. Most of them are just shells, but M and A – it stands for Mumbai and Antwerp – seems to be fully operational. Certainly, Mr Biswas uses an M and A bank account to pay some of his business expenses. A company credit card was used earlier this week to pay for a room at the Imperial Court Hotel in St James's.'

'I know the Imperial Court.' Carlyle sat up.

'The booking was for three nights,' Gloria continued, 'the last one being tonight.'

'He's still there, then?'

'We don't know that,' Gloria said. 'All we know is that a room has been booked using that card.'

'I'd better go and check it out.' Carlyle tried to come up

with the name of a contact at the Imperial Court but his mental Rolodex was currently out of service.

'I hope that's useful.'

'Very. Thanks.'

From somewhere in the background, Dudley boomed, 'The bill's in the post. Cash only. No discounts. No refunds.'

'Dad,' Gloria groaned, 'stop it.'

'Dudley's right,' Carlyle offered. 'You can't keep doing stuff for free.'

'I know, but still.'

'I'll see about raiding the Met research budget in the next few days. Give your dad my best in the meantime.'

Stepping into the empty lobby of the Imperial Court Hotel, the first thing that Carlyle noticed was a large poster advertising a *Berlin in the 20s* themed party. Better than *Berlin in the 30s*, he supposed.

Making his way to the front desk, he picked out the most docile-looking of the receptionists on duty, a short guy operating from behind a pair of thick acetate spectacle frames. The name badge on his uniform said 'Graham'.

'Can I help you, sir?' Graham asked, not quite managing a smile.

'I'm looking for Duncan Monroe.' A couple of quick calls on the way over had ascertained Monroe was the hotel's head of security and that he was considered a reliable enough sort when it came to assisting the forces of law and order as they went about their business.

Graham looked flustered. 'I'm sorry?'

'Mr Monroe.' Leaning forward, Carlyle lowered his voice a notch or two. 'Your head of security.'

A pained expression clouded Graham's face. Then he started to blush as violently as if Carlyle had just propositioned him in the Gents. 'Are you a guest?'

The inspector's scarce reserves of good humour evaporated as he considered the dullard in front of him. 'No.'

'Then can I—'

Carlyle took out his ID and laid it on the desk. 'Just get the gentleman for me, please.'

Pushing his glasses up his nose, Graham looked at the photograph on the warrant card, then at Carlyle, clearly unsure if he was looking at the same person. 'So you're a police officer?'

'That is correct.' Carlyle resisted the temptation to reach across the desk and give the idiot a firm slap.

Sensing the physical threat, Graham stepped away from his station and bolted towards a side door. 'Hold on one moment, please.' When he reappeared, it was with bad news. 'I'm afraid that Mr Monroe isn't on duty.'

'Who *is* on duty, then?' Carlyle hissed.

'That would be me,' said a voice behind him.

Turning on his heel, the inspector came face to face with an Asian woman, name tag 'Fiona'.

'Can I help you?'

Biting his upper lip, he gave serious consideration to arresting both members of staff on the spot. Give it one last go, he told himself, summoning the patience of Job. 'I'm looking for whoever is currently responsible for hotel security.'

'That would be me, 'the woman repeated, her voice betraying no accent. 'Fiona Chambers. Mr Monroe has the night off.'

'John Carlyle.' He offered a limp handshake. '*Inspector* John Carlyle.'

'Yes.' Chambers gestured in the direction of a door marked *Staff Only*. 'Please, come with me.'

A dimly lit corridor led to a large room at the back of the building. It was decked out like an old-school library – all dark-wood panelling, floor-to-ceiling bookcases and leather furniture. The inspector scanned the obscure titles of the tomes on the shelves and thought of Grom – the professor would doubtless have loved it in here.

'This is one of our private meeting rooms,' Chambers explained.

'Very nice.' Carlyle's gaze alighted on the drinks trolley at the far side of the room.

'Please,' said Chambers, following his gaze, 'help yourself.'

'No, no,' Carlyle said. 'It's a bit early for that.'

'Well, if you change your mind, feel free to help yourself at any time.'

'Thank you.'

Placing her hands behind her back, Chambers finally got down to business. 'What can we do for you, Inspector?'

'You have a guest by the name of Bob Biswas. I need access to his room.'

'Hm.' Chambers let her gaze drift off into the middle distance. 'Do you have a warrant?'

Carlyle pushed back his shoulders and launched into his pitch. 'This is a very serious and fast-moving investigation.'

'You don't have a warrant, do you?'

'Do you want me to get one?' Carlyle asked. 'And bring a couple of vanloads of uniformed officers onto the premises in order to enforce it?'

'Not really.' The woman's expression didn't change. 'Give me a couple of minutes. Let me see what I can find out about Mr—'

'Biswas.'

'Let me see what I can find out about Mr Biswas.'

While she was gone, the inspector reviewed the extensive contents of the drinks trolley. Refusing to yield to the siren call of a fifteen-year-old Speyside malt, he took refuge in a leather armchair by a window looking out over a small internal courtyard.

After a few minutes, Chambers reappeared. 'Mr Biswas is booked into the KitKat Suite for three nights.' She paused. 'That's one of our premier suites – it costs almost nine thousand a night.'

'*Pounds?*' Carlyle let out a low whistle.

Chambers nodded. 'He's due to check out tomorrow.'

'Is he there now?' Carlyle asked hopefully.

Chambers shook her head. 'He left the hotel this morning and has not been back since.' She waved the mobile in her hand. 'Guests unlock their doors with their smartphone. It allows us to track their movements in and around the building.'

'Is it legal?'

'Perfectly. The guests accept our use of the system as part of the terms and conditions when they book a room.'

'Handy.'

'I worked for the Chinese company that developed the software technology. I spent the last two years rolling out the system across the Imperial Court chain – four hundred and fifty-nine properties in seventy-two countries. Six months ago, the Imperial Court asked me to come and work for them. It gave me the chance to spend some time in London, so I took it.'

'And now you do security?'

'It's all part of the same piece. Data collection, data analysis, data deployment – it's all about data now.'

Carlyle stifled a yawn.

'We can predict problematic bookings with almost seventy-seven per cent accuracy. We build a profile of our guests. All companies do it. It helps us target priority customers and screen out less optimal opportunities.'

'Undesirables,' Carlyle translated.

'These days, everyone is the sum of their data.'

'Yes, I suppose we are. But what about Mr Biswas? If he's booking the KitKat Suite he must be a priority customer.'

Chambers's eyes narrowed. 'Confidentially?'

'Nothing we discuss goes any further.'

'Mr Biswas is a Tier One guest.'

'That's good?'

'That's *very* good. He regularly uses this hotel and others in the chain.'

'And you have lots of data on him,' Carlyle probed gently.

'Lots of *confidential* data,' Chambers asserted. 'We take data-protection issues very seriously.'

'As you should,' Carlyle said solemnly. 'It's a very important matter.'

FIFTY-FOUR

It took the inspector little more than five minutes to stick his nose into the various nooks and crannies of the KitKat Suite. Returning to the sitting room, Chambers pointed at a framed print standing on a sideboard. 'Is that what you were looking for?'

Carlyle squinted at the splodges of grey. For some reason, they looked familiar. 'Not really, I don't think.' Stepping over to the sideboard, he picked up the picture and turned it over, smiling when he saw the sticker on the back bearing the logo of the Molby-Nicol gallery. '*Death Smiles IV*,' he read from the descriptor, 'a special-edition print from the workshop of Ting Sasse.'

'Is it valuable?'

'Knowing where it came from, I would say it was expensive.' Carlyle sensed the germ of an idea forming in his brain. 'I'm going to take this with me.'

Chambers looked unsure whether she should try to stop him. 'Doesn't it belong to Mr Biswas?'

'If he comes back looking for it,' the inspector said, 'please ask him to get in touch.'

'If you need to ask the price, you can't afford it.' Dominic Silver placed *Death Smiles IV* on a shelf in the storeroom next to his office at the back of the gallery. 'But, between you and me, Mr Biswas ended up shelling out the thick end of twenty-five grand on it.'

'The guy certainly likes spending money,' Carlyle said, envious of his disposable income.

'Ting Sasse is hot right now. We've sold almost a million quid's worth of his stuff this month alone.' Ushering Carlyle out of the room, Dom locked the door and led them back into the office. 'You found it in his hotel room?' He reached for the whisky bottle on the back shelf.

'He'd done a runner.' Carlyle dropped into the seat in front of the desk. 'Looks like he'd just abandoned it.'

Dom shook his head as he poured two large measures. 'Strange bloke.' He handed one of the glasses to Carlyle. 'If the cleaners had found it, it could have ended up in the rubbish.'

The inspector took a mouthful of Scotch. 'Or in some flea market, on sale for a tenner.'

'Twenty, surely.' Dom chortled. 'Can you imagine? The artist would have a fit at the very thought. He's even more temperamental than Biswas.'

Lifting his glass, Carlyle gestured in the direction of the storeroom. 'What will you do with it?'

'I'll keep it here till I can speak to Bob. If he really doesn't want it, I can try to sell it for him. He'll have to take a hit on what he paid for it – plus my commission, of course – but at least he'll get some of his money back.'

'What a business.'

'Just like any other, there are a lot of variables.'

'*Caveat emptor.*'

For a short while they drank in companionable silence.

'Helen told me about your dad's funeral,' Dom said finally, reaching for the bottle again.

'Hm.' Carlyle realised guiltily that he had paid no attention whatsoever to the details.

Dom refilled his glass. 'Don't worry, we'll be there on Tuesday.'

'Thanks,' Carlyle said. 'I appreciate it.'

'We have to pay our respects.'

'Yes.' Carlyle didn't want to think about it. Grieving wasn't really his kind of thing. 'Meantime, I was wondering, maybe you could do me a favour.'

'Me? Do you a favour?' Dom rolled his eyes. 'That makes a change.'

'I want you to try to get hold of Biswas and tell him you've got his painting. Tell him the hotel returned it to you for safe keeping and he needs to come and collect it because you haven't got any storage space or something. Then let me know when he turns up.'

'So that you can nick the guy?' He stared into his drink.

'He's involved in some serious shit,' Carlyle said.

'Okay.' Dom sighed. 'I'll try to lure him here for you. But do *me* a favour, try not to nick him on the premises. That kind of thing gets around and it's bad for business.'

FIFTY-FIVE

Carlyle smeared some butter across a slice of toast, shoving it into his mouth while waving his knife in the air. They were sitting in a café on Bedfordbury, east of the Charing Cross Road. After his flying visit to see Dominic Silver, the inspector had waited for Alison Roche to finish her interview with Melody Rainbow, then marched her out of the police station in search of both sustenance and a place suitable for a quiet natter. The café – the inspector could never remember the name – ticked both boxes, even if it wasn't one of his favourite haunts. It was just about far enough off the beaten track to be largely empty most of the time and the coffee was acceptable.

'It's a bit late for breakfast.' Roche restricted herself to a small pot of green tea and a chocolate bar.

'Breakfast can be enjoyed at any time of day.' Returning the knife to his plate, Carlyle munched happily. 'It's the most unpretentious meal and also the best.'

The sergeant carefully removed the wrapper from the chocolate before taking a dainty nibble. 'Good to see you've made such a speedy recovery from your blunt-force trauma,' she said acidly.

'You have to move on.' Raising an arm in the air, Carlyle signalled to the girl behind the bar that he needed more toast. 'Setbacks are part of the job.' He had decided that he was not going to let 'the Bole incident', as he had come to think of it, get him down. After all, he had solved three murders.

261

'You should know,' muttered the sergeant.

'What?' The more her mood darkened, the cheerier Carlyle felt.

'Nothing.'

'It's just one of those things.' Carlyle slurped his coffee and contemplated the poster on the wall behind Roche's head. It was advertising a play on the South Bank that Helen had expressed an interest in seeing. Carlyle himself had no intention of going. 'No sign of Mr Bole yet, I suppose?'

'What do you think?' Roche huffed. 'The ports and airports have been alerted, the usual drill, but nothing.'

'Don't worry, he'll turn up.'

'*I*'m not the one who needs to worry.'

'You have to remember that I managed to track him down in the first place.'

'And here I was, imagining it was Adam Palin,' Roche responded drily. 'Wasn't he the one who made the big breakthrough?'

'What makes you think that?' Carlyle squirmed in his seat, his good humour suddenly gone. 'What's the little scrote been saying?'

'Relax, relax.' Roche managed to shake her head and sip her tea at the same time. 'Palin seems a very nice young man. Not the kind to try to steal your glory.'

'He's been a big help,' Carlyle said grudgingly. 'It's a team game, after all.'

'Except when you go off on your own and allow a killer to escape.'

'Manny Bole'll definitely turn up,' Carlyle repeated, determined not to let her wind him up.

'You hope.' Roche took a large bite of chocolate and chewed dolefully.

'In the meantime, how did things go with the pink-haired bruiser?'

'Pretty much as expected. Melody's got her story off pat, and

262

she's sticking to it.' Roche watched idly as a woman walked past the window pushing a young child in a buggy. 'You were going to tell me how you knew Karen Jansen.'

'Karen Jansen, yes.' Carlyle rubbed his chin thoughtfully. Where to begin? The waitress arrived with the toast, giving him a couple of moments to prepare the framework of his narrative.

Roche poured some more tea from the pot and sat back in her chair, waiting for him to begin.

'Well, Jansen worked for Harry Cummins.'

'The posh pimp?'

'There was only one Harry Cummins, thank God.' The inspector took a moment to remember the life of the thirtysomething club owner, *habitué* of the gossip columns and, briefly, owner of one of the most successful escort agencies in the city.

'And you were after him?'

'No, no,' the inspector corrected her. 'Our paths never really crossed. But Umar ended up working for Harry after he got kicked off the force.'

Mention of their ex-colleague caused Roche to wrinkle her forehead. 'I heard that you didn't exactly do much to help him when he was facing that misconduct charge.'

Spare me, Carlyle thought. 'Umar Sligo was the author of his own misfortune,' he said firmly. 'He wasn't the best sergeant I ever worked with – that would be you, of course . . .' he paused to let Roche graciously accept the compliment '. . . but he had his moments. All in all, I would have been prepared to stick with him. Under the circumstances, however, there was precious little I could do to change the ultimate outcome. If you manage to get done for sending pictures of your willy to a selection of less-than-delighted co-workers, there's not a lot that anyone can do to save you from getting shown the door, one way or another.'

Grunting, Roche grudgingly conceded the point.

'In the end, he jumped before he was pushed.' On a roll, Carlyle pressed on: 'Anyway, what would you have done if the stupid bugger had sent you a snap of little Umar?'

'I would have told him to behave. As long as he only did it once, I wouldn't have been that bothered. You've seen one knob, you've seen them all.'

Carlyle did not have an opinion on that particular topic.

'Men do stupid things all the time. Anyway, I imagine I've seen a lot worse over the years.'

The inspector didn't wait for her to offer up any examples. 'Not everyone is as thick-skinned as you are. Things are different, these days. People are quick to take offence and quick to complain. They want to be able to express their hurt and embrace victimhood. They want their feelings to be recognised. They want those who have wronged them to be punished for the upset they cause.'

'Yes, but we're the police,' Roche pointed out, 'not a bunch of – I dunno – Brownies or something.'

'It doesn't matter. The police are just the same as anyone else. People are soft – both physically and mentally.' He realised he was sounding like a grumpy old man but he ploughed on. 'The Job has changed out of all recognition since I started. The snowflakes have taken over. You have to be so careful these days – they can kick you out for anything. It'll happen to me one day.'

'Be careful what you photograph,' Roche advised.

'Just as well I'm not that good with technology.' Carlyle laughed. 'Umar was asking for trouble. But I think that was the point. In the end, like I said, he walked before they could sack him. I think he just wanted the excuse. He'd had enough. He basically trashed everything, walked out on his job, walked out on his family, and ended up working for Harry Cummins.'

'Unlucky.'

'Self-destructive, more like. Literally. Both of them ended up destroying themselves. Harry spent so much of his time off his face that he barely noticed he was in a turf war with an old-school gangster called Vernon Holder. Then, surprise, surprise, one day Harry is found shot in the head in his club. Umar, who, true to form, was shagging Harry's girlfriend, was offed – along with the girlfriend – a few days later. We never properly got to the bottom of who did it but I have my suspicions.'

'Which are?'

'Which are for another time.' Carlyle finished his coffee. 'Anyway, just before Umar was killed, Christina turned up at the station with Ella. Umar wasn't paying his child support and she wanted me to talk to him about it.'

Roche made a face.

'Happy families, right?' A thought popped into his head. 'Tell you what, if you and Shaggy are doing well, stick with it. So many people manage to royally fuck things up, it's amazing. If it ain't broke, don't fix it.'

Roche shot him a look that said, *That's none of your business*.

Carlyle moved quickly on. 'Anyway, Christina put me on to Karen Jansen. I think Jansen was kind of her spy, feeding her updates about what her old man was up to. Which intel must have pissed Christina off no end. In a way, I was surprised she didn't kill Umar herself.'

Roche glanced at her watch, telling him to get on with it. Pick-up time at the nursery was little more than an hour away and she would need to be on her way imminently.

'Fast forward to now and Jansen is working for the new boss, Vernon Holder, the poor man's Harold Shand, and managing Melody Rainbow, the world's most dangerous pink-haired hooker.'

A look of confusion crossed Roche's face. 'Who's Harold Shand?'

Carlyle couldn't be bothered to explain. 'Google it. The point is that—' His mind went blank. 'Well, I'm not quite sure what the point is, but it's time for us to take the wins on the table and move on.'

'What about Holder?' Rising to her feet, she lifted her bag from the floor. 'Is he involved in any of this?'

'That's what we're going to find out.'

Roache groaned 'What happened to taking the wins and moving on?'

'Where's the fun in that?'

'But you just said we should take the wins,' the sergeant said stubbornly. 'Then you contradicted yourself with almost the next words out of your mouth.'

'I'm getting on a bit.' Carlyle fished in his pocket for some cash to pay the bill. 'Consistency goes out the window.'

'You're taking the piss,' was Roche's verdict.

'Never.' Carlyle counted out the right amount, plus a modest tip. 'Just stick with me, kid, and you'll go far.'

'I'll be happy just to get back to Charing Cross, full-time,' Roche reminded him.

'Your wish is my command. Meantime, let's just find Manny Bole and put the bastard firmly behind bars, where he belongs.'

Muttering to herself, Roche headed for the door.

'It's really great to have you back,' Carlyle called after her. 'Things just haven't been the same without you.'

FIFTY-SIX

'Let me get this right,' Bob Biswas grumbled down the line. 'It's gonna cost me the best part of ten grand, *sterling*, for you to sell that damn print?'

Sitting in his office, Dominic Silver stifled a grin. 'I'm afraid that's just a provisional estimate. I can't guarantee the resale price. The market for Ting Sasse is obviously going to be a little soft at the moment, what with the exhibition and all the new material that's come on the market recently. We can set a minimum price, should you wish, but in that case, realistically, I would not advise that we go as high as fifteen thousand.'

The dealer paused, listening to the cogs whirring in Biswas's brain as the man came to terms with the consequences of his twenty-five-thousand-pound impulse buy. Ten grand was neither here nor there but the idea of losing money on the deal would irritate him beyond belief. Some guys could accept crystallising their loss. Others couldn't. Bob Biswas fell into the latter category. 'We will,' he added, 'of course, endeavour to get the best possible price for you that we can.'

'I'm not going to give the damn thing away.'

Although you did leave it in your hotel room, Dom reflected. 'Of course not. Apart from anything else, it's a very nice piece of work. If you were to keep it, I'm sure it will give you much pleasure over the years to come.'

'Hm.'

'If you're still in London, I can have it brought over to you. That might make more sense than having it shipped. Belgian Customs have been known to be quite tricky recently and I wouldn't want you facing a large tax bill, not on top of all your other expenses.'

'Fine,' Biswas huffed.

'The Imperial Court was worried you'd forgotten it. I have to say, it was good of them to go to the effort of tracking me down. They said you'd checked out.'

'I was planning on going home tonight but now it looks like I'll be staying an extra day or two anyway.'

'Do you want me to send it back to the hotel?'

'No, no. I'll pick it up from the gallery tomorrow.'

'I'm afraid the gallery will be closed tomorrow, due to staff illness. However, if we can agree a time, I'll come in personally to make sure you can get your print.'

There was a pause. Then Biswas said, 'Five.'

'Perfect,' Silver purred. 'I look forward to seeing you then.'

With a grunt, Biswas hung up. Sitting next to him in the back of the car, Elke Poosen watched him put the phone away. 'Who was that?'

'My art dealer. I think I mentioned him before. The guy's a complete charlatan. I wouldn't use him if I were you.'

'They're all complete charlatans.' Elke shrugged.

'No concept of proper customer service.'

Elke stared out of the window. 'I think we've got more important things to worry about than paintings, don't you?'

'It's a print. If it had been an original painting, God knows how much the thieving bastard would have taken me for.'

Surprised by the level of Biswas's irritation, Poosen gave a sympathetic cluck. 'Art is like any other game. It takes a while to learn how to play properly. In the meantime, you inevitably have to learn a few expensive lessons.'

'Bloody crooks,' Biswas whined.

Whatever. 'Manny gave me the stuff,' Poosen continued, keen to get down to business. 'You saw the list?'

'Yes.'

'There are some nice pieces.'

Gerry Durkan's wife, or partner, or whatever she was, clearly had an eye for that sort of thing, Biswas mused. 'I'm not a jewellery man,' he proclaimed. 'I prefer cash.'

'It will take a little while to get everything properly processed.'

'Of course. I hardly expected cash on delivery. But I know that you won't let things drag on for too long.'

'This meeting should help speed things up,' Poosen gestured at the traffic ahead, '*when* we get there. Elliot is looking forward to meeting you.'

The lights finally, finally, finally turned green. They had been red for so long Biswas had begun to wonder if the computer system controlling the traffic had been wrongly programmed. As the cars in front started to move forward, he tried to calculate if they would make it through the intersection before they changed again. 'I'm perfectly happy to meet your man but I don't really see why a face-to-face meeting is necessary.'

'Relationship-building in business is so very important,' Poosen said calmly, 'as you know better than I.'

I know a lot of things better than you, Biswas thought.

'Elliot Monk is the man who will get you the best price with the minimum of fuss. He has an excellent network of buyers at the top end of the market.'

'But he's not working for me, he's working for you.' Biswas noted with satisfaction that their driver had slipped across the junction, despite the light reverting to red.

'That's not how Elliot sees it.'

Why was he arguing? The fact that he was sitting next to her in the car meant that he had already conceded the point. 'Very well.'

'It's important to Elliot that he knows you personally. He's very traditional like that.'

'Old school,' Biswas grunted.

'Exactly. Like all of us, Elliot has his own ways of doing things. And, if he does a good job, it will make a significant difference to the final sum you receive from this windfall. Enough to cover the cost of plenty of paintings.'

'Prints.' Biswas wanted to call Manny, but by now his bodyguard should be on a plane, on his way home to Mumbai. Bloody airlines. The sooner they allowed people to make calls while they were in the air the better. Everyone knew it was safe. Why couldn't they just get on with it?

FIFTY-SEVEN

The Daimler rolled down a narrow lane. Biswas peered out at the vista of warehouses and light-industrial units on either side. Whatever part of London they were in, it wasn't one that figured in the tourist guidebooks. 'Nice neighbourhood.'

'Elliot likes to meet prospective business partners on home turf,' Poosen cooed. 'It adds to his sense of wellbeing.'

'We wouldn't want to upset his sense of wellbeing,' Biswas mumbled sarcastically.

'First impressions count. Elliot wants it to be a memorable meeting.'

'Everyone wants to put on a show these days.'

They pulled up in front of a small warehouse. A faded sign over the main entrance bore the legend 'F. Monk & Sons, Greengrocers'.

Biswas raised an eyebrow. 'Greengrocers?'

'Ferdinand Monk was Elliot's grandfather,' Poosen explained. 'He passed the business on to his son, Cyril. About twenty years ago, Cyril had a massive heart attack at four one morning while haggling over the price of a box of avocados with a bunch of Afghans in New Covent Garden Market. That's how Elliot likes to tell it, anyway. He inherited a business that was on its last legs so had to diversify. That was how we met. Elliot never gave up on the family business, though. It's even enjoyed a bit of a revival in the last few years — one of Elliot's sons runs the wholesale side, supplying a couple of top-end hotels and a number of restaurants in Knightsbridge, including mine.' Biswas noted the use of the word *mine*. Kaplan's had very much been Kevin Lamoot's vanity project. For all her talk of selling it, though, Poosen seemed happy enough to continue dabbling in the restaurant game. 'The other son has a chain of high-end designer flower shops in Chelsea, Fulham and Clapham.'

'Fascinating.' Biswas was beginning to wish he was on his way to India with Manny.

'There was even talk of opening one in Paris. Remind me, I must ask Elliot how that's coming along.' The driver opened the door and a blast of cold air invaded the back of the Daimler. Grabbing her bag, Poosen struggled out of her seat. 'Come on, let's go in and say "hello".'

When it became clear that the driver wasn't going to open his side, Biswas fumbled with the door and pulled himself out of the car. Allowing himself a stretch, he shivered against the cold. In the middle distance, he spied a row of lock-ups and idly wondered about making an addition to his portfolio.

'We'll use the side door.' Poosen disappeared round the corner of the building.

'Okay,' Biswas called after her. Pointing at the garages, he turned to the driver, who was leaning against the Daimler, lighting a cigarette. 'Let's go down there on the way back. I want to check something out.'

'Yes, sir.' Smiling, the driver took a long drag on his cigarette and tilted back his head, blowing a stream of smoke into the air. 'No problem at all.'

You're definitely getting a tip, Biswas thought as he headed inside.

FIFTY-EIGHT

On first inspection, Elliot Monk looked like an architect in a TV advert for some midlife-crisis motor-car. Dressed entirely in black, a pair of rimless spectacles perched on his nose, he had a shock of pure white hair that looked as if it had been expensively coiffured only that morning.

'Mr Biswas,' Monk purred. 'Thank you for coming all this way out here to see me.'

'The pleasure is all mine.' Biswas didn't care if the insincerity in his voice was obvious. For all that Elke Poosen had talked him up, Monk was only a glorified middle-man.

'Elke explained that I like to do business face-to-face?'

'Yes.' Biswas looked around the large empty space. 'Where is she?'

Monk gestured towards a door in the far corner of the room with his chin. 'Gone to the bathroom.'

'Ah, yes.' Arm extended, Biswas stepped forward, hand outstretched. As he did so, his shoe caught on something on the floor, pitching him forward.

'Careful,' Monk said solicitously. 'You don't want to injure yourself.'

'No.' Regaining his balance, Biswas looked down at his feet. A length of heavy plastic sheeting had been laid out on the concrete floor. It covered a space of maybe ten feet by four.

Just the right size for wrapping a body.

'I do that myself all the time.' The sickly grin on Monk's face told Biswas all he needed to know. Turning back towards the door, he saw his escape was blocked by the driver. The cigarette had gone. Instead, a hammer swung menacingly from the man's hand.

So much for a tip. Biswas felt his bowels begin to loosen.

'Elke wanted you to know that it's nothing personal.' Monk sounded amused rather than apologetic.

'And Manny?' Biswas clenched his buttocks tightly together. 'What about him?'

'As long as your man doesn't come back to London, he'll be left alone.' He signalled to the driver. 'Let's get this thing done.'

As he braced himself for the first blow, Biswas was surprised to find himself thinking about his garages. It looked like there'd be no further additions to the portfolio now.

'I realise it's not up there with what you'd usually charge your commercial clients, but it's the best I could manage. If nothing else, it's a token of my gratitude.'

Not to mention cash in hand.

Carlyle placed the slim packet on the desk and stood back.

'How much?' Dudley Carew asked, frowning.

'It was as much as I could get,' Carlyle repeated. Scratching his ear, he tried not to look too sheepish.

With a heavy sigh, Dudley opened the envelope with a pearl-handled paper-knife.

Carlyle shot a glance at Gloria, who looked on, amused.

After noisily counting the notes, Dudley grunted his extreme displeasure and shoved them into the pocket of his jacket. 'We're not a bloody charity, you know.'

'At least it's cash.'

Dudley didn't smile. 'Are you inviting me to conceal that income from the Revenue, Inspector?'

'Not at all,' Carlyle lied.

The old man made a noise like a motor dying. 'The amount's too bloody small for even them to worry about.'

Smiling wanly, the inspector held up a hand. 'I know it should be more but my access to funds is severely limited. What I've handed over is basically my informant budget for the next three months.'

'You must get shit tips.'

'Money's tight,' Carlyle repeated.

'Hmph. Last time I looked, the Metropolitan Police had a budget of billions.' Crumpling the empty envelope in his fist, Dudley dropped it into a metal bin sitting on the floor. 'You can't spend it all on overtime and sick leave, surely.'

Behind her computer, Gloria shook her head. 'What my dad means is that we're always very happy to assist the police, and we appreciate you helping to offset some of our costs to the extent that you're able to do so.'

'Thank you.'

'You owe me a favour,' Dudley grumped, returning to his crossword puzzle, 'a bloody big one.'

'I think he owes *me* the favour,' Gloria pointed out.

'Any time,' the inspector said happily. 'You always know where to find me.'

'We do,' Gloria agreed.

Dudley muttered something under his breath.

Carlyle hesitated. He wanted to ask if she'd dug up anything more since their last meeting but he didn't want to push his luck too far.

'I'm still keeping an eye out for your Mr Biswas,' Gloria continued, reading his mind. 'There's been no sign of him since the booking at the Imperial Court. But there's no evidence of him having left the country either. He seems to have gone to ground.'

'We'll get him.' Carlyle felt sure Bob Biswas would be safely ensconced in Charing Cross before the end of the day. He had spoken to Dom and agreed he would arrest the Indian crook when he left the gallery – having collected his print – making as little fuss as possible.

'Mr Bole, on the other hand, arrived at Chhatrapati Shivaji International Airport a couple of hours ago.'

'Where?'

'Mumbai. He managed to get on a plane to India before his name appeared on the No Flight list. And no one seems to have stopped him at the other end.'

'Fantastic,' Carlyle said sarcastically.

She gave him a look that said, *These things happen.* 'He hired a car at the airport using a credit card in his own name.'

'Not very professional,' Dudley observed. 'If you're chasing this guy, just sit back and relax. He'll land in your lap soon enough.'

Which was basically what I told Roche, Carlyle reflected. Now that Bole had made it safely back to India, the inspector felt his confidence in such a laissez-faire approach begin to waver. He wondered what this latest development would mean for the different murder investigations. Was there an extradition treaty with India? He had no idea. On the other hand, that would be someone else's problem.

Gloria idly tapped at her keyboard. 'Given what we know about Mr Bole's associates and employment history,' she offered, 'I would wait for him to return to Europe. Involving the Indian authorities may only serve to complicate matters.'

'In other words,' Dudley harrumphed, 'they're useless buggers. And bent as a nine-bob note.'

'Thanks for the tip,' Carlyle replied. 'I'll bear it in mind.'

FIFTY-NINE

At the station, Carlyle found Adam Palin enjoying a bacon sandwich in the canteen. 'Did you ever track down Martin Grom's cleaner?'

The sergeant wiped brown sauce from his chin with a napkin. 'No,' he admitted, through a mouthful of food. 'I got caught up on other things.'

'It doesn't really matter now.' The inspector brought him up to speed on developments, leaving out the details of his run-in with Manny Bole at St Mary's.

'How's the head?' Reaching for his mug, Palin took a mouthful of tea.

'Eh?' The inspector tried to feign ignorance.

'Didn't the Indian guy knock you out with a bedpan?' The sergeant struggled to keep a straight face. 'It's the talk of the station.'

'The head's fine,' said Carlyle, through clenched teeth. 'And we'll have Bole back in custody soon enough.'

Realising that this was not a suitable topic for further conversation, Palin asked, 'Meantime, presumably, with this thing more or less wrapped up, it's okay for me to ask Hana out on a date?'

'Sorry?' This time the inspector's confusion was genuine.

'Hana Curkoli. The daughter of Professor Grom's cleaner. I told you about her.'

'Erm, yes, sure. Be my guest.'

'Great.'

'I hope you guys have fun.' Carlyle retreated to his desk and called Karen Jansen.

'I wondered how long it would take you to get in touch.'

'You did?' For a moment, the inspector wondered if she had mistaken him for someone else.

'Umar always said you were tenacious.'

'He said that?'

'Among other things.' She mentioned the name of a hotel a ten-minute walk from the station. 'I'll see you there in an hour. In the bar.'

Carlyle looked at his watch. There was plenty of time to speak to Jansen and still reach the Molby-Nicol to pick up Bob Biswas. 'That works. See you there.' Ending the call, he sent Roche a quick email update. Then, after some further pottering about, he switched off his computer and headed out.

In the event, Jansen was fifteen minutes late. After buying a glass of wine at the bar, she headed over to his table. 'Sorry. I got delayed.'

'No problem.' The inspector sipped from a glass of carbonated water; there was still enough time to make it over to Cork Street to grab his man. Patiently he waited for Jansen to taste her wine. 'You worked with Umar after he left the police?'

'He was such a dog.' Jansen gave a rueful smile. 'Always trying it on, never taking "no" for an answer.'

'That sounds like Umar.'

'I can look after myself, though, so it wasn't a problem. That was the thing with Umar. You just had to be firm with him.'

'I tried.'

'It was like dealing with a kid.'

'You're right enough there,' Carlyle agreed.

'I didn't realise you two were so close.'

'We weren't. We just worked together for a while. He arrived at Charing Cross when he transferred down from Manchester. That was the only known case of him running *away* from a girl.'

'Oh?'

'Long story,' Carlyle said hastily. It didn't need to get back to Umar's widow. 'Do you still keep in touch with Christina?'

'Now and again. Last time I spoke to her, a few weeks ago, she was talking about going back to the US to be closer to her parents.'

'Makes sense.'

'Yeah, but Ella's doing well at school, so they were probably going to stay put. Chris doesn't want her to suffer the upheaval of having to move schools, make new friends . . .'

'I can understand that.'

'I moved around a lot as a kid,' Jansen offered, 'and it never really bothered me that much. But I can see where she's coming from.'

'How long have you been in London?'

'Long enough,' said Jansen, with feeling. 'It wears you down, you know?'

Carlyle, the London lifer, made a noncommittal gesture.

'I'm thinking about going back to Australia. We'll see.'

'Hm.' Carlyle glanced at the clock behind her head. She clearly wanted to tell him something, but he didn't have all day.

'That's the thing about this city, everybody talks about leaving but no one ever does.' Taking a gulp of wine, she suddenly changed tack. 'You never did find out who had Umar killed, did you?'

Carlyle stared at the bubbles in his drink, choosing his words carefully. 'Well, it wasn't really my case, but Ronnie Score was the guy who shot him.'

'Ronnie worked for Vernon.'

'I suspected as much.'

'Vernon was taking over Harry Cummins's operation and wanted to tidy up the loose ends.'

'And Ronnie himself ended up just another loose end, like Umer?'

'I guess so. In the end, Vernon went into business with Harry's widow.'

Carlyle raised an eyebrow.

'He imagined she was going to be a sleeping partner but Vicky had other ideas. She's quite a woman.'

The inspector wondered what he was supposed to do with this information. 'And you? Where do you fit into the operation?'

'Middle-management.' Jansen took another mouthful of her wine. 'I made my way up from the shop floor, as it were. Having to manage the likes of Melody Rainbow can be a pain but it's rather better than the alternative.'

'Ah, yes, the pink-haired ninja.'

Jansen sniggered. 'She's going to Tibet, you know. For her studies. That's the plan, at least.'

Another one trying to leave London, Carlyle thought. But Melody Rainbow didn't interest him all that much. Instead, he wondered how a woman like Karen Jansen had ended up in such a murky business in the first place. 'You had no problem about going to work for Vernon Holder?' he asked.

'I didn't see that I had much choice.' Jansen polished off her wine. 'I think I need another drink. Want one?'

Carlyle looked again at his watch. 'I've got to get going in a minute. Was there something you needed to discuss?'

Jansen fixed him with a hard stare. 'I want to give you enough to put Vernon behind bars, where he belongs.'

'We're still waiting for Mr Biswas.' Dominic Silver stalked the gallery, phone attached to his ear. 'There's no sign of him yet.' He peered out of the window, in Carlyle's direction. 'I tried calling him earlier to confirm but his phone was switched off, so we'll see. In the meantime, I hope Becky's looking after you.'

'She is.' Rebecca Moore owned the Pretoria Gallery across the road from Dom's shop. Rather confusingly, the Pretoria specialised in art from Central and South America. It was currently hosting an exhibition of sculptures by a Costa Rican artist. A competitor of sorts to Molby-Nicol, it was ideally located for keeping watch on the comings and goings at its rival.

'Becky's a good girl,' Dom observed.

'Yes. She's very kindly let me hang around inside, till closing time at least.'

'Don't worry. If Biswas isn't here by six, he won't be coming at all.'

'It's twenty-five grand's worth of painting,' Carlyle stated hopefully.

'Which he left in a hotel room,' Dom countered.

'Fair point,' Carlyle conceded. 'If he's not here by six, the beers are on me.'

'Deal. I'm going into the back to catch up with some paperwork. Remember the plan: if he turns up, let him pick up the painting and make sure he's at least round the block – or in a taxi – before you nick him.'

'Yeah, yeah. Don't worry, I won't drop you in it.' Watching Dom disappear into his office, Carlyle glanced at his watch. Biswas was already more than fifteen minutes late for his appointment. However, the inspector remained confident that he would get his man. Over the years, he had developed a sense for such things. The guy would turn up, for sure.

SIXTY

The Windmill pub was surprisingly quiet for the time of evening. Making his way back from the bar, Carlyle placed a couple of pints on the table. His profound irritation at Bob Biswas's no-show was yet to wear off. Pulling up a stool, he sat down, relieved, if nothing else, to finally take the weight off his feet.

Placing his phone on the table, Dominic Silver reached for his pint. 'He's not answering – call's still going to voicemail.'

'I guess he really doesn't like the painting, then.'

'Clients can be funny like that.' Dom took a sip of his lager and gave a small sigh of approval. 'When he bought it, he couldn't hand over his credit card quickly enough.'

'He paid for it on his card?' Carlyle was genuinely shocked.

'I think it's safe to say his credit limit is considerably higher than yours.'

'And they say crime doesn't pay.'

'If it makes you feel better, he couldn't just tap and pay, he had to put in his PIN.'

'Makes all the difference in the world,' Carlyle groused.

'It was just about the easiest sale I ever closed. I remember thinking at the time that our Mr Biswas would probably have paid double to get his hands on it. He was almost as bad as any junkie I've ever met. And then, a couple of days later, he can't bear the sight of the thing.'

Carlyle supped his pint. He wasn't much of a lager man but,

after the aborted stakeout, the crisp taste hit the spot nicely. 'I always wondered about that. How do you decide what these things are worth?'

'It's what the market can bear.'

'What you can get away with, you mean.'

'More or less.'

'It's all a bit of a con.'

'Not at all.' Dom looked vaguely offended. 'Like most things, the art market relies on basic market forces. In this case, limiting the supply stimulates the demand. If you're a dealer, you want to have enough product but not too much.'

'Are we talking about your current job or your old one?'

'Both. Back in the day I didn't want to be left with stuff I couldn't sell. Not only did it tie up working capital but there were the risks of having the drugs in your possession.'

'Of getting nicked.'

'Obviously. These days, the risks of getting nicked aren't there, but cash-flow is a much greater issue. I can't have all my cash tied up in one artist when I'm trying to plan the next show for someone else.'

Carlyle tried to look interested.

'I have to think about the artists, too. They want their prices to grow in a sustainable fashion. You don't want too much on the market too quickly or prices could go south.'

'Which impacts your commission.'

'Which impacts my commission,' Dom admitted, 'and also the resale value. The buyers want to know a piece will work as an investment as well as a work of art.' He took another mouthful of lager. 'They want to feel in the know . . . special.'

'And you make them feel special by charging them a shed-load of money.'

'You're getting the hang of it.'

'I don't know about that.' Carlyle imbibed more of his beer. Such things had always been far beyond his ken. Even if he – by some miracle – ever found himself with more money than he knew what to do with, he couldn't imagine spending twenty-five thousand pounds on a painting.

'Ting Sasse is being carefully promoted. He's currently got exhibitions in London, LA and Miami, with others in Dubai and Shanghai later in the year. The Americans in particular love him. It's clear that he's on the cusp of being really quite big. The irony is that Bob Biswas probably made quite a shrewd investment. Even if he didn't want to have to look at the damn thing, he could have stuck it in storage and just sat tight. *Death Smiles IV* is probably going to be worth north of a hundred grand in a few years' time.' He took a moment to reflect on his prediction. 'Well, maybe in a decade.'

'Bloody hell,' Carlyle mumbled into his pint. 'It didn't look all that much to me.'

'Ultimately, this guy could be as big as Ai Weiwei.'

The name meant nothing to Carlyle but he knew better than to ask. Dom could be a bit of an art bore once he got going. 'That would be good, huh?'

'That would be *great*,' his friend enthused. 'First and foremost because I would make a bloody fortune.'

That's why you made such a smooth transition from drug-dealer to art-dealer, Carlyle reflected. You always focus on the numbers, rather than the product. 'What are you going to do with the painting?'

'It's a limited-edition print. Not the same thing.'

'Whatever. It's twenty-five grand's worth of something that no one seems to want.'

'Twenty-five's the retail price,' the dealer pointed out. 'If you were going to convert it into cash, you'd end up with a lot less than that.'

'Still, a tidy sum.' An idea popped into Carlyle's head. 'Maybe you could donate it to the Police Benevolent Fund. Begin to reha-bilitate your reputation among your ex-colleagues.'

'My reputation hardly needs rehabilitation,' Dom said haughtily. 'And, anyway, you're just about the only one of my ex-colleagues who's still around. All the others had the good sense to grab their pension and bugger off.'

'Still,' Carlyle persisted, 'it could be the star prize in the Christmas raffle.'

'Maybe.' Dom's tone suggested that would never happen. 'For the moment, it can stay in the storeroom at the gallery. I'll have to keep it for a while at least. The owner will probably collect it sooner or later.'

'If I don't arrest him first.'

'There is that.'

'Maybe he's gone back home to Belgium.' Carlyle wondered about checking in with Gloria to see if she'd managed to pick up Biswas's tracks.

'I don't think so. His phone had an English ring tone.' Dom finished his pint. 'He'll turn up.'

'Yeah.' Carlyle swirled the liquid around in the glass. 'In the meantime, sorry to drag you into work for nothing.'

'No problem, my friend. I needed to sort out a few things anyway. I like pottering about in there when it's closed. It's nice and quiet. My private domain in the heart of the city, the only place where I can get any real peace.' He waved his empty pint glass. 'Want another?'

Carlyle shook his head. 'Make it a Jameson's instead.'

Each item had been numbered so it was easy to see that the single sheet of A4 paper listed a total of eighty-two separate items of jewellery. Next to each one, scribbled in pencil, was a price. At the bottom of the page, the total represented a large, if not massive, number.

'Is this in sterling?'

'That's right. No more than half a dozen pieces per customer. We made sure that they've been spread around among reliable buyers. No one who might flash stuff about in an inappropriate manner.'

None of the stuff is that unique, anyway, Elke Poosen

reflected. No one's going to be trying to recover it. She pointed at the total at the bottom of the page. 'And this is the net figure?'

'That's gross. You have to deduct the usual commission.' Elliot Monk mentioned a figure. 'The balance will be in your designated account by close of business tomorrow at the latest.'

'Good.' The contents of Gerry Durkan's safety deposit box, briefly in the hands of Bob Biswas, was providing a nice little earner, as the British liked to say. Staring into the fireplace, Poosen allowed herself a moment to consider how she might deploy the funds.

'It excludes the seventeen pieces you wanted to hold back. They were by far the best of the bunch, probably worth more than all of the rest put together.'

'Yes.' Poosen took a sip of her single malt and purred happily. 'But don't worry. I have no problem with the numbers. It's more than enough.'

'It's not bad for such a quick turnaround.' Monk finished his own whisky and signalled to a nearby waiter for another. 'You could probably get more if I made a few more enquiries. With the right buyer, given another week or so, I could possibly get another twenty per cent, maybe thirty.'

'Better to get it done quickly. I make it a point of principle never to be too greedy. It's always best to leave something on the table for the next man.' Poosen scanned the list one last time. Then, crumpling the paper in her fist, she tossed it into the fireplace, watching as it quickly turned to ash. 'No, you've done a great job at such short notice, Elliot.'

Delighted with the compliment, Monk gave a small bow. 'My pleasure.'

'Not to mention the other thing.'

'Happy to be of assistance.'

'And how much do I owe you for the other piece of work?'

'Oh, no,' Monk replied, 'there's no charge for that. On the house.'

Poosen was surprised by the offer. 'Are you sure?'

'It was a relatively small matter,' Monk explained, 'given that you'd set everything up perfectly. All in all, just a few hours' work.'

'And the body will never be found?'

'There's nothing left to find.'

'Bob Biswas RIP.' Poosen took another taste of her Scotch. 'One less thing to worry about.'

'It's always good to tidy up loose ends,' Monk agreed.

'Bob was more than a loose end,' Poosen muttered, more to herself than to her associate. 'He was a creep and a liability.'

'You need a bit of churn or the talent pool becomes stagnant. The corporate DNA needs constant refreshing.' The waiter reappeared, presenting Monk with his Scotch on a silver salver before slipping away.

'That sounds like the kind of thing you learn in business school,' Poosen said drily.

'I went to INSEAD,' Monk said proudly.

'Impressive.' Turning away from the warmth of the fire, Poosen contemplated the wider room. 'You know, I've been past this place many times over the years, but this is the first time I've ever been inside. I thought it was only for men.'

'They let women visit the club as guests,' Monk explained, 'but they won't let you become a member.'

'Ah.' Poosen looked around at the wood panelling and the over-stuffed sofas. Kevin would have loved it.

'It'll happen eventually.'

'In a few centuries, perhaps.'

'One thing at a time. Getting through the door, even as a guest, is progress.'

'Yes, I suppose it is.' Poosen glanced at her watch. She really should be going. 'You English never do anything in a hurry, do you?'

'It's safer that way.'

'Perhaps, but moving at a snail's pace you never really get

anywhere, do you?' Getting to her feet, she started towards the door. 'That's why the world is leaving you ever further behind.'

'Perhaps.' Monk followed her across the room. 'Speaking of moving on, I might have an interesting new proposition for you.'

Keeping her eyes focused on the exit, Poosen did not break her stride. 'I'm always happy to explore interesting business opportunities, Elliot. You should know that by now.'

SIXTY-ONE

Karen Jansen looked dolefully at her phone. Flights to Sydney were so bloody expensive, even one-way.

'Something the matter?'

'No,' Jansen quickly closed the web page, 'not at all.'

Vernon Holder dropped into a leather armchair, which squeaked in protest at his bulk. The old gangster was dressed formally, in a navy three-piece suit with a white shirt and a dark tie. What was left of his grey hair was slicked back across his skull. In the gloom of the office, he reminded Jansen of nothing so much as a feral version of Alfred Hitchcock.

His watery blue eyes considered her carefully. 'Business is slow.'

'It ebbs and flows,' Jansen ventured. 'I'm looking at revamping the website and we're evolving our social media strategy.' *Our social media strategy.* That kind of thing always shut him up. 'Google have changed their algorithms again,' she shook her head sadly, 'which accounts for most of the drop in online bookings.'

'Google.' Holder had no clue how the internet giant could have had such an impact on his custom.

'It's annoying, but we'll be okay.'

'And the girls? How're they doing?' Holder steered the conversation back to matters that he could more easily relate to.

'We're fine. To be honest, we have more girls than we need at the moment.'

'We always need more talent.' Sitting back in his chair, Holder pulled open a drawer in the desk. After some rummaging, he came up with a thin box of elongated matches and a fat cigar in a cellophane wrapper.

Please don't start smoking that thing now, Jansen prayed.

Tossing the matches onto the table, Holder began unwrapping the cigar.

'There's always plenty of talent in this city,' she opined, hoping to bring the conversation to a swift conclusion. 'We'll never have any problem on that score. And it might seem slow, but business is holding up quite well. In terms of the revenue numbers, we're down less than four per cent, quarter on quarter.'

'Year on year, it's closer to ten per cent.' Holder placed the cigar between his teeth.

This time last year, Holder had not been running the business. Not wishing to make that point, Jansen simply observed: 'The comps are tough. Last year we had a big boost from the G8 summit in London. You have to take that into account.'

'Hm.' Holder reached for the matches.

Keeping her expression neutral, Jansen mentioned several upcoming trade fairs. 'They'll bring something like seventy thousand extra visitors into town, which will be good for business.'

Holder took a match from the box, but didn't strike it.

'Plus, Parliament is finally back in session next week.'

'Useless buggers,' Holder observed, 'always on holiday.'

'Very good customers, though,' Jansen pointed out.

Holder waved the match in the air. 'Did you speak to the cop?'

'That's all done.'

'And?'

'And he lapped it up. I imagine he'll be coming after you over the Ronnie Score thing sooner rather than later.'

'Good.'

Jansen watched in dismay as Holder finally lit the match and lifted it to the end of the cigar. 'What I don't understand is why you want him to come after you.'

Holder puffed thoughtfully on his cigar. 'Loose ends.'

Jansen pushed her chair a few inches away from the desk. 'Loose ends?'

'This guy Carlyle, he had a run-in with Score. I assumed he would still have an interest in Ronnie's disappearance. I wanted to know if he was still on the case.'

'He is now.'

'That's fine. Better to know than to spend your time guessing.' Holder blew a column of smoke into the air. 'People spend far too much time speculating and far too little acquiring the facts.'

For a moment, Jansen had the horrible sensation of being back in business school. *Management Strategies 101 with Vernon Holder.* No doubt you could charge a fortune for a course like that.

'Inspector Ronnie Score,' Holder chuckled, 'he was a right sod.'

Realising that her boss was talking to himself, Jansen stared at her lap.

'If anyone's still looking for him, we need to deal with them sooner rather than later.'

Jansen let that sink in. If Holder was thinking about killing a second cop, she thought grimly, it was time to head home, whatever the cost of the damn flights.

Holder blew a stream of smoke towards the ceiling. 'And the girl?'

Wrinkling her nose, Jansen looked up. 'Which one?'

'The one with the pink hair.'

'What about her?'

'Is she going to be a problem?'

Knowing how Holder liked to deal with problems, Jansen stiffened. 'No,' she said quietly. 'Melody's not going to be a problem.'

Holder's eyes narrowed. 'Are we sure about that?'

'Yes,' Jansen said calmly. 'She doesn't know anything about

the business. Anyway, all she wants to do is go to, erm, China to finish her degree.' Technically it was true, Tibet being part of China, without giving her boss much of a steer.

'China, eh?' A disgusted look crossed Holder's face. 'What's the point of that?'

'It's part of her degree course.'

'Is she there now?'

'Yes.' Jansen crossed her fingers. 'She left a couple of days ago.'

'If she's over there, no copper's gonna track her down, so she can't really cause me any trouble, can she?'

'No.'

'Good.' Holder took a contented puff on his cigar. 'So, that just leaves you.'

'You don't have to worry about me, Vernon.' Jansen hoped the smoke helped to disguise her unease at being put on the spot.

'I hope not.'

'As far as I'm concerned, it's business as usual. We could do with a period of quiet around here. There's lots of work to be done.'

For a moment, the old gangster looked lost in thought. 'True enough,' he said finally. 'True enough.'

SIXTY-TWO

Hands thrust deep into his trouser pockets, Carlyle looked out across the grey London skyline, trying to think of something useful to do. 'Why are we back here?' he asked.

From behind the desk of the late Gerry Durkan, Alison Roche muttered something inaudible.

'I've got things to do.' Carlyle stopped short of mentioning his father's funeral. The service was only a couple of days away and he was supposed to be sorting out the final details, along with the outstanding paperwork. Helen had told him, in no uncertain terms, that it was time to stop hiding behind his work and get on with it. Unable to argue, Carlyle had promised to head straight home from the station and do as instructed. Instead, however, he had allowed himself to be waylaid by Roche. The sergeant had come up with a new, unresolved, aspect of Gerry Durkan's killing and now they were back in Docklands, searching the dead man's office.

'Don't you have to pick up young David?' the inspector asked hopefully. He had been studiously ignoring his wife's calls on his mobile and was increasingly concerned about the potential consequences.

'Shaggy's picking him up.' Roche cursed under her breath. 'I mean Alex,' looking up she glared at her boss, '*obviously*.'

'It's an affectionate nickname,' Carlyle insisted. 'It suits him.'

'It's a put-down.' Roche slammed one drawer shut and yanked open another. 'The poor boy has enough problems with his self-confidence as it is. His parents were very critical of him when he was a kid and his self-image is fragile. We need to build him up, rather than knock him down.'

A lawyer with self-confidence issues, Carlyle mused, now that really is a first. He glanced through the open doorway and into the reception area. From behind her computer, a weary-looking Delia Sansom, Durkan's executive assistant, shot him a hostile glare. Lifting his gaze beyond the secretary, the inspector could see that the main office floor was largely deserted. Most of the staff had left for the evening. Many of them were probably networking, looking for new jobs. The word was that Durkan's widow wanted a quick sale. The traders weren't going to sit around and wait to see who walked through the door next.

'Camila Steinbrecher.'

'Sorry?' The inspector turned his attention back to the sergeant.

'Camila Steinbrecher – the head of security – I told you already.'

'Hm.' The name vaguely rang a bell.

'She's vanished too – the latest senior member of staff to disappear. A girlfriend reported her as missing last night when she didn't turn up for a trip to the theatre.'

Having mentally put the whole investigation to bed, the inspector struggled to think of something useful to say. 'What were they going to see?'

'Does it matter?'

'No reason to assume so,' Carlyle conceded.

'Camila's not been seen in the last forty-eight hours. Given everything else that's been going on, there seem to be reasonable grounds for concern.'

'You think it's linked to her boss being drowned in a pot of soup?'

'It's got to be a distinct possibility, seeing as his killer is still on the loose.'

Carlyle winced at the low blow. 'Last heard of, Manny Bole was back in India.'

'Good luck trying to get your hands on him, then,' Roche scoffed.

Ever the pragmatist, Carlyle was quite happy for the brute to stay where he was. It might not represent justice in its purest sense but at least Bole was a safe distance away. 'I thought maybe we could send you over there to track him down,' he joked.

'Fuck off.' Roche chuckled. 'I'm not going to bloody India to try to save your skin.'

Carlyle faked a look of bemusement. 'My skin doesn't need saving.'

'The powers that be might not see it that way. You could well end up carrying the can for letting him slip through our fingers.'

'Institutional failings,' Carlyle stated. 'We would be doing a disservice to our various stakeholders if we went searching for scapegoats.'

'Fuck off,' the sergeant repeated.

That's exactly what I'm trying to do, Carlyle thought. 'I hope you don't use that kind of language at home,' he teased.

'Like Alice didn't learn any swear words from her dad.'

'She didn't. Well, maybe one or two.'

'I'm not taking any lectures on parenting from you.' Roche plonked herself in Durkan's chair and placed her hands on her head, considering her next move.

The inspector pointed to the sleek, aluminium-encased screen sitting on the desk. 'Have we checked his computer?'

Roche's look said, *Of course we have.* 'According to the IT boys, it seems that all he used it for was porn and horse-racing. So much for the business big-shot, playing the markets every waking hour of the day.'

Sounds like he was a pretty normal bloke, then. Carlyle was surprised to feel a twinge of sympathy for the dead Irishman. For all his roller-coaster life, good old Gerry had indulged in some fairly simple pleasures.

'Odious little prick,' said Roche, with feeling.

'Me?'

'No. Gerry Durkan.' Taking one hand from her head, Roche scratched her nose. 'My dad was in the army in Belfast in the seventies. He never talked about it but it was obviously grim. In some ways, he never really got over it. He would have gone spare to think of a scumbag like Durkan sitting in an office like this.'

Carlyle had never heard Roche mention her father before. 'He would probably have appreciated Durkan's unfortunate demise.'

'Maybe.' Leaning forward in the chair, Roche pulled open another desk drawer and brought out a small photograph.

For several seconds the inspector watched her scrutinise it. 'What've you got?' Roche handed over a picture of an Oriental woman standing in front of the Eiffel Tower. 'Is that her?' He tried to remember the woman's name but his mind had gone blank. 'The head of security?'

'I wouldn't have thought so. Camila Steinbrecher's Portuguese. Anyway, it's clearly a holiday snap.'

'Maybe they were having an affair,' Carlyle postulated, 'and he took her to Paris for a dirty weekend.'

'Very imaginative.' Roche groaned. 'It's badly faded – an old picture. It might even have been taken before Camila was born.'

Carlyle shoved the photo into his pocket. 'Who is it, then? Gerry's wife?'

Roche shook her head. 'He wasn't married but I've met the long-term partner, Rose Murray. She's English, nothing like the woman in the picture.'

Carlyle recognised the name. 'Rose Murray was a bit of a minor celebrity back in the day. If I remember rightly, she was an English society gal who joined the Irish Republican cause.'

'Well, these days,' Roche observed drily, 'she seems more concerned about recovering her stolen jewellery than anything else.'

'No sign of any of that, I suppose?'

'Nothing so far.' Roche slipped out of the chair and started investigating the contents of a sideboard behind Durkan's desk.

'The man liked a drink.' She held up an almost empty bottle of Scotch. 'There's enough in here to stock your own bar.'

'One of the privileges of being the boss,' Carlyle observed.

'How much do you think this one's worth?' Roche held up a bottle with a blue label.

The inspector recognised the brand, although he had never tasted the product. 'About a hundred and fifty quid, something like that.' The possibility of trying a little nip crossed his mind until he remembered the prying eyes of Delia Sansom.

Roche put the bottle back in its place.

'We're not going to find anything in here,' Carlyle said. The phone started ringing in his pocket. Inevitably, it was Helen. Knowing he would have to talk to his wife sooner rather later, he hit the receive button. 'Sorry, I got delayed.'

Helen's response was vigorous and direct. Flinching at the hostility pouring into his ear, Carlyle turned away from the gaze of Roche.

'Yes,' he muttered, 'I know, I'm coming . . . Right now . . . Yes . . . Of course.'

After a final blast of complaint, Helen rang off.

Contemplating the floor-to-ceiling windows, the inspector gave silent thanks for the fact that they didn't open. Otherwise he might have given serious consideration to jumping out of one.

Now it was Roche's turn to smirk. 'Trouble at home?'

'A bit. I need to get going.'

Stepping away from the sideboard, Roche pushed out her arms and stretched. 'Don't worry,' she yawned, 'I can handle it here. Like you said, we're not doing much, only snooping around in the hope of turning up some kind of clue.'

'Let me know if you find anything.'

'Sure.'

'I'll see you back at the station tomorrow.'

'Maybe not. I need to put in an appearance at Limehouse. Detective Inspector Wrench is on my case.'

'Ah.'

'Have you spoken to Simpson yet?'

'She's proving elusive.'

A grave expression crossed Roche's face. 'The word is that the commander's ill.'

'Oh?' The inspector wondered why he was always the last person to hear of these things.

'Cancer.'

The single word was a broad term for a range of potential conditions, all of them sufficiently unpleasant to have him shifting uncomfortably from foot to foot. 'Bugger.'

'Sorry,' Roche said abruptly, misreading his expression. 'I forgot about your dad.'

'No problem.'

'How are you doing with all that?'

'Fine, fine.' It struck him that Roche hadn't asked him about the funeral. Not that he held it against her: he wasn't keen on talking about it himself. 'I do have to get going, though. Stuff to sort out and all that. Let me see what I can find out about Simpson. Whatever the problem is, it can't be too serious if she's back at work.'

'Maybe not.' Roche was clearly not convinced.

'I'll see what I can find out,' Carlyle repeated.

Leaving the office, he ignored Delia on his way to the lifts. Out on the street, he was about to enter the tube when he received a text from Susan Phillips: *Don't forget tonight!*

Cursing, Carlyle almost walked into a woman handing out free newspapers. Dancing away from her, he hovered on the pavement while he tried to recall the details of the pathologist's leaving party. 'The Monkey in Orbit.' Pleased at his powers of recall, he decided he had time to show his face, have one quick drink and still make it home in reasonable time.

SIXTY-THREE

Standing at the bar, whiskey in hand, the inspector surveyed the packed room, pleased there had been such a good turnout for his old friend. Susan Phillips was in one corner, talking animatedly to a group of men, none of whom he recognised. Looking up, the retiring pathologist caught sight of Carlyle and gave him a thumbs-up then returned to her conversation. Enjoying a taste of the Jameson's, he spied Superintendent Maria Lockhead nursing a large glass of white wine. Sliding along the bar, he moved out of her line of sight.

'I was wondering if you'd turn up.'

Feeling a hand on his shoulder, Carlyle turned around and smiled. 'Never in doubt, boss.'

On first glance, Commander Carole Simpson looked tired and maybe a little thin but, basically, the same as he remembered. Waving a twenty-pound note at the barman, she ordered a mineral water. 'And another glass of Jameson's for my colleague here.'

With a nod, the barman went about his business.

'I heard you were back.'

'Not for long.'

'Sorry?'

'I've quit.'

Carlyle felt a jolt in his chest.

'I'm retiring, didn't you hear?'

'No.' First Phillips and now Simpson. Maybe the writing was on the wall for him as well.

The barman placed their drinks in front of them. Simpson paid the man and handed Carlyle the whiskey.

'I was only going to have the one.'

'Don't be silly, it won't kill you.' Simpson's face darkened as she realised what she'd said. 'Sorry, that came out wrong.'

'It's fine.' Carlyle poured it into his existing drink. 'Thank you.'

'I was very sorry to hear about your father.'

'Thank you. It'd been on the cards for some time. In the end, it went as well as you could hope, if you see what I mean.' He thought of Stine Hassing and wondered what she was up to right now. If what Roche had told him was true, Simpson herself might be in the market for the services of a death doula soon enough.

'Yes.' Simpson lifted the glass to her lips without taking a drink. 'Have you had the funeral?'

'Yes,' Carlyle lied, not wanting Simpson to feel obliged to come.

'My apologies for not attending,' Simpson said stiffly.

'It was just a small family affair.' Carlyle took another drink. 'It's good to see you.'

'I bet that's the first time you've ever said that.'

'Well, you've been away for a while.' The noise and heat of the room were becoming oppressive. Glancing at the stairs, the inspector planned his escape.

Simpson cleared her throat. 'I'll be gone for good by the end of next month.'

Bloody hell. Carlyle gave a nervous laugh.

'I'll be going quietly, without ceremony. No speeches.' She cast a glance around the room. 'No leaving dos. It's easier all round that way. You understand?'

'Yes.' Carlyle nodded. 'I understand.'

'It's time to let someone else take over.'

She had raised it, so he asked the obvious question: 'Any idea about who might be the new boss?'

A mischievous smile spread across Simpson's lips. For a

fleeting moment, the years fell away and he imagined he could see the girl behind the woman. 'From what I hear,' she said quietly, 'I think there's a chance it might be you.'

'I had to go.' Carlyle lowered himself onto the sofa, next to his wife. 'And I only had the one.' Helen was about to complain but he added quickly, 'I saw Carole Simpson. She's retiring next month. And she reckons *I* might get her job.'

Helen's mouth fell open.

'I know. A promotion after all this time. They must be desperate.'

'You deserve it as much as anyone else. More, probably.'

'Yeah, but after that business with Manny Bole, you'd have thought my card was marked.'

'Your card's been marked for decades,' Helen pointed out.

'All the more reason why I wouldn't expect to get the call now. And commander, bloody hell, that's quite a jump.'

'If you've learned one thing in the Met,' his wife reminded him, 'it's that being promoted – or not – has got absolutely bugger all to do with whether you've done a good job or not.'

Carlyle could only agree.

'If they're thinking about giving you Simpson's job, it must be for some bureaucratic convenience.'

'If it were to happen,' Carlyle mused, 'it means, of course, that I'm one step closer to being kicked out.'

'If you want to look at it that way,' said Helen, exasperated by his negativity, 'every day leaves you a day closer to being kicked out. Everybody gets kicked out in the end.'

'Hm.'

'In the meantime, they'll pay you more. God knows, a bit of extra cash would be welcome, especially with university looming for Alice.'

'I thought Dad had sorted the university fees,' Carlyle mumbled, still not quite convinced that Alexander would come through.

'Yes, but still, a bit extra would always be useful. And if your salary goes up, when the time comes to leave you'll end up with a bigger pension.'

'But I don't want to spend the next few years sitting behind a desk, bored out of my skull.'

Slipping her arm through his, Helen pulled him close. 'John Carlyle, you're such a terrible pessimist.' She gave him a peck on the cheek. 'If you're the boss, you can stick your nose in wherever you like. There's no one better on this planet at seeking out trouble than you. Whatever they give you, you won't just sit there like a lemon, shuffling papers.'

The thought cheered him a little. 'Maybe not.'

'Anyway, they haven't offered you the job yet. You can worry about it later. For the moment, let's just get your dad's funeral out of the way and take it from there.'

'Okay.' Resting his head on her shoulder, Carlyle breathed in her smell. 'That sounds like a plan.'

SIXTY-FOUR

It was his second funeral in a fortnight, at the same north London crematorium. They even had the same priest, Father Connelly from St Etheldreda's. Carlyle stared at the empty pews, waiting for things to get started. At least his dad had enjoyed a rather better turnout than this. He had counted a grand total of twenty-six mourners at Alexander's service. Today, there were just the two of them paying their respects.

'How did you know Professor Grom was a Catholic?' Karen Jansen whispered, although there was no chance of them being overheard.

'I didn't,' Carlyle admitted, 'but we needed someone to fill the slot and Father Connelly was available.'

Jansen looked vaguely nonplussed. Then she said, 'I don't suppose it matters.'

'The professor certainly isn't bothered,' Carlyle muttered.

With no need to stand on ceremony, the priest gave them the express service. In less than ten minutes, they were back outside, strolling through the Garden of Rest. Happy it was over, Carlyle breathed in some fresh – by London standards – air. 'Vernon Holder didn't feel like paying his last respects, I take it?'

'Hardly.' Jansen laughed. 'For a gangster, Vernon can be a tad squeamish. I guess, at his age, death's becoming a bit less of an abstract concept.'

'I was surprised the cleaning lady didn't turn up.'

'I imagine she couldn't get the time off.'

'That's probably it.' Carlyle pointed to the car he had waiting by the gates. 'Can I give you a lift?'

Jansen readily accepted the offer. Heading back into the city centre, she pulled up a photo on her phone and showed it to Carlyle.

'Melody Rainbow.' That was one name he wouldn't forget in a hurry. He pointed at the golden temple in the background of the picture, three-quarters hidden by the girl's pink hair. 'Where's that?'

'Lhasa. Some Buddhist temple, I think. The kid finally made it to Tibet.'

'Good for her. I hope she enjoys it.'

'So do I.'

'What about you?' Carlyle handed back the phone. 'Still want to put Vernon Holder behind bars?'

'I've been thinking about going back to Oz.' Jansen pushed out her lower lip. 'We'll see.'

Carlyle didn't push it. 'You should get away from him,' he suggested, 'one way or another.'

'I can handle Vernon,' Jansen insisted. 'He talks up all that gangster stuff but he's not stupid. He knows he needs reliable people to work for him. Reliable people like me.'

She made working for a criminal organisation sound like running a bookshop. 'Would he try to stop you leaving?'

Jansen shot him a look that said, *It's none of your business.* 'If I were to leave, I wouldn't tell him in advance.' Conversation closed, she began checking her emails, then got the driver to drop her at the first tube station they came to.

Carlyle spent the rest of the journey staring vacantly out of the window. Back at the station, he wasted twenty minutes clearing the build-up of detritus on his desk. Going the whole hog, he emptied out his pockets as well. The haul from his jacket included various receipts, a tube ticket, a pencil, two pens and

305

a paper clip, plus the photograph taken from Gerry Durkan's office. Tossing it onto the desk, he stared at the Japanese woman standing in front of the Eiffel Tower. It was a summer's day. The woman was holding a guidebook. She was smiling into the camera. Carlyle smiled back. 'I hope you enjoyed your day out in Paris,' he said quietly, 'whoever you are.'

Alison Roche appeared at his shoulder. 'Have you worked out who she is yet?' She placed a plastic bag full of papers on the desk opposite, along with a shoebox.

'Doesn't really matter now, does it?' Carlyle nodded at the bag. 'I hope that isn't a load of unsolved cases you've brought from Limehouse.'

Roche reassured him that it wasn't.

'Good. Welcome back.' Roche's return to Charing Cross had been assured once Adam Palin had decided to take a sabbatical in order to go travelling with Hana Curkoli. Not surprisingly, Hana's mum was none too happy about her daughter abandoning her studies to run off with a policeman. Niza Curkoli had rung Carlyle to complain and was deeply unimpressed by the inspector's unwillingness to get involved.

'Thank you.' Roche looked weary but her smile was genuine. 'It's good to be back. Especially as things seem to be falling apart in E14.'

'I heard about that.'

'It's the talk of Docklands.' Roche chortled. 'I don't think the estate agent's recovered from walking in on Wrench shagging his girlfriend Ingrid Yates, doggy-style, in the living room of Balthazar Quant's flat.'

'I heard it was the kitchen.'

'You know what it's like with these things – they take on a life of their own.'

'Don't let the facts get in the way of a good story.'

'Wherever they were doing it, they were busted.' Roche couldn't have sounded any happier if she'd won the lottery. 'The detective inspector's been suspended for using a victim of crime's flat for his trysts with a colleague. Yates has been sent on unpaid leave, too.'

'Will Wrench lose his job?' Carlyle asked.

'Probably not. But I've heard that his wife's already filed for a divorce. And he and Yates'll be split up. They won't be allowed to stay at the same station.'

'No.'

'Just as long as neither of them ends up here.'

'No danger of that,' Carlyle reassured her. 'This is a plum posting. We take only the best of the best.'

'Right,' Roche said sarcastically.

'It is,' Carlyle insisted. 'I had to fight to get you back in.'

'And I'm very grateful, which is why I brought you a present.' Roche gestured at the box.

Carlyle looked at it suspiciously. 'What is it?'

'The remains of Camila Steinbrecher,' Roche said. 'Gerry Durkan's security chief.'

'Urgh.' Carlyle scowled. 'What happened?'

'They found a piece of jawbone and a few teeth among some rubbish that had been fly-tipped by the railway tracks near Victoria. We were able to make an identification from dental records.'

'And that's it? Where's the rest of her?'

'That's all that's been found, so far. We're still looking for more but someone's going to have to notify the next of kin.'

'I'll leave that to you,' Carlyle said hastily. 'After all, you've got the better social skills.'

'Thanks a lot,' Roche complained.

'Could be worse,' he reminded her. 'You could still be back in Limehouse.'

The sergeant rolled her eyes. 'Why do I think I'm going to be hearing that a lot from now on?'

'Because you are,' Carlyle admitted cheerfully. 'I see it as my job to keep reminding you of just how lucky you are.'

SIXTY-FIVE

The Promotions Board hearing will run for approximately ninety minutes . . .

When was the last time he'd been up in front of the Promotions Board? It was so long ago that he'd been made inspector, Carlyle couldn't even remember if he'd had an interview at the time. And, now, here he was, looking at the possibility – maybe even the probability – of being plucked from utter obscurity and handed Simpson's job.

The commander had left without fanfare some weeks before. Her whereabouts were unknown and, as far as he could see, there was no obvious successor waiting in the wings. The timing was perfect: one of the Met's periodic scandals had just exploded into the public domain, leading to the hasty retirement of a group of more qualified colleagues. As of now, he was looking very much like the last man standing. Even Carlyle, the inveterate pessimist, could see the path to preferment opening in front of him. It would easily be the biggest break of his career. If offered, he would have to take it. Put simply, it was a no-brainer.

Yet the prospect left him with a vague sense of doom. He felt as if he was looking at a postscript to his career, rather than a new chapter.

'Now's not the time for daydreaming.' Helen tapped him on the shoulder. 'Alice is waiting for us. If we're not careful, we're gonna be late.'

'They'll hardly start reading the will without us.' Getting to his feet, Carlyle folded the Board notice and shoved it into his pocket.

'There's no reason not to be on time,' Helen said briskly. 'Alexander went to a great deal of trouble over all this. We should show some respect.'

'We should,' he agreed. 'Under the circumstances, it's the least we can do.'